'In the race to be first in describing the lost generation of the Eighties, Geoff Dyer in *The Colour of Memory* leads past the winning post. 'We're not lost,' one of his hero's friends says, 'we're virtually extinct.' It is a small world in Brixton that Dyer commemorates, of council flat and instant wasteland, of living on the dole and the scrounge, of mugging, which is merely begging by force, and of listening to Callas and Coltrane. It is the nostalgia of the DHSS Bohemians, the children of unsocial security, in an urban landscape of debris and wreckage – 'the one thing we really know how to manufacture'. Not since Colin MacInnes's *City of Spades* and *Absolute Beginners* 30 years ago has a novel stuck a flick-knife so accurately into the young and marginal city. A low-keyed style and a laconic wit touch up *The Colour of Memory*.'

The Times

'Dyer's narrator is a garrulous soul, and doesn't take exception to many of the people he meets. He's an ex-student type of fellow who wanders aimlessly through the DHSS-imposed black economy with a care-free ingenuity. He and his mates fix the electricity meters so that they run backwards; play Ludo for 10p stakes; get mugged; do shit jobs for shit pay; paint and write; read Calvino and listen to Callas; go to dreadful parties and sometimes have a bunk-up. Every-day sort of stuff, really; but Dyer observes it all with such humour and gusto that he makes it matter. Without labouring the politics, he gives us a London that refuses to lie down and die in the face of the late-'80s depredation.'

City Limits

'The narrator's real love affair is with Brixton itself. He is a camera, snapping away obsessively, recording and preserving, and he does take some marvellous snaps capturing the vigour and life of Brixton ... There are vivid tableaux of street life, shot through a compassionate lens ... *The Colour of Memory* demonstrates that Dyer can write. The transitory nature of happiness is his theme, and the book is an elegy for a time when friendship and belonging were paramount ... The writing, as the narrative moves towards its dying fall, is sustained and powerful.'

Sunday Times

'Dyer writes crisp Martin Amis-inflected prose, full of acute perceptions and neat phrases; he works hard to maintain a neutral, dispassionate voice, but also to put spin on his locutions. The book abounds in colourful descriptions of familiar aspects of London life, from racist taxi drivers to pub-knifings.'

Times Literary Supplement

THE COLOUR
OF MEMORY

Geoff Dyer is well known as a writer and critic. His articles and reviews have appeared in the *New Statesman*, the *Listener* and *City Limits*, amongst others. He is also the author of *Ways of Telling*, a critical study of John Berger. He has recently been in America researching a new book.

Geoff Dyer

THE COLOUR
OF MEMORY

VINTAGE

VINTAGE

20 Vauxhall Bridge Road, London SW1V 2SA

London Melbourne Sydney Auckland Johannesburg
and agencies throughout the world

First published by Jonathan Cape Ltd 1989
Vintage Edition 1990

The passage by Friedrich Nietzsche is from *The Gay
Science*, translated by Walter Kaufmann, New York
1974, reprinted by permission of Vintage Books ©
Random House Inc., 1974

The passage by Italo Calvino is from *Invisible
Cities*, translated by William Weaver, London
1974, reprinted by permission of Martin Secker
& Warburg Limited © Giuilio Einaudi Editore
s.p.a. 1972 English translation © Harcourt Brace
Jovanovich Inc. 1974

Draft versions of a few paragraphs of this book first
appeared in very different form in *New Society* and
New Statesman

Set in 10$^{1/2}$/12 pt Sabon by
Falcon Typographic Art Ltd

Printed and bound in Great Britain by
Courier International Ltd, Tiptree, Essex

ISBN 0 09 9775603

FOR MY
SOUTH LONDON FRIENDS

There are happy moments but
no happy periods in history.
Arnold Hauser

What remains of our hopes is a long
despair which will engender them again.
John Berger

The pages were bathed in the yellow light of the reading lamp. I read a few phrases at random, flicked through some more pages and then turned back to the beginning and read the first sentence:

060

IN AUGUST IT rained all the time – heavy, corrosive rain from which only nettles and rusty metal derived refreshment. The sky was a grey sea with no tide. Gutters burst their kerbs. When it didn't rain it drizzled and when it didn't drizzle the city sweltered under a thick vest of cloud. Even the clouds looked as if they could do with some sun. The weather was getting people down. I wasn't keen on the rain either but what really put a damper on things was being thrown out of my house and sacked from my job.

Being evicted from a house was a new experience for me but getting sacked was something I'd always had a talent for. I started early, when I was still at school. On Saturdays I worked in a sports shop and was laid off because there was a question mark against my honesty. Called in to the manager's office at four o'clock, I left for good at quarter past, helping myself to a generous silver handshake from the till as I went. A few years later I was fired from an insurance company for lack of attention to detail. My work involved checking someone else's figures for errors and I tended not to bother. There was no point; my checking was checked by somebody else and before anything went through the computer it was double checked, cross checked and double-cross checked by two or three other people. Would you have bothered? Of course not; you'd have been down in the basement playing in the ping-pong tournament like the rest of us.

Next I was sacked from a place before I'd even started working there. Now that takes some doing. Apparently there was a little problem with one of the references – I'd drawn up some headed notepaper and written it myself – and my future employer felt that under the circumstances they would have to withdraw their conditional offer of employment. It turned out to be a blessing in disguise. A week later I was taken on at a civil engineer's. Before they had a chance to sack me I trashed my leg in an industrial accident and picked up a thousand pounds in compensation. Easy money.

Cursed with a track record like that and tainted by several years of unemployment it seemed unlikely that I would ever get a job. Experience is all important as far as employers are concerned and since my only experience was of un-unfair dismissal it came as quite a surprise to find myself in a proper job with a regular wage, luncheon vouchers and everything. I thought I'd finally got a foot on the ladder. The job turned out to be a real ladder on the foot number but at least it took my mind off having nowhere to live. A week before starting work myself and the five other people who also lived there were thrown out of the crumbling cesspit on Brixton Water Lane where we had lived quite happily since the riots. Discourteous visitors assumed it was a squat but no self-respecting squatters would have lived there; in fact we were legitimate, rent-paying tenants. We had a rent-book to prove it. We *didn't* have a rent-book to prove it but Len said we could have one any time we wanted. In the meantime we handed Len's dad a total of five hundred pounds a month cash (it made no difference to us: we were all claiming housing benefit anyway). Len didn't own the house – he owned the motor repair shop next door – and neither did his dad. It was Len's brother Stass who actually owned the house. There were three other brothers as well but at any one time at least two of them were in gaol. Stass himself wasn't in prison; he was in the nut-hutch. Unlike his brothers Stass wasn't a bit violent; he was very violent – that's what his father, Anastassi, told us the day before Stass got his discharge. The first thing Stass did when he got out was tell us to get out. There was no reasoning with him. I started to explain how we, as tenants, had certain rights. Stass looked at me with eyes like dead planets and asked if I'd seen his brain anywhere.

'Whose brain?' I said.

14

'Mine.'

'No. Why?'

'See I took a big shit and realised I'd shit my brain down the bog,' said Stass and then just stood there.

Bewildered but unable to counter this belligerent interpretation of the Rent Act we all moved out at the end of the week. A week later I started my job.

The night before my first day at work I crashed at a friend's house and went to bed early to make sure I got up in time. I set the alarm for seven-thirty. Jesus! How did people ever get used to getting up at that kind of time? Slightly drunk, I got into bed and thrashed around for a couple of hours without feeling sleepy, got up to go for a piss, crawled back into bed and lay awake until four o'clock. In the morning the alarm split my sleep like an axe. More than anything in the world I wanted to go back to sleep, to call in sick and say I'd start tomorrow. All around was the wireless crackle of rain. The room was full of early morning light that seemed both brighter and darker than the sort I was used to. In the bathroom I slapped my face with cold water and took a joyless shit before running out of the house to catch the bus. The sky was pigeon-coloured and sick-looking. The pavements were already swarming with people splashing through the drizzle to work. And this, I remembered with a jolt, was going on every morning: the busy hum and honk of the metropolis.

All that first day and for most of the ones that followed I longed for time to pass and dreamed of doing fuck-all. Typically I spent a good part of any morning trying to tunnel my way out of a hangover before getting down to the serious business of skiving and flat-hunting. I was in no shape to work: being homeless, I slept at the flat of whichever friend I happened to be seeing on a particular night, went into work, changed into a suit and slowly assumed the identity of a diligent employee as the morning wore on. Sometimes I didn't make the transition until the afternoon; sometimes I didn't make it at all. If I was out very late I let myself into the office at two or three in the morning, slept on the couch in reception and then shaved in the washroom and clambered into my suit before anybody else arrived. The good thing about this arrangement was that by the time anybody else turned up I was already beavering away like a going-places company man. The bad thing was that it was difficult to sleep properly on the couch and by eleven in the morning I felt like Lazarus.

I was in even worse shape than usual on the Wednesday morning when Mr Caravanette said he wanted to have a word with me in his office. The night before I'd had a brief glimpse of what the ten-to-six lifestyle entails. Having got to work dutifully enough at ten fifteen I left at five thirty and met people for a drink in Soho. Swilled out by eight o'clock, I stayed on for another hour's dousing and then travelled up to Highbury to crash at a friend's place. On our way we called in at the local pub, stayed till eleven and then dropped in at the chippie. I woke up on the sofa the next morning with my suit for pyjamas and a half-eaten bag of cod and chips for a pillow. I got into work smelling like I'd washed my hair in salt and vinegar shampoo and dried it in the deep frier.

As I tidied myself up before going to Mr Caravanette's office I thought it was highly unlikely – all things considered – that he would offer me a seat on the board. I knew I was going to get a dressing down and a strip torn off but that was fine by me. Getting told off had quite a lot going for it: it didn't hurt and it didn't cost money. Getting told off I could handle.

Mr Caravanette was a self-made man with a face like a toupee, a silver-haired slug stuffed into a fat pink shirt with his initials embroidered over the left tit. The shirt fitted him like a bun fits a burger and ketchup: he was squeezing out of it any way he could.

Mr Caravanette was a busy man. His time was so valuable that he didn't want to waste any of it walking to the kitchen (where I had been known to take up to twenty minutes to make a trayful of coffee). He had a kettle in his room and he switched it on as I sat down. His desk was crammed with stacks of correspondence, memos, intercoms and telephones, all this clutter indicating my comparative unimportance in the face of the many and varied responsibilities that converged here.

The problem, he said, was my attitude. Now attitude, I knew, was shorthand for 'bad attitude'; a good attitude was like a bad guard dog – invisible and inaudible. Mr Caravanette then outlined exactly what he meant: I was slovenly round the office, I took a long time to do things, my letters needed correcting . . .

'No they don't,' I said.

'. . . And your office is a mess.' (Dead right – it didn't even look like an office; it looked like the bedroom of a rebellious adolescent. Being homeless I'd ended up keeping most of the things I needed on a day-to-day basis – clothes, tapes, books, squash racket and so on – in a filing cabinet but gradually they had spilled on to the floor. My filing wasn't all it could have been either.) As he continued with his list of grievances I got the first inkling that maybe I was on the brink of a sending off or a disqualification, not the booking or public warning that I'd first imagined. Meanwhile the catalogue of breached office protocol continued:

'You don't even wear shoes in the office.'

'They were pinching my feet,' I whined.

'That's not my problem.'

'I know it's not. That's why I took off my shoes not yours. Besides, what difference does it make? The only people who see my socks are the people who work here. Has somebody complained about my socks?'

'Look I'm not here to argue about your socks . . .'

I think he was about to call me 'sonny' but changed his mind, possibly because the kettle, after a lot of huffing and puffing, had managed to work itself up to a steamy climax.

'As I say, I'm not here to argue with you,' he said, absent-mindedly taking a book from his shelf and weighing it in his hand as if he might, at any moment, throw it at me. 'Things aren't working out as we hoped and I think it's best for all parties concerned . . .'

And that was that. He was giving me a month's money. I could leave in the afternoon. Maybe with a month's money I could sort myself out . . .

'Sort myself out?'

'Get a grip on things.'

'Get a grip on things?'

'Pull your socks up?'

'Pull my socks up?'

As the kettle subsided into sighs and rattles I looked at Mr Caravanette, at the boardroom glaze of his glasses, at the hands sitting heavily on the desk in front of him. Eventually I said, 'Is that all?'

He said it was.

I left his office shaking slightly. It was a piss-bin job but you always feel demoralised and foolish when you've been sacked. It's like getting punched: by the time you see it coming it's too late to do anything about it.

My workmates all wanted to know what Caravanette had said. I told them about it through a half-hearted grin. They all said how unfair it was but there's something about losing your job that makes people take a step back in case it might be catching. The swish of the guillotine generates excitement, fear and, at the same time, a sense of relief – that it's you not them – which also serves as a warning.

I didn't want to stick around. I went into the office of the old toad in accounts to get my month's money. I'd heard from someone that I ought to watch out for her, that she'd said a couple of things to Caravanette. Now she uttered a few sympathetic murmurs.

'Just give me the fucking money will you?'

What with all my stuff in the filing cabinet and desk and everywhere it was less like getting sacked from a job than being evicted from a flat. I packed a small hold-all and arranged to pick up everything else some other time.

I left before lunch. Everybody said stay in touch.

From a Payphone I called Fran's house but nobody had seen her for a couple of days.

'D'you want to leave a message?'

'Yes ... No ... If you could just say her brother called. I'll try her again.'

I wandered round Soho in the rain for a while, unsure what

to do next. Getting fired was bad news. It wasn't something I'd counted on or planned but at least I had a month's money in my pocket. I'd have some spare time again as well. During the time I'd been working I'd badly missed the life I'd been leading for the two or three years before: signing on, doing casual jobs when they came up. Getting sacked meant a return to normal life.

I walked up Charing Cross Road, past Leisure Hell or whatever it's called where the noise of electronic whooping and cascading money rushed out on to the wet street from the flashing, purple interior. The kids in there looked like ghosts, their pale faces tattooed by agile shrieks of light.

WHEN I WOKE up the next morning I had no idea where or who I was. Gradually I realised I was at Freddie's — he'd gone away for a few days and had lent me his keys — and that I was someone whose circumstances were enviable only from the perspective of total dereliction. No job and nowhere to live. The slippery slope. I lay in bed and wondered at what point somebody actually becomes derelict? You can see how it starts (a run of bad luck; losing your job, having nowhere to live, slipping through the social security net) and how it ends, but the long interim tends to take place invisibly. That is probably the most painful part: when you are still tormented by the thought that one last effort of will might improve things. From then on time means nothing; there is only weather, benches and booze.

With this in mind, I spent the rest of the day re-activating my social security claim. Since I'd last been to the DHSS offices a month before, they'd spruced the place up a bit. In particular they'd put in a thicker plate-glass partition and lowered the claimant's side of the counter so that you actually ended up on your knees and yelling, as if praying to a deaf and bureaucratic God.

I left the dole office and shook my head at the pavement-faced guy selling a revolutionary tabloid. Across the road the pale sun brightened the colours in the huge Nuclear Dawn mural showing a spectral figure of death clad in stars and stripes, striding over the dwarfed, fish-eyed landmarks of London. Bricks, their colours slowly warming in the weak sun, would have looked nicer but that was probably not a relevant consideration any more.

Immediately behind the mural was the railway bridge. After the uprisings the local traders paid for huge 'Welcome to Brixton' hoardings to be hung from the bridge. Now only a few tatters were left to cover the blank boards. A train clanked overhead, pulling a long freight of dangerous-looking, toxic-coloured containers towards some unspecified zone where no one was sure what happened. An innocent possibility of horror, the train clunked and screeched past. Further off, visible over the moving freight, were the large letters ATLANTIC forming a balcony on the roof of the pub.

Outside the pub Luther shook his coffee jar and asked for money. Years ago I used to see him in the George Canning, wearing a combat jacket and selling his paintings which were bright and colourful. People who hadn't seen him before were fascinated and he always managed to shift a few. Then, after seeing him in the boozer selling the same paintings night after night people stopped taking any notice. The more trouble he had selling paintings the harder he hustled. The landlord barred him and things began going badly. I saw him in various places, wearing the same green combat jacket but looking less like an artist and more like somebody with time not paint on his hands. By the time of Band Aid he was reduced to roaming around Brixton with a coffee jar, an optimistically wide slot cut into its green lid and a label saying BAND AID: PLEASE GIVE GENEROSLY. ETHIPIA FAMINE. The jar was never quite empty; there were always a few bronze coins in the bottom like half-an-inch of beer in a glass. After Band Aid he rationalised his enterprise still further by taking off the label and throwing away the lid. He looked worn out from tramping the streets all day. He had that fucked-up look in his eyes.

Until today I hadn't seen him for a couple of months and in that time he'd slid a few inches nearer to destitution. His combat jacket had big rips in it; one sleeve was in shreds as though he'd been mauled by a spiteful dog. He shook the tin at me, still trying to maintain that he was not begging but collecting.

'Who's it for?' I asked.

He paused for a moment, looked me up and down and mumbled, 'Nicaragua.'

I dropped some coins into his jar.

Back at Freddie's I circled the phone and played the start of some records, looked out of the window at the nothing-happening grey of the sky, turned a tap on and off, read one and a half lines of the paper and then put it down again. I turned on the TV and found horse-racing on both sides. I watched for about twenty minutes, ignoring the horses and concentrating instead on the suburban hinterland in the background: a place where it always drizzled, a place that didn't look like anywhere. I turned the TV off, picked up one of Freddie's books and studied the Olympic coffee rings on the cover. I rehearsed things I might say if someone turned up. I rang Fran and left another message. I called Freddie, heard the engaged sound, tried again and then remembered that I was actually at Freddie's and had dialled my own number. I called Steranko and a voice said he was out. I called Carlton but there was no answer. Where was everybody?

The doorbell rang just as I turned on the TV to watch the news. I trudged along the hallway and opened the door.

'Fran!'

'Hi!'

We kissed and held each other.

'How did you know I was here?'

'I was in Brixton anyway. I called home and they gave me your message.'

'I'm so glad to see you. I'm so miserable.'

'Why?' We were walking back along the corridor to Freddie's kitchen.

'I got sacked from my job.'

'Again?' Fran laughed. I nodded. 'You're going to end up in the Guinness Book of Records.'

'It's not funny.'

'No, I know. I thought you said it was an awful job though.'

'It was. Now I'll have to get an even worse one. What will I say when a prospective employer asks what I've been doing

22

for the last two years? That I've been in prison, studying for a sociology degree with the Open University?' I put my arms around Fran: it couldn't be described as a hug – I just put my arms around her and leaned.

'You feel thin,' she said.

'So do you.'

'We're a thin family.'

'Built for speed,' we said together, quoting our mother.

Fran was wearing a beat-up suede jacket, very baggy light trousers rolled up above her ankles, old suede shoes and faded yellow socks. Her hair looked like it had just been cut. I filled the kettle through the spout and sat down, resting my head on my hands.

Fran and I didn't meet up regularly. Often I wasn't even sure where she was living and would go a couple of months without seeing her. Then, just as I was beginning to wonder what had happened to her, when I was wanting quite badly to see her, she'd turn up or we'd run into each other.

'Why are you holding your head?' she said suddenly.

'Not because I've got a headache.'

'That's a weird answer. OK. Why *aren't* you holding your head?'

'I *am*,' I said and stood up to make the tea.

'What were you doing?' Fran said. 'When I arrived, I mean.'

'Lamenting my lot – my little. And thinking about the slippery slope.'

'What about it?'

'I was wondering where you slipped to.'

'A blind alley probably – through there to a park bench and meths. What else were you thinking about?' She was leaning against the door frame, one foot resting on the thigh of her other leg.

'Nothing really. I was just waiting for time to pass.'

'Time is money,' said Fran. 'I saw that sprayed on a wall near my house a couple of days ago. Then today I saw that somebody had changed the 'is' to an 'isn't'. People spray weird things these days. You see something like that sprayed on a wall and suddenly it looks like some kind of prophecy. You wonder if you know what it means.'

'Well, if time was money I'd have paid this afternoon into my account. I bet there are people who'd give their right arm for an extra couple of hours. I'd have been happy to loan them a couple of mine – I'd have *given* them away. Anything to have got them off my hands.'

'You should have been with me yesterday,' Fran said. 'I was sitting on a park bench and this man asked me where some road was. I didn't know exactly where it was but I pointed in the general direction. Then about ten minutes later the same man came charging up in an absolute fury. "You sent me the wrong way you silly bitch," he was saying. Absolutely furious. "You owe me ten minutes. Ten minutes, and I want them now!" I thought he was going to kill me.'

'What did you do?'

'I jumped on a passing bus.'

As I washed out some cups Fran walked by the kitchen table and banged her hip on the fridge.

'Ow! That hurt,' she said, absently rubbing her hip and sitting down. She was always banging into things or knocking them over. When we were kids our father used to tell her not to be so careless and to look after things but you could tell that really he was worried about Fran hurting herself. As Fran got older this concern subsided into a bemused and tender attention to the way she navigated her way through the world. I had more or less inherited this tendency of his and often found myself fascinated by her movements, wondering what would happen next. There was something graceful about her awkwardness. Several times I'd seen her knock a bottle off the edge of a table and then catch it before it hit the ground. For her part Fran paid little attention to these bruises and knocks – as if even when things hurt her there was some level at which she didn't feel them.

I poured the tea. Fran took off her jacket and threw it on the floor (something else she used to get told off about). She was wearing a dark blue T-shirt and men's braces.

'What's this?' she said suddenly, turning up the volume on

the TV. 'Oh it's that Van Gogh painting they're auctioning at Sotheby's.'

The bidding got up to eight million fairly easily, stalled for a few moments and then soared upwards again.

'He ought to make a special offer: for fifty million you can have the whole of England too – industry, agriculture, health service, the lot,' I said.

The bidding continued for a few more millions and when it was over no one knew who had actually bought the painting. It was as if the escalating logic of the auction had generated this final bid independently of human intervention so that the painting was now the property of the auction.

'A bid without a bidder,' said Fran. She was sitting on the chair with her legs tucked up under her, sawing away at a loaf of bread. I watched the muscles move in her arms, heard her bracelets jangling together.

'Have you got any butter?'

As I reached inside it the fridge shuddered and rumbled quietly.

'Have you heard of this new kind of butter that you don't even have to spread?'

'No.'

'It's part of an exciting new range of products.' I watched her scrape the cold butter on to the bread.

'D'you want some jam?'

'Hmmn. What sort have you got?'

'Apricot.' There was something unusual about the word as I said it, as if there were more sounds in it than could be logically accounted for.

Splodges of jam dropped on to the kitchen table as she hooked it from the jar and on to the bread. In a moment of sudden clarity I said, 'I hate stickiness.'

'Me too,' said Fran, sucking jam from her fingers. 'What about this evening? Have you got any plans?'

'None at all.'

'Let's have dinner then. I'll pay. That bread's made me hungry. We can drive somewhere in your car. Is it working?'

'After a fashion. You know what it's like. It won't get out of second gear but the bloke at the garage reckons there's no mechanical fault – I'm thinking of having it psychoanalysed.'

I'd bought the car for seventy pounds – while the balance of my mind was temporarily disturbed – from an unscrupulous drug dealer in Tulse Hill who felt it was time to expand and diversify. Most of the time people like Freddie and Steranko used it as a wastebin for tins of beer or a mobile observation lab in which they could get stoned and see the capital rush past in a blur of colours and near-misses. As far as I was concerned it was a millstone round my neck. Actually that's not true. A millstone around my neck would have felt like a loose-fitting polo-neck by comparison. I couldn't go out in it without getting lost and I couldn't get lost without losing my temper in sympathy. I often lost my temper almost as soon as I'd folded myself into the driving seat – only a few seconds after it had broken down, in other words. The only time it didn't break down was when it wouldn't start.

As luck would have it, on the night of Fran's visit it was working perfectly – so perfectly that the kids who stole it made barely a sound as they drove off. I must have only missed them by five minutes which is a shame because I would like to have thanked them personally.

While I got changed Fran went down to get the A–Z to work out where we were heading. When we left the house a few minutes later the car was gone. It's odd, that elusive sense of non-presence when something just disappears. It takes time to establish that something's not there and for a couple of minutes we paced up and down the street as if the car had just been mislaid – Fran even peered beneath another parked car as though it had rolled under there like a lost coin. Maybe the car was around somewhere and we couldn't see it. Maybe it had never been there. Maybe it was somewhere else.

'It's been stolen,' said Fran eventually and we set off for Brixton police station to report it. Only a few minutes from the house we ran into a policeman who put out an A.P.B. on the missing vehicle. I started to explain that it was extremely unlikely that the culprits could travel more than a couple of miles in it, that it was a fucking useless car and I wished I'd never bought it but the cop held up his hand in a halt sign and said there was no time for that because I still had to go to the nick and report the theft officially. We hopped on a bus to save time.

'It's like a Hitchcock film,' said Fran. 'Always a bus when you need one.'

I jumped off at the traffic lights opposite the police station. A few seconds later, as the bus accelerated away, Fran jumped off too, crashing into the arms of a moody-looking guy with long locks.

'Man, you ought to keep her on reins,' he said.

They were doing a lot of business at the police station that night – so much that you wondered if somebody was selling grass under the counter as part of the community policing project. The queue was pub-sized, hardly a queue at all, just a scrum of bodies, three or four deep, pushing to the counter. It took me fifteen minutes to get to the bar – the counter, I mean – and as I began telling my story the message crackled over on short-wave that a squad car was pursuing my vehicle down Streatham Hill.

'You can listen to it happen,' said the lager-complexioned copper behind the counter. 'Just like on the telly – metaphorically speaking anyway.'

On the wall to my right was a noticeboard covered with MURDER posters. In Westerns, posters like these always showed the murderers; here it was the victims, all but one of whom were black. Men and women; one aged nineteen, another in his forties, the rest in their twenties. Stabbings, an axe murder, someone beaten to death, a shooting in the early hours of the morning. The faces of the victims had something of the random, anonymous quality of their deaths. None of the photographs had reproduced properly; they looked like photocopies of photo-fit assemblies. The format made the victims look guilty, as if they were being sought in connection with their own deaths.

The airwaves sang with the crossed wires of distress and crime, the coughs of static giving way to the delta-tango zero-niner dialect of break-ins, pub fights and muggings. Then in a rare burst of clarity it came over the radio that my car had been brought to a standstill by a brick wall. A few minutes later we heard that the two kids who had ripped off the car were unhurt but the car had taken it full in the face.

The loss of his first car is a big moment in a man's life and as such he is entitled to a lavish display of grief. Since I appeared totally unmoved by this mechanical castration it was assumed that the trauma had already plunged me into deep shock. A policewoman offered me a cup of tea with lots of sugar. As we left she whispered to Fran that it might be a good idea to keep an eye on me for a few days.

'Well that's a load off my mind,' I said as we stepped through the door.

Outside I caught a quick glimpse of a twitching grey squirrel, high up in the dusk of a tree.

'Look,' I said, touching Fran's elbow and pointing. At school they had taught us that the red squirrel was cuddly and lovable but that it was being forced out of business by vicious greys. I couldn't remember ever having seen a red squirrel but as we watched I was struck by how cute this grey one looked with its munching jaws and bushy tail.

'Soon it'll probably turn out that even the greys are endangered, that their survival is threatened by a new, savage mutant of the species, perfectly adapted to life in the inner city,' I said.

'The scag squirrel,' said Fran in the hushed tones of a TV naturalist. 'Capable of living off dustbins and the dried blood from old syringes, its graffiti-patterned coat enabling it to blend in perfectly with its natural habitat of windswept tower-blocks and crumbling window sills.'

As we walked on it occurred to me that in the last month I'd lost my home, job and car. Each loss bothered me a little less than the previous one. I mentioned this to Fran as we sweated over plates of chicken madras in the local Indian.

'I'm becoming immune to catastrophe,' I said.

'There's a good side to all of this as well.'

'How?'

'The house was terrible, the job was boring and the

28

car hardly worked,' she said, reaching out and touching my hand.

'Thanks Fran, I appreciate that. Hey, I thought you were a vegetarian.'

'I am – a meat-eating vegetarian.'

'Is that possible?'

'Yes. Hitler was a vegetarian. Did you know that?'

I shook my head. Then Fran told me about her latest scrapes.

Fran had a knack of getting into scrapes and then slipping out of them, bewildered but no worse for wear. A couple of months ago she had popped out from her house to buy some milk and had ended up on the outskirts of Barcelona. Most of the time Fran emerged from her encounters completely unscathed but I was always worried that one day something was going to happen that she couldn't handle, that she was going to find herself completely out of her depth. Whispering over our curry she told me how she'd stolen a hundred pound necklace on impulse from a jewellers ('the next thing I knew I was out of the door') and sold it to someone she happened to meet in a nightclub. I made a point of never going shopping with Fran; it was too nerve wracking. She regularly lifted clothes, shoes and books from shops and had always told me stories of scams, deals and stealing but this was on a different scale altogether. It was when she told me things like that that I wondered what was going to happen to her.

I looked at her face, at her brown eyes and the tiny scar just above one eye. When she was nine and I was eleven she banged her head on the corner of a table and I wrapped a clumsy bandage around her. Later she had four stitches above her eye in hospital. We sort of looked alike. I looked at her and saw myself reflected in her eyes. In her face I saw our history, our parents.

'What now?' said Fran, hands on her stomach and tilted back in her chair. 'God I'm full.'

'Up to you.'

'I'd like to go back to the place you're staying and get really wasted,' she said. 'How about you?'

'That's great. There's an offie just round the corner.'

Fran insisted on paying for the meal and for the expensive Japanese lager we picked up from the off-licence. Even as a kid she was generous with money. Our father used to call her a windfaller.

Lugging our booze back to Freddie's we saw a guy up ahead smashing a four-foot plank into the corrugated iron that fences off the old synagogue on Effra Road. We crossed to the other side, keeping an eye on him as we drew level. As he hurled the plank round his shoulder and crashed it into the metal he screamed and shouted: Nyaargh! Nnnnagg! His head must have been like a shaken can of beer, ready to explode all over the place. We walked fast, not wanting to attract his attention, the bash and clatter of bent metal ringing in our ears as the distance between us increased.

Back at Freddie's we drank beer and smoked Fran's sinsemilla until we were almost legless. Just as there was an odd combination of elegance and gawkiness in Fran's movements so her fine-boned features concealed a considerable physical resilience. She looked like a dancer and had the constitution of a pit pony.

We listened to early Coltrane, moving fast and easily through the contours of bop. We played one record after another, concentrating hard until we were existing only in the music and pursuing whatever train of thought came into our heads. We danced to whichever song came next and bottles got kicked over. When I say we danced I mean we hung on to each other, slugging back beer and crashing over the sofa or on to the floor. Neither of us cared. Then we sat down again for a few songs. Fran's eyes were shiny and wet from laughing.

'You OK Fran?'

'I can feel a lot worse than this and still feel fine. How about you?'

'I can feel a lot better than this and still feel bad,' I said as I got up and lurched to the toilet.

'I hardly know where I am,' said Fran when I got back. 'I've been looking forward to this point.'

Eventually the beer ran out. Neither of us threw up. I drifted off to sleep and woke up in bed, unable to remember how I got there. It was six a.m. and my bladder felt like a hot-water bottle that had been filled to bursting. In the bathroom I pissed and gulped down mouthfuls of water. I looked in the main room and saw that Fran was asleep under a sleeping bag.

FRAN HAD ALREADY gone by the time I got up the next morning – sleep was something she snatched at odd intervals like coffee from a vending machine. Propped up against an empty packet of Rice Krispies was a note scrawled in her appalling handwriting:

'Had to rush. See you soon. Don't worry about the slippery slope. Love F.   PS: That Japanese beer! I've got a hangover like Pearl Harbour.'

I felt pretty bad too – like a toilet full of unflushed shit – and if my current form was anything to go by I'd be lucky not to finish the day feeling a good deal worse. Extrapolating from the events of the last few weeks it seemed likely that I would end up either in prison or hospital within a month. The only good thing about the way things had worked out was that in my current circumstances it was logically impossible to get burgled.

Joints creaking like floorboards beneath the weight of my hangover, I made my way to the bathroom and stood beneath the tepid drizzle of Freddie's so-called shower for ten minutes. Back in the kitchen all I could find to eat were eggs. I swallowed one raw and began pouring hot tea down my throat. It wasn't until the fourth cup that I noticed a letter addressed to me lying on the table. It was from Enterprise Estates: I'd applied to them for a flat in one of the blocks nearby and given Freddie's as my current address. I ripped the envelope apart and there it was: the offer of a flat I'd looked at a couple of weeks ago, just around the corner from where I used to live. I raced through the details: unfurnished, bedroom, living-room, hundred pounds a month, vacant as of now.

Saved! Saved! I thought to myself and for the next half an hour I paced around Freddie's flat, clutching the letter in my fist like a prisoner's news of reprieve.

FREDDIE GOT BACK a couple of days later, just as I was locking up to go round to Steranko's.

'I'll come with you,' he said. 'Just give me a couple of minutes.' He dumped his bags in the hallway, pulled off his shirt and sweater at the same time – something he always did – and tossed them to one side. After putting on a new shirt and blowing his nose on some toilet paper he was ready to leave.

'How are you feeling?' I asked as we walked away from the house.

'Tired. I think I've got bus lag.'

'What was the cottage like?'

'Damp,' he said blowing his nose again.

'You sound like you've got a cold.'

'I have. It rained all the time. I arrived there soaking wet and woke up with a cold the next morning. I spent most of my time snivelling by the pub fire, drinking hot toddies and listening to people talking about their walking boots. It turns out that there's a lot more to walking boots than meets the eye.'

'Did you do any writing?'

'None at all.'

'Too ill?'

Freddie nodded and smiled. He'd gone to Northumberland to try to make some headway with the book he'd been writing. Off and on he'd been working on it for a couple of years but it didn't seem to be progressing very fast. He wasn't exactly a slave to his art – he once said he'd done nothing on it for a week because he'd been unable to find a pen – but to Freddie this didn't matter. The important thing at this stage, as far as he was concerned, was to *act* like a writer. In recent months he'd taken to wearing jackets, cotton work-shirts, baggy trousers and food-stained ties – clothes, as he said, with an element of intellectual pretension – and these, together with the black-framed glasses and hair swept back towards one ear (it wasn't quite long enough to be swept back *over* the ear) gave him that air of the young would-be often associated with Paris cafés of the 1920s.

The door of Steranko's house opened just as we arrived and one of his flatmates stepped outside, engulfed by a wave of hot air that swept out into the street.

'He's upstairs,' she said. 'I've got to rush.' The hallway was as hot as the underground in a heatwave. A three-bar electric fire stood guard at the foot of the stairs and as we walked up it became even hotter. Steranko's door was wide open. Like most of the other people in his squat he'd knocked two rooms into one: divided by an assortment of structural props, one half of the room was a kind of sleeping-living area and the other half was a studio which refused to keep to its side of the bargain. There were cans of paint and brushes all over the place. Canvases were stacked up against the wall; smaller drawings and paintings on paper were stuck to the walls with adhesive tape. In a corner was a paint-splattered easel. The most striking thing about the room was the heat. All the windows were open but it was hot as a steel works. Slumped in a chair and swigging water from a bottle, Steranko was dressed for the beach. He was wearing a vest and boxer shorts, his long arms and legs covered in a thin film of sweat. I was sweating too.

'Oh hi!' he said, getting up.

'Why's it so hot in here?' Freddie asked.

'Probably because all these fires are on,' Steranko said laughing. I looked around: there was an electric-bar fire full on, a radiator that was too hot to touch and a small fan heater that emitted a parched breeze.

'How come all the fires are on?'

'The meter is due to be read in a couple of days and

we've got to use up as many units as possible to get the bill down.'

This made perfect sense to me. I'd been here on the day Steranko had first tried to fix the electricity meter. It was surprisingly easy. All you had to do was insert a copper pin into the meter and it stopped working.

'Simple as that,' he'd said, delicately inserting the pin. The meter stopped quietly without even a murmur. Five minutes later it blew up and there was a total power cut.

'Well that's one way of keeping bills down,' I said. The meter itself was blackened and showed obvious signs of having been tampered with. To remedy this Steranko smashed it to pieces with a hammer – he had an approach to home improvement that was utterly his own – and called the electricity board. One of the people doing work on the house, he said, had accidentally knocked the meter with a metal ladder, thus touching off a potentially dangerous short circuit.

Somebody from the Electricity Board came round within the hour but after taking one look at the meter it became obvious that he wasn't going to have any of this shit about accidentally breaking it with a ladder.

'Shall I tell you what happened?' he said.

'Yes,' said Steranko while I looked on.

'You shoved a copper pin into the meter, the meter bust and so you smashed the meter with a hammer. Am I right?'

'No you're not right, Sherlock Holmes. You're fucking wrong,' said Steranko. 'It's like I told you . . .'

In the end Steranko's household only narrowly escaped prosecution and were made to pay a huge deposit for a completely impregnable meter. Undeterred, Steranko got in touch with Erroll, a guy with singed eyebrows who, for twenty-five quid, showed him how to disconnect and reverse all the leads so that after running the meter forward for six weeks you could then run it back for another six, thereby cancelling out the units used. The only problem with this technique, Erroll pointed out casually, was that since it involved holding about six thousand volts of raw power in your hands it was an extremely dangerous operation. It was therefore important to get things right and not get anything muddled up. It was advisable to wear Doc Martins but even then, he concluded, they probably wouldn't do you any good.

What had happened now, Steranko explained to Freddie and I, was that after about six weeks of running it forward he had switched the meter round and run it backwards. Without realising it, though, they'd used up enough units to take the meter back to less than zero, to about 9000 units, close to the maximum.

'With the clock like that we'd have a bill of about five thousand pounds – probably more than the whole of the street put together so I had to reverse the leads to send the meter back past the other side of zero, zero, zero. The meter man's due any day now so we've got the house on full steam ahead, fires, lights, everything, twenty-four hours a day. Even when we get it into positive figures we've still got to nudge it just past the previous reading. It's fucking dangerous too. The wiring in this house is pretty dodgy. Feel that wall there.'

We touched the wall which felt hot as a potful of tea.

'Jesus,' said Freddie. 'I think you're getting close to meltdown.'

We sat sweltering for a few minutes and then Steranko – unusually, I'd not seen him for a week – asked what had been happening to me.

'My life plummeted to an all-time low,' I said. 'I was on the edge of the abyss.'

'You should have looked over the edge,' said Freddie. 'You'd have seen me lying at the bottom of it. You could have dropped in for tea.'

'I got fired from my job,' I said.

'You're kidding,' said Steranko, laughing. What was it about my getting sacked that everyone found so funny? There had been some amazement when I'd been offered a job in the first place and even more when I accepted it. It was as though getting a job was a temporary illness from which I had now recovered.

'What were you sacked for?'

'Oh it was a whole load of things: attitude, skiving. I don't know what it is about me and work. As soon as anyone pays me to do anything I devote all my energies to skiving. A lot of the time skiving's even more boring and tiring than doing the work but the urge to attempt it is irresistible.'

'That's why people work,' said Freddie. 'Employment is a prerequisite for the truly fulfilling task of skiving, of feeling that you're screwing your employer. Even heart surgeons probably try to find some way of leaving out a few valves and the odd stitch so they can knock off half an hour early. *Homo skiver*: man the skiver. Man must work to provide himself with opportunities for skiving.'

'But the good news — the news so great that I hardly care about losing my job — is that I've got somewhere to live.'

As I finished telling him about my new flat the phone rang. Steranko went to answer it and after a moment shouted upstairs to ask if we wanted to go to a party with Carlton.

'Where is it?' Freddie shouted back.

'Near Euston. We've got to meet him in a pub in Stockwell if we want to go.'

'When?'

'Now.'

I said I'd go; Freddie said he might be along later which was the nearest he ever got to saying no.

The pub was one of those grim boozers where people go to quench their misery rather than their thirst. The bar was full of red light and air so thick you felt insubstantial, as if at any moment you might fade away. Steranko and I waited to get served. Two bar-stools along a man with arms the colour of raw sausage was telling an anecdote.

'So I got the cunt by the lapels and whump! Straight in with the head.' His companion nodded, a gesture that echoed softly the action being described. 'Then one in the side of the fucking head . . .' He smacked a fist into his palm for emphasis. Yelps and flashes from the fruit-machine were the only other signs of life.

The barman came over. He had an old linoleum face — years ago someone had cut it up with a stanley knife and then walked all over it, now it didn't fit properly. I ordered two pints of Gutmaster and tried to imagine a pub where no one talked about fighting. Carlton arrived and put his hands on Steranko's and my shoulders. We shook hands as the barman trudged off to the beer pump.

'D'you want a drink Carlton?'

'No I'm OK . . . So you got somewhere to live yeah?'

'I move in next week.'

'Nice.' The barman dumped our drinks in front of us, glancing at Carlton as he did so. I handed him some money and we moved further along the bar.

'Some pub isn't it?' Carlton said.

'Fucking awful.'

'It was the only place I could think of round here. You know my brother-in-law's been in hospital, yeah? So I been at my sister's place helping her out. She lives on the top floor of this tower block a couple of minutes walk away. Incredible place: you see everything — rainbows, lightning, shafts of sunlight bursting through the clouds, amazing sunsets. And the noise, man. Traffic, music, sirens all night and then at seven in the morning the pneumatic drills start. I couldn't work out where they were coming from. It sounded like it was coming from up above so I went up in my dressing-gown and that's where they all were, about ten geezers from the council digging up the roof. It was like they were going to build a road across the roof.'

Steranko took a gulp of beer and grimaced.

'Shit. It tastes like it's been wrung out of a bar towel.' I took a small sip from my glass and asked the barman to change them for two new pints. He said there was nothing wrong with the ones we had.

'Nothing wrong with them? There's nothing right with them,' Steranko said. In a dark corner someone with a double barrel gut sucked at his pint like a dinosaur cooling its head in a mug of mud.

'It's not cloudy, it's within the sell-by date. And everyone else is drinking it,' the barman said. The expression on his face was as dead as a creature floating in a jar of alcohol.

He didn't bother looking at us and we didn't bother slamming the door when we left.

We walked to Stockwell tube, moaning about what a piss-bin country this was, and how fucking crazy we were to still live in it. We picked up some drink from a store by the underground station where the video security camera was backed up by a uniformed guard and an alsatian dog with bad teeth. Most of the customers had dogs too.

There was a long wait for the tube. We watched two men and two women about our age, dressed up to go dancing, not drunk but already having a good time. We took the tube north, yelling at each other above the clatter of the train. Sitting opposite us was a bap-faced guy who stank of mayonnaise.

Suddenly a middle-aged man a couple of seats down erupted in a fountain of sick. Then he just sat there while the tube hurtled on through the tunnel. Two stops later we got out. He continued sitting their stoically, drenched and stinking.

The party took some finding. After a quarter of an hour we were still walking through an area of abandoned factories, rubble-strewn yards and rusting metal lying in puddles. A little further on there was a new-style post-industrial estate with small freshly-painted corrugated metal manufacturing units making hi-tech software for video games. A few moments later we were back in the derelict landscape of empty factories with broken windows and black chimneys silhouetted against the blue-streaked night sky. It was difficult not to feel a loyal affection for these ugly smoke-blackened buildings when faced with their modern counterparts, the clean, lightweight computerised factories.

'Nostalgia,' said Steranko. 'That's one thing we really know how to manufacture.'

The party was being held in the grounds of an abandoned school, sealed off from the street by high sheets of corrugated iron. The only entrance was through the cab of a lorry which had been driven up alongside a narrow gap in the fencing. Since there was only room for one person at a time to scramble through the cramped cab it served as a very effective turnstile. A large crowd of people pushed and shoved and spilled back on to the pavement.

Inside there was pandemonium. Here and there the darkness was slashed by swirling lights so bright that it was difficult to see anything except the edges of buildings and the dark shape of a gasometer that loomed huge and solid over the whole scene. As our eyes got used to the combination of dazzle and darkness it became possible to make out angular constructions of scaffolding and industrial metal. Music was throbbing around but it was difficult to say from where. We passed through a gap between two buildings; through the steam-coated windows on each side you could see figures packed together and writhing around in yellow light as thick as mustard. Music thumped on the window panes; faces, lit by a lash of red and then an explosion of orange, appeared at the windows. There seemed to be no way in or out of the building. At the end of this narrow alley we stumbled down dark and slippery steps towards a courtyard enclosed by several buildings. Fires had been started. Planks, bottles and branches were thrown on. Groups of people staggered around and shouted or looked down on the scene from the sloping roofs of the school. A guy with a shaved head and a vodka bottle keeled over into the fire, sending up a great splash of sparks. His friends pulled him out and he lurched off again, smouldering. Someone leant over the bonfire and was sick.

Carlton and I lost sight of Steranko. Around another corner we found the entrance to one of the buildings and tried to get in but there was a huge scrum at the door. A great crush of people were trying to enter and as many were trying to leave. The more eagerly people tried to get out the more frenzied others became in their attempts to get in, like passengers on the *Titanic* rushing at a cruel mirror.

'Watch the fucking dog!' someone shouted. Carlton and I were in the middle, getting crushed from all sides. A foot from my face I saw the huge head of a dog, cradled against someone's chest, salivating and barking, frightened eyes shining red, tongue lolling. Someone screamed. Further on, in the swirling lights of the hall itself, it was just as crowded. The air was scorching hot. There was no music, only amplified noise echoing and thumping as if it was trying to get free of the hall by burrowing through the walls. I let myself get pushed out and watched as Carlton was spat out behind me, quickly jumping clear of those falling out after him. Fireworks and rockets shot horizontally past, exploding in bonfires and whizzing and cascading over everyone. There were more people on the roof, just standing, watching. Most people on the ground were watching everyone else. A body was carried towards some bushes and dumped there.

A group of punks had forced open the small window of an empty, dark building and were trying to climb in through the gap. The window was about five feet above the ground. Once one of them had got his head and chest through, his friends pushed at his legs until there were only shins and feet sticking out and then these disappeared suddenly and there came a loud crash and laughter from the other side. Then it was someone else's turn. When they were all in this black, empty room all you could hear was more crashing and shouting. Then one of the other windows of the room exploded like a firework around our heads, big fragments of glass angling through the night and splashing everywhere. A few moments later there was a barrage of broken glass as bottles from inside were hurled out through the windows. We scattered to one side. There was a pause and then, from the roof opposite, two bottles were lobbed gently through the windows of the room. There was a crash and shouts from inside. Two sizzling fireworks were dropped like grenades through the broken windows and went off with a huge *kerrumf* that echoed round the empty room. Smoke swirled out of the windows. No sounds from inside.

Things were burnt and broken, people ran around in the dark. Two policemen appeared, one of them shaking his head and not quite sure whether it was worth anyone's while to do anything about whatever it was that was happening here.

By now, like sand slipping through an hour-glass, the level of the gasometer had fallen and a vast cylindrical web of spars was silhouetted against the dim sulphurous sky. I saw Steranko sitting on an upturned crate close to a bonfire, his face bathed in the deep red light of the flames. The burning frame of a chair toppled down the slopes of the fire and rolled, still burning, to the ground. A momentary sense of *déjà vu* surged through me and vanished as I called Steranko's name.

42

Some friends of Carlton's came over. They were going to another party and asked if we wanted to come with them.

'What do you think?' Carlton said.

'I'm tempted to abandon the evening,' Steranko said.

'Yeah, me too. What about you?'

'I might go along for a while,' Carlton said. 'Sure you don't want to come?'

'Yeah.'

'OK, I'll catch you later.'

'Yeah, see you next week.'

'Take care yeah?' We waved goodbye, another burst of fireworks exploding low overhead.

After clambering through the exit Steranko and I began walking silently to Trafalgar Square to catch a night bus. Halfway there, feeling drained and worn out by this shitty evening, we hailed a cab. We climbed in and shut the door before the driver had time to ask where we were going.

'Brixton, please.'

The driver grunted and the cab began bumping its way reluctantly south. It was the first time I'd travelled by taxi in about six months. Trees slurred by as clouds slipped past the indifferent moon. The driver tugged back the glass partition. His neck was red through years of vigorous scrubbing.

'What part of Brixton?'

'If you go via Stockwell – then we can direct you,' Steranko said.

'What's it like there then?'

'Where?'

'Brixton . . .'

'It's OK.'

'No trouble?'

'Some. Not really.'

'Yeah?'

'You know, like everywhere. Most of the time it's fine.'

'You don't mind living there?'

'Not really. No, it's fine.'

'Rather you than me. I wouldn't fancy it.'

'No?'

'Nah. Not me. All those . . .'

'I tell you what, man,' Steranko said. 'You just keep quiet and get us there in one piece and we won't piss on your seats OK?'

The driver stopped the cab on the spot, brick-walled it then and there.

'Right! Out!'

'Forget it.'

'Get out you filth.'

'Fuck you.'

'Out!' He turned round uncomfortably in the front seat as he said this and opened the door on Steranko's side.

'Let's get out,' I said.

'Jesus.' We got out. The guy wanted the money for the journey so far.

'One ninety,' he said. 'That's what's on the clock.'

'You must be fucking kidding,' I said.

'Yeah, fuck you scumbag,' said Steranko. (We'd seen 'Mean Streets' a couple of days previously.) We walked off.

'Oi!'

We stopped and looked round. He was standing there with a jemmy in one hand. He didn't need anything in the other. We stood still as the trees shaking slightly in the breeze. In the cab his radio cleared its throat and crackled out into the night.

'Now you slags give me my money.'

The money was the least of our worries now but handing it over involved getting near him. Steranko gave him two quid at arm's length. The jemmy remained where it was, carving out a hook of sky over his shoulder.

'You cunts,' he said and walked back to the car, arms at his side.

'Hey!' said Steranko as the guy was getting back into the cab . . . 'Keep the change.'

I was already running.

MOVING MY STUFF in to the new flat took less time than the paperwork: signing the lease, filling out a claim for housing benefit, applying for exemption from rates, registering the rent – all the fraying strands of state support had to be twisted, tugged and woven together in a secure financial safety net.

The flat was on the top floor of a five-storey block, protected from the outside world by a security door which was rarely closed – someone had ripped off the self-closing hinges. The area just outside reeked of drains, a damp, heavy smell that made you think of typhoid and cholera epidemics. On the stairways and landings the smell was a mixture of animal shit and piss. On hot days you made your way up and down the stairs through buzzing flags of flies. The flat itself was fine: spacious, light, and smelling like the previous tenant was decomposing beneath the floorboards. The living-room was covered in that slightly faded wallpaper associated with cases of suspected child abuse.

I spent my first morning there doing a bit of home improvement. I woke up early, full of anticipated achievement and in such good spirits that I gromphed down a breakfast at Goya's, the faded fry-up cafe on Acre Lane. On the way back I bumped into Freddie and asked if he wanted to help.

'I'd love to but you know how I am with things like that. I get toolbox envy, the fear that your toolbox is much smaller than other men's. It's quite a common worry apparently – more men than you might think suffer from it – Fear of DIYing.'

'I know what you mean. I'm not that well equipped myself,' I said. A few petrified paintbrushes sculpted in a jar of turps, a roller you could make pastry with and an assortment of screwdrivers, bent nails, and inappropriate hammers were all I had in that department.

Steranko, on the other hand, had all sorts of tools and accessories scattered around his studio and I dropped in to borrow his drill and anything else that looked as if it might come in useful. Back home half an hour later I realised that the drill wouldn't reach from the socket without an extension lead so I headed back to Steranko's, slightly frustrated but still looking forward to the labour ahead.

Extension lead in hand, I stopped off at the DIY shop. I hovered around waiting for my turn and then realised that the guy behind the counter – a big white bloke with a triple chin and piss-coloured hair – had been waiting for me to say what I wanted. He didn't say 'next please' or 'can I help'; he just leant forward, both hands on the counter, jutting out that gut of a chin a fraction of an inch and raising his eyebrows as if to say 'yeah? Fancy your chances do you?' His face was clean-shaven, red and sore-looking as if he used a sandpaper flannel and Ajax aftershave.

I made him even more sore by not knowing what I wanted. I knew what I wanted but I didn't know what it was called in the hermetic argot of the building trade and as far as he was concerned that meant I was wasting his time. He assisted reluctantly, all the time making me feel like a piece of china in a bull ring. He threw screws from his hand into a bag, trudged around the shop heavily and yanked stuff out from dark recesses as if I was making him late for the heart attack that he'd planned on having for elevenses. When I'd got everything I wanted he did the eyebrows and chin bit again and stood his ground like a nightclub bouncer.

'That's the lot,' I said.

He took the pencil from behind his ear and added everything up. It came to a small fortune. Then he slapped VAT on top and the total took another leap upwards. I handed over the money and the guy said 'thankyou', pronouncing it so that it sounded like rhyming slang for 'wanker'.

46

Back home – Jesus, I seemed to have been in and out of the flat about ten times already – I set about reinforcing the door. At the old house we'd been burgled so many times that by the end of our stay we'd turned cut-price home security into a science. Other people knew about parquet floors, loft conversions and double glazing; what I knew about was low-budget impregnability. With a top-floor flat like this it was no problem: most of the kids who broke into places resorted to the simple expedient of kicking the door down and that was easily remedied. I fixed a long metal strip up the entire length of the door-frame with three inch screws every six inches so that the frame wouldn't give way. Once that was done the problem was that the lock itself could get kicked through the door so I fixed two large metal plates around the lock. That left the other side of the door as the weak point and I screwed two heavy right-angled brackets into the wall so that they rested against the hinges. Finally there was the door itself which I reinforced with a thick metal strip down its entire length.

The whole business took close on two hours and by the time I stepped back to admire my handiwork my arm was aching and I'd lost a good deal of my earlier enthusiasm. It didn't look pretty – with all those rusty metal strips and protruding screws it looked like nothing else so much as a medieval dungeon – but it certainly was secure. A bit *too* secure I discovered a few moments later when I tried to open the door and couldn't. I'd screwed the brackets so close to the hinges that they wouldn't rotate so the door could only open a couple of inches.

Rectifying things took another hour and by that time both arms were numb with fatigue; all that remained of my earlier enthusiasm was the spreading sweat patch on my shirt. Shelving my plans to put up shelves I put on a clean shirt and went round to see Carlton instead.

Carlton lived in a large, bare flat in a house near Brixton prison. The front of the house was white except for a band of about two feet just below the roof, which had been painted red. Before the paint had dried it had bled down into the white in deep arterial drips along the entire length of the house.

'Welcome to the House that Dripped Blood,' said Carlton in a creaky hinges voice as he opened the door. 'The landlord's trying to do the place up.'

'Nightmare on Jebb Avenue. You busy?'

'I've got to go out in a minute but come in. We've got time for a coffee or something . . . What you been doing?' Carlton said as I hurried up the stairs after him.

'Trying to sort my flat out. What a headache. Somebody ought to come out with one of those magazines: Yoga and DIY in fifty weekly parts building up into a complete encyclopedia of how to remain calm in the face of mounting chaos and runaway expense. I'd fucking buy it.'

Music was playing quietly in Carlton's flat. I finished making the coffee and picked up some small barbells while Carlton searched for a pair of socks. He was wearing jeans and a T-shirt that looked dazzling white against his dark arms. There was a mattress on the floor, a stereo, some open drawers, a rail of clothes; nothing on the walls.

'What's the record?' I said, pouring coffee into large white mugs. 'You have about five sugars don't you?'

'Roland Kirk,' said Carlton tying his shoes and tossing me the album cover. 'Three. I've cut down. You know about Roland Kirk?'

'No.' I picked up the cover which showed him in profile, playing about four saxophones at once.

'He went blind soon after he was born,' called Carlton from the bathroom. 'When he was in his late thirties he had a stroke that paralysed one side of his body. Even after that he kept playing. He died when he was forty-one. You could start a religion with a life like that.'

The music twisted and writhed and breathed, searching for a way out of itself.

'There's something I've always wanted to ask you Carlton,' I said. 'And this seems as good a time as any.'

'Go ahead.'

'How come there's never any dust in your flat? How come your clothes never smell? How come your cups and everything are so clean? Are you a closet cleansomaniac?'

'It's my insomnia. I tidy up my flat when I can't sleep and I'm too tired to do anything else.'

'How often d'you have trouble sleeping?'

'Every night virtually. I can only sleep if I'm stoned. I tell you, a squeal of brakes or a shout from the street at the vital moment make all the difference between about four hours sleep and none at all.'

'Shit. Sleep is something I have no trouble with – I can do it with my eyes shut. Sometimes I think I only get up to get tired enough to go back to bed again.'

'I only go to bed to get restless enough to get up again. Even when I'm asleep I sometimes think I'm awake.'

'D'you dream?'

'I haven't had one for a while – not a new one anyway. They're all repeats. I know them off by heart. Sometimes I nod off in the middle of them, they're so fucking boring.' As he spoke, Carlton – like me – was lifting a mug to his lips with one hand and a barbell to his shoulder with the other. It was as if we were in an advert for strong coffee.

'I got these homoeopathic tablets from the hippy shop. They had three kinds. I went for the ones that sounded like wholewheat Mogadon. They didn't do anything at all. Rubbish.'

'What d'you think about when you can't sleep?'

'My flat.'

'What about it?' The doorbell rang.

'I wonder if it's clean enough,' he said, going to answer the door. I heard voices on the stairs and then Belinda followed Carlton into the room. She wore glasses and used foul language and after five minutes in her company you felt as relaxed as if she'd seen you pee your pants in infants' school. She had beautiful manners. We said hello and smiled.

'Are those new trousers Lin?' Carlton asked.

Belinda stepped back and twirled round. She was wearing a pair of blue silky trousers with a low gusset, very loose around the hips and legs and tied tight at the ankles.

'You like them?' she said, smiling.

'Very nice,' I said.

'Thank you.'

'They make it look like you've got a turd hanging out your bum,' Carlton said. Belinda's laugh was like gold coins pouring from a fruit-machine.

'No, I'm only joking Lin. They're terrific.' Belinda and I talked for a few moments while Carlton opened and closed drawers and cleared stuff away.

'Hey, listen, I'm sorry I've got to rush you both but I've really got to get a move on,' he said. Belinda handed him a bag of grass.

'Thanks a lot. How much do I owe you Lin?' he said.

'Twenty-five. Plus ten for being so rude about my trousers.'

'Can I owe you?'

'What a cheek.'

'Thanks.' Carlton pulled some notes out from behind a book and eyed them like a disappointing hand of cards before shoving them in his pocket.

'Where are you going?' Belinda said.

'My brother's for lunch. I'm supposed to be there already. Right: keys, money, bike-lock . . .'

'And you're coming to Foomie's on Saturday?'

'Yeah. Right, let's go,' Carlton said, wheeling his bike backwards out of the door. We followed him out and waited while he went through the lengthy procedure of locking up his flat.

'I don't know why you bother. You've got nothing worth nicking.'

It was a warm, clear day; litter caught the sun and shone. Belinda and I walked along the pavement while Carlton skooted along beside us.

'Where you going Lin?' he asked.

'I'm meeting Foomie, Carmel and Manda for a rehearsal.'

'A rehearsal for what?' I asked.

'We're starting a rap group.'

'They're always starting something. First they were going to make a film then it was something else. Now it's this,' Carlton said. Belinda had put on a pair of sun-glasses. I was still squinting at the glare.

'It's a good idea isn't it,' she said.

'Old hat,' Carlton said, laughing.

'I wasn't speaking to you.'

'I think it's a great idea.'

'He's only saying that. He hates all that kind of music.'

'You don't do you?'

'Well . . .'

'Well, you're *square* . . .'

'I'm going to have to get on. I'll catch you later yeah?' Carlton said, leaning over to kiss Belinda on the cheek. He waved to me and cycled off.

Belinda said I should come along and meet the other people in her group if I wasn't doing anything. We made our way down Brixton Hill and past the town hall. Ahead of us a tall guy in a check sports jacket and baseball cap sprang along, trousers flapping round his ankles, walking as though each step had been astonished by the previous one. Outside Red Records we bumped into Luther and his coffee jar.

'What's it for?' Belinda asked. Luther looked up, saw a white man and a black woman, and said, 'Mandela.'

Inside the cafe a woman was trying to serve food and hold on to a baby at the same time. It seemed certain that either the baby or the contents of its stomach were going to end up in the stew before the day was out. Service was understandably slow. Belinda tapped her feet. The sun blared through the large plate glass roasting bag of the window. Belinda's friends hadn't showed up yet. We ordered a pot of tea and went outside and shared a table with a white rasta. He had a wispy beard and sunken, kidney-problem eyes. There was only one person in the world who didn't think he looked like a jerk and we were sitting next to him. After a couple of minutes he unlocked his bike and left. A damp waitress brought out tea and we drank it, sweating, in hot gulps.

'Nice shirt,' Belinda shouted to a young punk who slouched past with 'Sceptic Death' printed on the back of his black shirt. He took it as a compliment. Carmel and Manda showed up together and Belinda introduced me. They were both wearing sun-glasses.

51

'No sign of Foomie?' Manda said, taking her glasses off.

'You know what she's like.'

They ordered some cold drinks and sucked at them through straws.

'Here she is,' Belinda said, laughing and waving. Foomie walked slowly towards us, smiling. She had on a T-shirt, large black shorts, red ankle-socks.

'Where've you been Foomie?' Carmel called out.

'An *hour* late,' said Belinda, smiling.

Foomie came over and kissed all three of them. Her arms were thin and muscular. Her hair was pulled tight to one side of her head and tumbled down like black weeping willow over the side of her face. She looked sleepy but her eyes were unhurried and calm as water in a glass.

'I'm never drinking again,' she said, holding Belinda's hand. 'My head. It feels like it's made of tupperware.' Carmel shifted over so that Foomie could share her seat. She ordered mineral water and siphoned off an inch of Carmel's orange.

Belinda introduced Foomie and me and we shook hands for a moment. She smiled but there was something instantly different in her manner. She was friendly but formal, not at all like she was with her three friends and not at all like Belinda who was abrasive and funny from the moment you met her. I'd heard of Foomie but this was the first time I'd actually met her. Previously, she'd either just left before I arrived somewhere or she was meant to have turned up at a party but had got side-tracked and ended up somewhere completely different.

Foomie's water arrived. She drank it in one gulp, gasped and ordered another. The four of them talked about what they'd been doing, laughing loudly and sipping drinks. I laughed and smiled but didn't say anything. I was sitting there but I was like a guy at another table hidden by his newspaper. I looked at Foomie, at her arms and hair, and had a sense of gravity rippling around her limbs.

'Steranko!' I shouted suddenly, seeing him cycling home from Brixton Recreation Centre in training shoes and an old tracksuit. He came over and leant against the crossbar of his bike. We joked for a few moments until Belinda introduced him to everybody. He noticed Foomie and she noticed him, his gestures, the way he moved. I watched how they shook hands and smiled at each other. His sleeves were pushed up above the elbows; the veins stood out on his forearms. He was unshaven, his body had that easy assurance that comes after intense physical exertion. There was a clarity about his movements. He ran a paint-splashed hand through his hair, dripping with sweat or water from a shower.

'What have you been doing?' Belinda asked.

'Squash,' he said.

'You're so fucking sporty Steranko.' At this point I wanted, quite badly, to point out that I'd absolutely fucking hammered him the last time we'd played squash. And tennis.

'We've got to go,' Carmel said. 'It's practice time.'

'Where shall we go?'

'Let's go to my house.'

'Why don't we go to my house. It's nearer.'

'My place is near too.'

'We never go to my house.'

'It's too far away.'

'No it's not and I've got a double-tape cassette player.'

'I've got a double cassette player *too* and it's much better than yours. I only bought it six weeks ago. Yours hardly works.'

'It works perfectly.'

'I don't care where we go.'

'Nor do I.'

'Let's just go.'

Steranko and I listened and grinned at each other. There was an elaborate chorus of goodbyes and then we watched them walk away. When they had gone it was as if their ghosts were still there in the chairs, as if the air was still used to shaping itself around them. I could hear their voices all over again like a perfect echo.

'Well . . .' said Steranko a few minutes later, holding the handlebars of his bike with one hand as we walked up the road together.

'Exactly,' I said.

'God, you take one look at her and all you want to do is cry.'

'She's got those kind of looks that make you feel really sorry for yourself,' I said as we manoeuvred our way through tired women clinging to their prams. 'Still, you seem to be taking it pretty well.'

'Taking what well?'

'Foomie. It's obvious it's me she fancies but you don't seem to be sulking about it or anything.'

'You took the words out of my mouth,' said Steranko and we both laughed like college boys.

STERANKO WAS LEANT up against the bar, studying the original gravity information on the beer pumps. He was wearing his working clothes – paint-splattered jeans, an old sweatshirt – and his fingers and nails were black with paint and grease. He bought me a drink and we sat next to two women who were quite often in the pub.

'I've got some good news and some bad news for you,' I said.

'Go on.'

'The good news is that Foomie – remember her, that gorgeous woman at the Jacaranda?'

'Yeah, course.'

'She's having a party this Saturday. In the afternoon.'

'In the afternoon?'

'Yeah.'

'What's the bad news?'

'You're not invited.'

'You're kidding.'

I shook my head: 'Fraid not.'

'Are you invited?'

'Very definitely.'

'Jesus.'

'It's alright, I'll tell you what it was like, what she was wearing, what she said to me – all that kind of thing.'

'Shit.'

'Yeah, I'm really looking forward to it. I bet you're really pissed off. I know I would be.'

We drank beer.

'And I'm really not invited?'

'Yeah, course you are. Carlton just phoned. She asked him very specifically to invite both of us.'

'Brilliant,' Steranko said, smiling.

'We can ask Freddie to come too,' I said.

Steranko nodded: 'She's so beautiful.'

'Yeah, isn't she.'

'What about Carmel? D'you fancy her?'

'No. Do you?' One of the women opposite us glanced across disapprovingly but didn't say anything.

'Not really. What about Manda?'

'Not really.'

'No, me neither.'

This was one of the irritating aspects of my friendship with Steranko. We both tended to fancy the same women – and they tended to fancy him. We looked similar but it was always Steranko they went for.

'I've got some good news for you too,' Steranko said after a while.

'What's that?'

'I've got that money I owe you.'

'Great.'

I swallowed the rest of my beer in a big gulp just as time was called. The two women next to us started putting on extra layers of clothing and then picked up two crash-helmets. We left soon after them, just in time to see them roaring off down the road, hunched over a powerful motorbike.

On the way home I stopped off at Steranko's to pick up the money he owed me. I put two ten-pound notes in my shoe and a fiver in the cheap wallet that I always carried. Apart from that fiver the only things in it were cancelled bank cards and library tickets. There was nothing paranoid about doing this – like taking a quick look down a dark street before turning into it or walking on the outside of the pavement, I did it as automatically as a driver putting on a seatbelt. It was always a good idea to have some money you could get at quickly if you got jumped. Unlike Carlton, Freddie and Steranko I'd never actually been mugged but I knew that nine times out of ten you handed over the money and nothing much happened. It was when you didn't have any money that things got nasty.

Pursued by the tolling of the town-hall clock I left Steranko's at midnight and walked home through drizzle so fine it was hardly more than a damp breeze. Behind me I heard the sound of running. I turned round, feeling the first warning shock of adrenalin, my arm half raised to protect myself, as someone charged past. A few seconds later he disappeared round a corner, still running, feet slapping hard on the wet pavement. My heart was beating fast. People tended not to run like that after dark round here. It was like a false alarm that set others on edge and made them nervous — it looked too much like you were running away from something.

054

THAT WAS ON Wednesday. On Saturday morning Carlton and Freddie called for me and the three of us called for Steranko.

We trooped up the stairs to his room, opened the door and found that everything in it had been moved round. Steranko did this from time to time, turning his room from a place of relaxation into an obstacle course for living in. There were coloured scaffolding poles everywhere, the bed was perched up on a platform of planks about six feet in the air and most of the other things he used regularly – record-player, books – were stored well above eye-level. If you went to bed drunk and got up for a piss in the night it seemed unlikely that you'd be able to find your way back to the bed. Steranko was nowhere to be seen. Freddie called his name and Steranko's head appeared over the side of the bed.

'Shit, what time is it?' he said, still half-asleep.

'Twelve thirty.'

Carlton dumped a pile of clothes on the floor and sat on the seat they'd been occupying. I looked out of the window which was thick with grime that the sun arranged in patterns. To the left of the window there was an easel with the beginnings of a painting. Propped up against one wall was a battered-looking cello. Steranko had lain back on the bed and disappeared from view. He reappeared a few moments later, yawning and rubbing his head.

'How come you're here so early?'

'You said come round for breakfast before Foomie's party.'

'Did I?'

'No but we came anyway,' said Freddie. There was some rustling up on the bed. Steranko pulled on a dressing-gown and swung himself down to ground level.

'So what's this supposed to be?' Carlton asked, gesturing towards the bed. 'Urban Tarzan or what?'

'It's my experiment in negative ergonomics. An attempt to turn the fabric of the everyday inside out. It's pretty exhausting.'

'I bet. So that's why the bed's up there . . .'

'A man's bed should be like an eagle's nest – Nietzsche said that,' explained Steranko.

'Did he fuck,' said Carlton.

'What he really said was only a fool goes to bed while he could still be working,' said Freddie. 'He used to sleep about half an hour a day in his bed and spend the rest of the time nodding off at his desk because he couldn't bear the idea of being proved stupid by his own logic. That's what I call will power.'

Steranko grunted and headed towards the bathroom.

'Have you still got that trumpet Steranko?' Carlton asked.

'It's over there in that case. You want to buy it?'

'Maybe.'

'I thought I was buying that,' I said. Hearing Carlton say he was interested in the trumpet made me suddenly certain that I wanted to buy it. Up until then I hadn't been bothered one way or the other.

'First come first served. Maybe you'd be better off with the cello,' he said, glancing towards it and then going out the door. A great variety of musical instruments passed through Steranko's hands. He picked them up cheaply, learned to play them a little, and then sold them.

Carlton took the trumpet from its case, inserted the mouth-piece and made a few screeching blasts. There was no hint of a note let alone a tune but he was wearing a suit and looked good ('a little like the young Miles Davis even,' said Freddie).

When he had finished I picked up the trumpet and blew loud and tunelessly. Freddie meanwhile was sawing away at the cello and by the time Steranko got back from the bathroom Carlton was banging out random notes on the out-of-tune piano in the corner.

'Jesus, what a fucking racket,' Steranko said, rubbing his face with a towel.

'It's free-form, man,' Carlton said. 'Collective improvisation.' Freddie and I sniggered; Steranko looked pissed off.

'I've only been awake five minutes,' he said.

'How much do you want for the trumpet then,' Carlton asked.

'Twenty-five quid.'

'Thirty,' I said, gazumping Carlton.

'Do I hear thirty-five?' Steranko said, buttoning up his trousers.

'You'll never learn to play it,' Carlton said.

'Probably not but at least I'll stop you getting it,' I said.

'You can have it,' said Carlton, 'and I bet in six months you still can't play anything remotely resembling "My Funny Valentine".'

'I only want to play "The Last Post" anyway,' I said. 'Something to bring tears to my eyes.'

'I bet a fiver you've given it up completely in a month,' Carlton said.

'You're on,' I said, extending my hand. 'Shake.'

'Two months,' said Carlton extending his.

'Actually now that you don't want it I'm not sure I'll even buy it,' I said, withdrawing mine.

'Jesus,' said Steranko, putting a record on the turntable. 'What a kid.' A few moments later the clean, intelligent emotion of Jan Garbarek's tenor filled the room. Audible landscapes formed and re-formed themselves around us. Morning music, mist melting in the sun.

'It's going to be a nice day,' Carlton said.

We went down into the kitchen where Steranko stirred a saucepan of porridge. He made porridge perfectly and patiently and ate it every day regardless of the weather.

When it was ready he filled four bowls. Carlton dumped in a lot of brown sugar and then some more after he'd taken one mouthful. It was still too hot to eat. We blew on it. Carlton poured more sugar in.

'I'm surprised you've got any teeth left. Jesus,' said Steranko.

We were all blowing on our porridge and taking gasped spoonfuls from round the edge. It felt like it was burning my stomach.

'Beautiful,' said Carlton when it had cooled down enough to eat.

'You sure it's sweet enough?'

When we'd finished Steranko chucked the bowls in the sink and we went back up to his room. While Steranko finished getting ready Carlton fiddled around with the cello.

'Can you play this?' he asked, leaning it back against the chair.

'Not really,' Steranko said. He reached for the cello, settled himself behind it, ran the bow across the strings a couple of times and then played what was recognisably the beginning of Bach's first cello suite. Freddie, Carlton and I clapped.

'That's all I know,' Steranko said, smiling.

Carlton had to call for Belinda but Steranko, Freddie and I arrived together at Foomie's place. The party was already in full swing. Foomie smiled warmly at both Steranko and me and said how glad she was that we could come. We introduced her to Freddie and they said hello and smiled at each other. Foomie was in a black sleeveless dress. Her hair was piled up and tied in a bright scarf and she wore big gold earrings. She asked if we wanted some punch but the three of us, at exactly the same moment, all said 'BEER'. The single perfectly synchronised syllable belched loudly into the room, followed quickly by three separate mumbles of 'please'. I could feel myself blushing.

'Help yourself,' Foomie said, pointing to the neat stack of cans on a sturdy table. The doorbell rang and she went to answer it, leaving the three of us standing in an awkward huddle.

'I think we really made an impression there,' Freddie said.

'Jesus, what a start,' Steranko said and then we just stood there, drinking fast and looking round. There was a lot to drink but there were a lot of people to drink it as well. I opened a second can. Soul records were playing in another room.

Steranko and Freddie drifted off. I stood in a corner, feigning intensity until Mary came over and handed me a joint. I remembered Mary from years ago when she would ask, wide-eyed, if Robert Mugabe was the fat one or the other one but in the last year she had suddenly got politics – it was like she'd received them in the post after a slight delay somewhere along the line. I liked Mary but her zest for arguing things through was sometimes a little wearying. After a film she always insisted that the sex scenes were pornographic, that the rape scene suggested that women liked being raped, that the husband's slapping his wife endorsed violence against women and so on. She recounted arguments with people where they had said they weren't interested in politics and she had responded by pointing out that everything is political. Her favourite expressions were 'offensive' and 'ideologically unsound'. The latter she used so often that it was virtually a form of punctuation, occasionally reversing its meaning and using it as an indication of unqualified approval as in 'ideologically sound'. Mostly, though, she preferred it in the negative mode when referring to buying Jaffa oranges, having service washes at the laundry or reading Martin Amis.

Now she was explaining to me how we were all bisexual really.

'But I don't want to sleep with men,' I said.

'How do you know you don't?'

'That's a daft question: you might just as well ask me how I know I don't want to eat concrete. I just don't want to.'

'That depends on how deeply you may have repressed the homosexual side of your character.'

'I think I'd know by now if I had any homosexual inclinations.'

'Not when you're brought up in a culture that makes you think of homosexuality as abnormal, wrong.'

'I still think I'd know by now.'

'How do you feel about gay men?'

'Fine.'

'Are any of your friends gay?'

'Not close friends really.'

'Are you homophobic?'

'No, I've just said: hardly any of my best friends are gay.'

'What?'

'Well all the time we're told that every anti-Semite or racist starts by saying that some of his best friends are Jews or blacks or whatever . . .'

'Very funny.'

'True too, actually. Almost all of my best friends are heterosexual.'

'D'you ever hug your friends?' (Talking with Mary I quite often had the impression that I was being vetted for membership of some obscure new men's group.)

'No.'

'What if one of them needed comforting?'

'Comforting and hugging aren't the same thing. Personally, I've never really taken much comfort from being hugged.'

'And what about kissing? When you meet women you know you kiss them. Why don't you kiss the men you know?'

'I don't always kiss the women I know. Generally I prefer to shake hands with people. The handshake is one of the great conventions of civilised living. Kissing is something else altogether.'

'In different cultures men kiss each other.'

'But we're in this culture. Men kissing each other in this culture is just an affectation.'

'What about crying? D'you feel embarrassed about it? D'you think men shouldn't cry?'

'I prefer it when they don't.'

'When did you last cry?'

'I can't remember. Ages ago.'

'That's terrible.'

'Look, I mean crying is not that easy. It's not something

that comes naturally. You have to work at it like everything else. What's so special about crying anyway?'

'There's nothing special about crying. It's just that men are conditioned to repress their feelings. Do you ever touch your male friends?'

'Well we touch each other for a drink now and again . . .'

'Now you're just being sarcastic.'

'No I'm not and no I don't touch my friends that much. But what's so special about touching? I hate this facile equation of tactility with intimacy.'

'Men are incapable of expressing affection for one another.'

'Listen,' I said, dimly aware that I was using the bigot's prefixes, 'look' and 'listen', as if I were issuing instructions on kerb drill. 'Look, women are always accusing men of reducing affection to sex, yeah?'

'It's true – they do.'

'But in arguing that men can't express affection for each other because they're frightened of touching each other you duplicate exactly that reduction of the expression of affection to the physical.'

'Rubbish.'

'Look . . .'

'There's no need to shout . . .' (A purely rhetorical ploy, this, designed to make me shout.)

'I'm not shouting,' I said, bait taken, voice raised.

'All men – or most men – it seems to me, are constantly competing, just like you've turned this conversation into a competition.'

'No I haven't.'

'Men are always bullying, either bullying women or trying to prove they've got a bigger dick than the next man . . .'

'These are just clichés,' I interrupted rudely. 'You think in clichés – more recent ones than those you oppose but they're clichés all the same.'

'You're the one that's coming out with clichés. And you're being rude . . .'

'No I'm not.'

'Anyway I'm bored with this conversation. Let's talk about

something else.' For the next couple of minutes we weaned ourselves off rhetoric and back on to pleasantries. We talked about what we'd been doing and stuff like that and then Mary went off to get another drink.

I crossed the room to where Freddie was talking energetically to someone about writing. You had to hand it to him: he really looked the part. He was wearing a corduroy jacket, suede shoes and a tie. Every now and then he took his glasses out of his jacket pocket, put them on and took them off again. ('My new affectation', he'd once described it as, 'one part Morrissey to one part George Steiner.')

'*I always wanted to be a writer*,' he was saying. 'Now that is the tense of great fiction. Only really great writers get a chance to come out with that kind of thing.'

'Did you always want to be a writer?' said the woman he was talking to.

'I got forced into it. I mean I got fed up doing nothing. Now most days I still do nothing but at least I feel I'm meant to be doing something. As an incentive I pay myself psychological overtime: time-and-a-half after seven o'clock, double-time after midnight, triple-time at weekends. So if I put in a good four or five hours on a Sunday I can take the rest of the week off,' said Freddie, pausing to swallow a mouthful of beer and then tossing away the empty can. 'And that's the really great thing about writing: you can take a whole week off and nobody is going to give a shit: that's the kind of powers writers wield. They can withdraw their labour at any moment – no need to ballot – and that's fine by everybody. Nobody's going to dock your wages, nobody's going to get shit-face if you turn up at your desk hungover or late and knock off at four o'clock after a two-hour lunch-break. A toss is exactly what no one will give about anything you do.'

At the end of this little speech – I'd heard earlier drafts at other parties – Freddie looked as if he would have appreciated a round of applause. I handed him a can of lager instead.

'You ought to read the book he's writing,' said Steranko to the woman they were talking to. 'It's a work of Tolstoyan banality. One of the few truly dispensable works of our time.'

'What's it about, your book?' the woman asked.

'It's a memoir of life at the eastern end of the Central line. I'm calling it "Look Back in Ongar".' At the very least I had heard Freddie make this joke ten times in the last two years. It was what he called one of his 'Classic Standards' and he showed no signs of ever getting fed up hearing himself say it.

'And what do you do?' the woman asked Steranko.

'I'm an artist,' he said.

'The only thing he's got in common with an artist,' said Freddie, 'is he gets cramp in the same wrist.'

'Jesus,' said Steranko.

Foomie came over, smiling, pouring wine and putting her arm around the woman Freddie and Steranko were speaking to.

'So you've met the beer boys Caroline?' she said, much less formal with us once she could mediate her comments through a friend. Steranko, Freddie and I stumbled over each other trying to make jokes.

'D'you three live together?' Caroline asked during a pause in all this verbal jockeying for position.

'We ride together,' said Freddie before going off to get some food.

Foomie talked to Steranko and me but however hard she tried to share what she said evenly between us it was obvious that the conversation was taking place on a slope, tilting away from me towards Steranko. If Steranko was talking to Caroline I could tell that Foomie was half listening to what they were saying. Her eyes lingered on Steranko when he spoke.

Someone tapped Caroline on the shoulder. I moved over to the drinks table where someone handed me another joint. The centipede rhythms of salsa snaked out from the room next door. Laughing loudly Belinda came through the door, followed by Carlton who was wearing the same dark suit he'd had on earlier. Picking up another can of warm beer I went over and kissed Belinda. As I shook hands with Carlton someone kicked me lightly on the back of the leg.

'Go on: give him a big kiss,' Mary said, winking and then walking off again.

Foomie came over and kissed Belinda and Carlton. Freddie came back, holding a plateful of chicken something.

'Look at Steranko,' Belinda said. 'In a suit he always looks like he's just got out of prison or the army.'

'What bollocks,' said Carlton. 'He looks like he's just got out of art school.'

'I tell you, I'd hate to live in a time when men didn't wear suits,' said Freddie who wasn't actually wearing one.

'I'd hate to live in a time when women didn't wear dresses,' said Foomie.

'Me too,' said Belinda. 'But I'd also hate to live in a time when you had to wear one.'

'Suits and dresses,' said Freddie. 'When I'm wearing a suit I always wish I was wearing a shoulder-holster too.'

'I even like the words connected with suits,' I said. 'Lapel, vent, turn-up . . .'

'You feel good in a suit,' Carlton said.

'Not as good as you feel in a dress on a boiling hot day,' said Foomie.

'I don't think I've ever had a suit that's quite fitted properly,' I said.

'A suit shouldn't fit properly,' said Freddie, a sudden gleam of illumination in his eyes. 'If it fits properly it doesn't fit properly.'

'What shit you talk Freddie.'

'Let's face it though,' said Carlton, buttoning up his jacket for emphasis. 'Suits only really came into their own when blacks started wearing them.'

'Just like everything else,' said Belinda.

'In fact, let's be honest about it: suits always look better on black people,' Carlton said.

'What about Lee Marvin in "Point Blank"? That's a great suit.'

'Not as good as Sidney Poitier's in "In the Heat of the Night".'

I went to the bathroom for a piss, leafing through a couple of pamphlets on cystitis and thrush while I was at it. When

I came back Freddie was giving everyone a lecture about Hemingway and the lost generation, leaning against a wall as though he needed to.

'It's meaningless. Every generation wants to think it's lost. Take us. Who could have been more lost than us? We're so lost we're virtually extinct,' he said and everyone laughed. 'As far as I can see there are only two things to be glad about. We were just old enough and just young enough to realise the full joy of short hair. And we were just about on cue for the jazz revival. Obviously it would have been better to have been in on it first time round but that's the way things happen these days. History is like the Cup Final: if you miss it in the afternoon you can always catch the highlights later on in the evening when it's shown again. As for politics, well, you might as well forget it. I mean I wasn't even able to vote in the last election . . .'

'Nor me,' said Foomie. 'I wasn't registered in time.'

'Nor me,' said Steranko.

'Me neither,' I said.

'What about you Lin?' She nodded and so did Carlton.

'Look at that. It's incredible. Four people out of six – two people out of three – don't even have the vote! Our being on the left means nothing. It means we hang around with certain kinds of people – people like us – but beyond that it means nothing. All it does is underwrite our friendships and provide a kind of shared language, a foundation of broadly shared values. None of us really has anything to do with politics. We sneer at the way the news is presented on TV but nothing we feel has any effect on anyone else. It's not our fault. That's just how things have turned out.'

I didn't know whether I agreed with this or not and Freddie probably didn't either.

'People of our generation aren't able to die for good causes any longer. We had all that done for us in the sixties when we were still kids,' said Steranko. 'There are plenty of good brave causes left but there's nothing we can do about them.'

The afternoon passed quickly as we all got more drunk and stoned. People kept arriving. Juggernaut funk, agile, cumbersome and moving at high speed, thumped around the flat. Carlton and I were in the kitchen with Belinda, scoffing French bread and hummus.

'How's your group going?' I said, searching through the kitchen drawers for a corkscrew.

'We split up,' said Belinda as someone else came into the kitchen. Belinda introduced her to Carlton and me. Her name was Monica and she was wearing a green cardigan. Her ripped Levis were three or four sizes too big, gathered in at the waist by a leather belt. She had light, wavy brown hair and wore earrings and no make-up. She talked to Belinda while I continued my hunt for a corkscrew.

Eventually I turned to Monica and said, 'I don't suppose you've got a Swiss army knife have you?' She reached into her pocket and pulled one out. 'You modern women.'

We talked for a while but by this time I was well past my best, not far off my worst in fact. I sprayed breadcrumbs when I spoke.

After not very long she said, 'I've got to go.'

'OK. I'll call you sometime maybe.'

'OK.'

'Have you got a pen?'

'No.'

'Nor have I,' I said, feeling in my pockets. 'I'll memorise it.'

'You memorise it, man,' Carlton laughed. 'You can't even remember your own phone number.'

'That's where you're wrong Carlton. My memory has never been in better shape. I answered one of those ads in the Sunday paper. Now I can even remember what I was doing on the day George Best quit football.'

'What were you doing?'

'I haven't the faintest idea. Now Veronica, go ahead.'

'Ready?'

'Sure.'

'Five . . .'

'Five . . .' I repeated.

'Five . . .'

'Five . . .'

'Five . . . Five . . .'

'Double five . . .' I said, concentrating hard.

'Five . . .' she continued. 'Five . . .'

'That's it,' she said.

'Hey, listen I know that's not a real number,' I said.

'Why?'

'It's only got six digits. London numbers have seven.'

'I'll see you around,' she said, smiling and leaving.

'I think you're in there,' Carlton said, watching her go through the door.

I looked out of the kitchen and into the living-room which had thinned out now. There were more empty bottles than people. Foomie was sitting on the arm of the sofa, talking to Steranko who had taken off his jacket and was propped up against a wall and drinking from a can like some swilled-out Valentino. She was laughing. Her hand rested on his for a moment as she said something I couldn't hear.

053

SOMETHING WAS HAPPENING. You could tell something was happening by the way everybody was asking everybody else what was happening. Railton Road was cordoned off. Police were everywhere. I was back in the DIY shop, wishing I measured things more accurately. Unable to find a tape measure I'd spent the morning calculating distances in terms of LP covers and Penguin books – quite a satisfying activity in an imprecise sort of way – and now, with the help of one of the assistants, I was busily converting everything back into feet and inches.

Ten minutes later all the stock from outside was bundled in and the shutters were yanked down.

'There's going to be a riot,' claimed the manager with conviction, ushering customers out of the shop. Hardly a day goes by in the summer without a riot being predicted: it's done like farmers forecasting the weather ('red sky in the evening, the ghetto is burning') but with less accuracy. Outside everyone just milled around while the diverted traffic congealed around them. I trudged back to my cave, eighteen foot (approximately) of shelving digging into my collar-bone.

From the roof of my block I looked out over the streets but everything was quiet, except for Concorde booming modernly overhead.

People were still talking about what had happened late that afternoon when I went over to Terry's, the greengrocer on Tulse Hill.

'The police raided a couple of houses on Railton Road,' Terry explained to a shopful of customers.

'They came down on the train,' said a woman with pink streaks in her hair. 'Like football hooligans.'

Terry was a big white guy whose thinning blond hair made him look older than he was. The shop was open till seven six days a week and until lunchtime on a Sunday. Terry was always there; even when he was out at the market picking up new produce in his van he was somehow still in the shop. Not only was he always there, he was always in a good mood. Whatever time of the day you went in he was joking or shouting hello to somebody. Such was the value everyone placed on Terry's high opinion of them that no one even dreamed of ripping stuff off or getting impatient or swearing because of the queue.

As well as all the usual fruit and veg he stocked a full range of West Indian vegetables and an array of wholewheat bread, natural yoghurt, free range eggs, tofu and vegan cheese. At the same time he kept an eye on tradition with a few packs of bacon and pork sausages stashed away in the fridge. Although it wasn't actually on a corner, Terry's was the heir to the idea of the corner shop but it also represented an unusual alliance of hard-working grocer shop economics with the anarcho-vegetarian culture of the inner city. One way and another he kept everyone happy.

I was just coming out of the shop when I bumped into Steranko and Carlton, both stoned and wanting something to eat. I offered to cook them an omelette and the three of us walked back to my flat. It was the first time they'd been there since I moved in.

'Shit, it smells like a skunk's toilet,' Carlton said as we made our way up the stairs, past marker-pen signatures and purple band-names in fluorescent Bronx script.

'What d'you call that?' said Steranko a few minutes later as the reinforced door clanged shut behind us. 'Lubyanka chic?'

Carlton laughed: 'Man, you might as well go the whole way – get yourself a drawbridge and portcullis while you're at it. Look at this,' he said, picking up the entry-phone by the door. 'When you get really paranoid you can just pick this up and *listen* to the outside world . . . Is there anybody there? Is there anybody there?'

With that they went through to the main room and lurched around there for a while. The day before I'd bought some flowers and put them in a jug on the window-sill: they had elegant green stems and purple petals with yellow dots. Carlton looked at the jug of flowers and said, 'Even *here* there is life.'

'Nice isn't it?' I prompted.

'Not exactly cosy is it?'

'Course it isn't cosy. It's cosier than that place you live in. All you've got in that room is bare boards. Besides, comfort can never do as verb what it boasts as noun.'

'Who said that?'

'Guess.'

'Freddie?'

I nodded.

'You know what sort of block this is?' said Carlton, gazing out of the window.

'Not really.'

'It's the kind of block where people draw their curtains early.'

'Look at this,' I said when we were back in the kitchen, turning on the hot-water tap and letting it run.

'So? You've got hot water,' said Steranko. 'Very twentieth century.'

'It's free. You can waste as much as you want. You can leave it running all night if you want . . .'

Later that evening, weighed down by large slices of an unappetising Spanish omelette, we walked down to the Atlantic. A lot of police were still around, walking the streets in twos and threes or waiting in buses parked some distance off in case anything happened. Groups of black and white youths were walking round too, falling silent as they passed the grim-faced police. The Atlantic was right at the focus of all this activity. It used to be a dingy boozer; then it got to be very popular as people were drawn there by the slight uneasiness as well as the fact that there was live jazz and the bar stayed open until midnight. After eleven it tended to fill up with people from the Albert, the pub across the road that was always packed with trendies complaining about how trendy and packed it was. The Atlantic was also well known as the place you could buy grass – an arrangement that suited everyone, dealers and punters alike, since the beer was awful and spilled out of the taps like watered-down piss. A lot of good musicians played there and even if they weren't so hot the place always gave an edgy intensity to their playing.

It was a warm evening and people had spilled out on to the pavement, the sheer sound of trumpet and saxophone slashing brightly into the dark street. The trumpet held notes that were long and high as a tightrope stretched out across the night.

When the band had played a quick encore more people came outside and stood around talking and drinking. Police vans cruised slowly past. No bottles smashed against their windscreens.

People began leaving the pub and we started walking home. Steranko turned right at the top of Cold Harbour Lane and Carlton dashed for a bus, waving to me as it pulled away. There was hardly anyone around. A few cars went past. It occurred to me that the whole idea of street life in this country came into existence at exactly the moment when, it was claimed, the streets became unsafe to walk in, when crime began destroying a way of life that had never actually existed.

A couple of young guys, one of whom I vaguely recognised, walked towards me. He nodded, 'Ah right.'

'OK.'

I walked slowly, enjoying the feel of the warm night and the clouds drifting like whales across the sky.

FOR THE REST of that week I had some work with a market research company. On the way home one evening I dropped in at the Effra. Freddie was there, pissed off and standing by the bar on his own. That morning he'd been burgled.

'What did they take?'

'Stereo, records, camera.'

'You insured?'

'Yeah. It's just the fucking hassle. They got in through the window and found a spare set of keys which they took so I had to spend the whole day getting new locks fitted. A hundred quid. Shit. I'm so fucked off. Guess how many burglaries there were in Brixton last night?'

'I don't know.'

'Twenty-five. That's what the cop who came round told me. He said he'd never known a night like it. I think there was even an element of pride in his voice as he said it.'

I laughed and bought Freddie another beer.

'This weather is so weird too,' he said, draining his old glass. 'Is it hot? Is it cold? It's not even that easy to tell whether or not it's raining. The seasons are all dissolving into each other. Look at it: it's supposed to be September and it looks like snow. I'm beginning to think the weather reports are government controlled, censored. They probably change the records to make out that thirty inches of rain is normal for August. I'm sure it never used to rain that much. People wouldn't have stood for it. There'd have been a revolution. They can't let the truth out because they know there'd be panic. The forecasts are just government propaganda. They say it's going to brighten up by the late afternoon and it's still pissing down at seven. The wonder is that people still go on believing them.'

Freddie was clearly in the mood to complain. I nodded my head in agreement.

'Mary says the weather is determined by the economic structure of society; it's all related to that economic base. We get the weather we deserve,' I said.

'Yes, we can't afford good weather anymore. We probably sold it all to America. That's why we get all this drizzle. It's the perfect weather for a declining industrial power,' said Freddie, groaning as he saw Ed making his way towards us. Ed was a manic depressive and like all manic depressives you never saw him manic, only depressed. You had to take his word for the mania and that was difficult because he communicated mainly in grunts and lumps of sentences that were swallowed as soon as spoken. Not only that but he never looked you in the eyes when he spoke; he looked at the rings and squiggles of beer that he traced on the bar with his fingers. He never bought anybody a drink and he always accepted one from somebody else grudgingly, as if he was doing so at considerable personal inconvenience. He never made jokes or laughed at other people's – as far as he was concerned, there was nothing much to laugh at, the state of the class struggle being what it was. The nearest he got to a smile was a sneer and for entertainment he rolled his own cigarettes.

Freddie slurped gloomily at his beer while I exchanged a few words with Ed. After a couple of minutes he trudged over to someone else.

'Thank God we didn't have to put up with him. He's like human drizzle,' said Freddie, putting down his glass. 'So what's this job like you're doing?'

'Boring as shit.'

'What d'you have to do?'

'Code and check questionnaires before the results are put through the computer. I'm working with this other bloke, a friend of Carlton's. There's no room for us in the main office so we have to work in the basement. The only time anyone comes down is when they want boxes of computer paper shifted so it's quite nice. It's so boring though. This afternoon we ended up playing Battleships. After that we just sat there and worked out how much money we were earning per minute.'

'Sounds a great job,' Freddie said. I went for a piss. When I got back Freddie's glass was empty and I asked if he wanted another. I had just ordered two more beers when Freddie touched my arm and gestured towards the door. Steranko was coming through the door – with Foomie. She was looking gorgeous and happy. I felt a jolt of shock and then a steady, draining sensation in my stomach. I was still looking at them when Steranko and then Foomie caught my eye. They made their way towards us; Freddie was already saying something to Steranko. It was one of those situations where you have either to conceal your reactions or conceal yourself behind your reactions. Smiling broadly, I leant towards them and asked what they wanted to drink.

THE GROAN OF thunder. Grey light. The cold smell of rain coming through the open window. There was the sound of a plane, soggy through the rain; the long swish and wince of cars, the sob of a police siren. I leant on the sill and watched the rain fall past the window, the trees below glistening and black. Suddenly I caught a blur of movement on the opposite roof, a shape indistinct in the drizzle. At that moment the rain began falling heavily again. I crossed the room and turned out the small reading light and went back to the window. I looked out again. For a long time I saw nothing and then, for a few seconds, I saw the shape of someone on the roof, smudged by the falling rain. The phone rang. I glanced towards it and when I looked up at the roof again there was only the rain.

I picked up the phone. It was Fran calling from a kiosk because her phone was broken. She was just calling to see how I was. Hearing the crackle of rain in the background I pictured her in the call box, hair dripping into the receiver, her hand idly wiping condensation from the fee-display.

I looked out again, my breath fogging the window. I wiped the cold glass clear, held my breath and stared out. The thump of my heart grew steadily louder. I turned my head, exhaled and breathed in deeply once again. The rain was as it sounded.

050

I DID NOT see Steranko or any of the others for several days. The market research company was conducting a survey for British Rail – What sort of tickets were people using? Where were they going? What did they think of prices? The buffet? – and I spent the next week shuttling up to Manchester and back four times a day, handing out questionnaires. On most trips it only took an hour to dish them out and then I sat back in the wide First Class seats and enjoyed the ride, reading and drinking, eating hot and cold snacks from the buffet bar, not thinking about Steranko or Foomie, just watching the damp landscape slide past the big windows.

On the last day of the survey I got back to the flat and found a note from Steranko pinned to my door: 'ON ROOF – S.' I chucked my bags in the flat and made my way up the stairs. The roof was the single best thing about the block. At the top of the stairs a door opened on to a flat concrete rectangle about the size of a tennis court, a low wall and railing running along the edge. At the other end the same arrangement was duplicated with an identical door leading to another flight of stairs and another lift. The roof of the lift-housing was also flat and since it was eight or nine feet higher it got another half an hour of sun at the end of each day – if there was any sun to have.

Steranko was reading by the light of a hurricane lamp that covered him in a warm tent of light.

'Hey, how's it going?' he said, looking up.

'OK.'

'Come over . . .' I sat on the rug next to him. Gnats

clung to the side of the lamp. Our shadows crawled the floor.

'Nice light, isn't it?'

'Beautiful. Where'd you get it?'

'This friend of Foomie's found it. She didn't want it so I cleaned it up and fixed it.' I wondered whether I should say something about Foomie and then decided against it.

'What are you reading?' I asked after a while. Steranko held up a battered paperback selection of Nietzsche.

'You read him?'

'Only odd bits.'

'Incredible. I borrowed it from Freddie. God, such a nutter.'

I flicked through some pages without reading them. The light from the hurricane lamp made the sky look dark as ink.

'You know there's football on Sunday?' I said.

'Yeah. You playing?'

'I think so, though my leg still hurts from the last game. That fucking guy.'

'Yeah it's a shame. There's nearly always somebody who's out to break your leg . . .'

We sat quietly for a few moments.

A few feet in front of us there was an unfinished sculpture of a woman, with rough-hewn head, arms and waist protruding from a block of white stone.

'Is someone who lives here sculpting that?' Steranko asked.

'Yeah, I don't know his name though.' On the afternoons that I'd been up on the roof I'd watched him work on it, enjoying the gentle tap of the chisel and the way the form of the woman slowly emerged from the hard block and the cloud of white dust.

Today had been the first time in several weeks that it had been hot and sunny; little progress had been made since I'd last seen the sculpture. The bricks of the low wall behind our backs were still faintly warm, breathing the last of their accumulated heat into the cool night air. On the roof of the opposite block I saw the dark shapes of a man and a woman, his arm around her shoulders. I waved at them and they waved back, the red glow of a cigarette tracing the movement of a hand.

'Shall we have a joint?' I said after neither of us had spoken for a while.

'Good idea.'

'Can you sort that out?' I pulled a bag of grass and some papers out of the pocket of my trousers. 'I'll bring some coffee up.'

'Hey, can you bring up your cassette player? I made this tape today – it's fucking unbelievable.'

'Sure. What's the tape?'

'It's a Mahler symphony. The third.'

Making coffee in the kitchen I thought about Foomie. There was an inevitability about her being attracted to Steranko that destroyed even the possibility of jealousy. Instead of wishing that Foomie was attracted to me I found myself wishing that I was more like Steranko. Just as there are individuals who are always on the periphery of a given group so there are those like Steranko who, you know, will always be at the defining centre of other people's lives.

By the time I came back up with everything Steranko had rolled a clumsy joint with the home-grown grass. Steam floated off the dark surface of the coffee.

We took turns pulling deeply on the joint and exhaling grey smoke that hung sweetly in the air for a moment and then disappeared. To the west the sky was tinted orange. I read odd pages of Nietzsche. My mind wandered. I imagined him in the American West selling miracle cure-all to dangerous outlaws and playing poker wildly. I pictured him on a bus, complaining that it wasn't going far enough, howling against licensing laws and not over-conscientious about getting his round in.

I was chuckling to myself, scalding my lips on the hot coffee.

'What's funny?'

'Nietzsche. Freddie ought to write a play about him and Van Gogh out on the piss together. Getting thrown out of bars and getting nowhere with women. Vincent cuts off his

81

ear and Nietszche tears off both of his own: "Just so I don't have to hear you whining!" '

Laughing, we sprayed coffee across the roof. Our giggling subsided and we watched clouds moving fast across the moon; the lights of a plane overhead. Neither of us said anything for a while. Steranko rewound and fast-forwarded the cassette player until he found the place on the tape he wanted.

'Right, this is the fourth movement: Vas meer die Nacht erzalt,' he added in Colditz German.

'What does that mean?'

'I dunno. Something, something, night, something.' Our laughter floated away and quietness gathered round us. The noise of the traffic was still there but quieter, further off, like the sea at low tide. Sheets hung out to dry on the opposite block, visible only as grey squares in the darkness, shrugged in the breeze. There was no sign of the couple we'd seen earlier. A few lights were on. The steady flame of the hurricane lamp, the tape running noiselessly. Then, hardly audible, barely distinguishable from the silence that preceded it, came the sound of a woman's voice.

Each syllable was like a breath, insubstantial as the night air. The voice was so frail a gust of wind could have blown it away. The singer's lone voice gathered the night's silence into itself and slowly overcame it, pulling itself out of the silence like the sculptured form of the woman, pulling herself clear of the rock. The voice continued its long, slow ascension, angular syllables stretched out and hanging for long seconds in the darkness.

O Mensch! O Mensch!
Tief! Tief! Tief ist ihr Weh!
Tief ist ihr Weh!

The voice came from the throat of the darkness. The light from the hurricane lamp wavered.

Steranko leafed through the grimy pages of the book, folded it back on itself and passed it to me without speaking. Half his face was in shadow. In the vacancy left by the music, in the silence that craved the lone voice of the woman, I read:

> What, if some day or night a demon were to steal after you into your loneliest loneliness and say to you: 'This life as you now live it and have lived it, you will have to live once more and innumerable times more; and there will be nothing new in it, but every pain and every joy and every thought and sigh and everything unutterably small or great in your life will have to return to you, all in the same succession and sequence – even this spider and this moonlight between the trees, and even this moment and I myself. The eternal hourglass of existence is turned upside down again and again, and you with it, speck of dust!'
>
> Would you not throw yourself down and gnash your teeth and curse the demon who spoke thus? Or have you once experienced a tremendous moment when you would have answered him: 'You are a god and never have I heard anything more divine.'

The words broke over me. I stared into the dark sky above and around us. The night remembered the voice. The night remembered how the voice had needed the night. There were no stars, only the red and white blink of a plane, the steady flicker of the hurricane lamp.

049

SOMETHING ABOUT THAT evening made me think of a day several years ago when I hardly knew Steranko. I was sitting in the Arizona, a cafe near the house on Water Lane where we spent a lot of time, reading the papers, chewing bacon sandwiches and ordering tea. Stan, who ran it, thought we were students who'd squatted a place nearby. To him that made us the lowest form of life imaginable, exactly the kind of people, in other words, that his establishment took pride in catering for. When we started going there builders from a nearby site would come in at about eleven thirty and start wading into cardiac-sized plates of eggs, chips, beans and fried ketchup. Gradually the reputation of Stan's cafe spread like the smell of eggs and soon its clientèle was made up entirely of squatters, students, anarchists and hopeful intellectuals looking for authentic proletarian experience. The builders drifted away; lorry drivers came from miles around to avoid the place. It got more and more crowded. One day the restaurant critic from *Time Out* showed up and selected it as one of the best vegetarian restaurants south of the river. It soon became the kind of place in which a working knowledge of the novels of Jack Kerouac was preferred if not actually required.

It was a freezing January afternoon when Steranko came round. He'd called at the house and been directed over to Stan's by our next door neighbour who said some of us were sure to be there. We shook hands and he ordered a plateful of everything.

At that time Steranko was living in a house near Vauxhall.

He suggested we spend the rest of the afternoon over there. I had nothing else to do so we paid and left.

Outside the wind cut through our clothes and crashed into our nostrils. As soon as you set foot outside what you most wanted to do was get back inside. Even the wind wanted to be indoors. It howled and twisted round blocks of flats, trying to squeeze through windows and force its way in through a few inches of open door. The sky was a charcoal smudge of clouds. A couple of blown-out umbrellas rolled around. What I thought was some new kind of bird – square, black, shiny – turned out to be a piece of black polythene kicked around by the wind. The restless sound of empty cans.

We saw a couple of buses coming and started to run for the stop. Two 3s and then, a little way behind them, another, hurtled past in convoy, half-empty.

'Shit.'

'Three 3s.'

'That's the best combination of buses you can get,' Steranko said, breathing hard. 'It beats anything.'

'There won't be any more buses for a couple of days now,' I said peering at the timetable. It was all pearled up with frost, impossible to read.

'Fuck it. Let's walk,' said Steranko.

We walked quickly, both wearing the same dark grey overcoats that were several sizes too big and weighed so much that you slouched under them. Mine had no buttons left; I kept it together with a massive old belt my grandfather had used to strap my father. We had our collars turned up against the wind; our breath clouded and disappeared quickly. The pavement felt hard, cold and brittle beneath our feet. Our shoulders bumped together. Steranko sniffed and wiped his nose with the back of his hand. Heavy with grit, the wind skated across the adventure playground and chiselled away at our faces.

'I wish I had my gloves,' I said. 'I left them at home.'

'At least you don't have to worry about losing them,' said Steranko.

We took a short-cut to Stockwell across the railway bridge which was covered in a caged hoop of wire netting, either to stop people throwing themselves under trains or to stop kids throwing bricks through the driver's window: both probably. A small boy trundled past us on one of those bikes that all the kids have. A white guy walked past looking desperate behind thick glasses.

The wind swept down on us like a slide as we made our way towards the tundra wastes of Vauxhall. By now we were feeling warm from the walk. The wind blew back Steranko's hair. His face looked hard and white, his lips pale. The sky was sooty with rain, full of all the misery of the city. It began to grow dark quickly. Bus windows became moving squares of light framing ghastly faces. Lights appeared in windows, brake lights left a ghost trail of red above the road.

At Vauxhall, where the streets widen and routes converge until there is nothing but roadway, the streetlights glowed red and then yellow. The wind, damp with spray from the river, stung our faces. I pulled the lapels of my coat together again, trying to seal in the warmth generated by the walk. My nose was running. I sniffed and my breath rippled and fanned out into the air like fog. The neon lights of a garage stood out brightly against the dark blue sky and the darker grey of the clouds. Cars hurtled past each other, across the river and down under the railway bridge.

Standing there, waiting for the lights to change, I felt a strong sense of converging definition. It was one of those moments which, even as experienced, is obscurely touched by the significance with which it will be invested by the future, by memory: this is how I was, this is how we were; this is how we spent our time, wasting whole afternoons and not caring because it was winter and there were so many afternoons still ahead.

Steranko touched my sleeve: 'Let's cross,' he said and we stepped out into the road, weaving our way between the red and white lights and the steaming breath of cars.

'Look,' said Steranko suddenly as we walked down a narrow street. A toy parachute was tangled up in some phone lines overhead. Lit by the yellow glow of a street-lamp the tattered parachute flapped quietly; hanging from damp strings a grey plastic soldier swayed stiffly in the wind.

As we walked the last few hundred yards to Steranko's house we passed the gas works. There were two gasometers, both full to the brim with gas and looking like huge, rusting drums.

By the time I walked home later that night, one of them had become a skeleton frame of metal spars that held only the empty sky. The tattered parachute still hung from the phone lines.

048

CARLTON, STERANKO AND I called for Freddie on our way to play football. His room was full of books and bits of paper; a record was playing so loudly on his new stereo – bought with the money from his inflated insurance claim after the break-in – that we all had to shout. Steranko had his football boots tied around his neck; Freddie was on his hands and knees, looking for his.

'Where the fuck are they? I think the animal they made these boots out of is still alive. They're always scurrying off somewhere.'

'What's this record?' Steranko asked.

'What?'

'What's this record?'

'The Art Ensemble of Chicago,' Freddie said, looking under his bed. 'It's a soundtrack for a film that was never made.'

'Ah the avant garde,' said Steranko. 'Those were the days.'

'I wonder if there's an avant garde now,' I yelled.

'We'd definitely have heard of it if there was,' Freddie yelled back. 'Where the *fuck* are they?'

'You reckon?'

'Yeah. We'd probably be it if there was one,' Steranko said.

'We'd be in the guard's van more like,' said Carlton.

'There's never been an avant garde in this country,' Steranko said.

'Is that true?'

'I don't know.'

'Bohemia is the last refuge of the avant garde,' said Freddie. 'Actually maybe I've got that the wrong way round.'

'How's the writing going then Freddie?' said Carlton, kicking the football skilfully from one foot to the other without letting it bounce.

'Terrific. If that ball lands on my new turntable, by the way, I'll be very upset. I've got some work writing copy for police Wanted notices. Apparently the police have decided that they need them done in a more punchy kind of way, a bit livelier and not so off-putting. Steranko's got some work there as well: he's assistant Photo-fit arranger. It's quite well paid.'

As Freddie finished speaking the ball bobbled awkwardly off Carlton's foot, hit the stereo and bounced towards Steranko.

'Must be the most creative thing you've done in about two years then Steranko,' said Carlton, glancing at Freddie who was storming round the room like a junkie, looking for his football boots.

'On the head, on the head,' said Carlton, gesturing at Steranko to throw the ball. Steranko did so and Carlton headed the ball as hard as he could into the door.

'Jairzinho!' he shouted. The 1970 World Cup in Mexico had made a deep impression on us all.

The music came to an end just as Freddie found his boots.

Steranko and Carlton were trying unsuccessfully to head the ball back and forth to each other.

'You nearly ready Freddie?' I asked.

'Fuck! Now I can't find my shinpads,' he said.

After the recent rain the grass was thick and green under the enamelled blue sky. Trees fanned the breeze. On the path beyond the touchline, old and young couples walked by or sat on benches.

I knew most of the rest of our team from around Brixton or parties or just from playing football. Some of us changed shirts with people in the other team until we were more or less in white shirts and they were in an assortment of colours.

I played as a sort of left-winger and after ten minutes I was breathing hard and starting to feel good. On the other wing Carlton tried to dribble past two or three men with occasional success; Steranko charged around the middle of the field (no one was quite sure where he was supposed to be playing); Freddie, who was surprisingly skilful and tenacious, played up front. As we rushed forwards and backwards my heart thumped in time with the pounding of our feet on the grass. Bracing my neck for the shock I headed the ball from a high clearance, catching it full in the forehead and hardly feeling it except for the sudden smack of impact. We dribbled, passed and ran back to tackle. Both teams clapped when their goalkeeper made a spectacular flying save from a shot by Carlton.

At half-time we drank water and didn't bother talking tactics. I lay on my back feeling the blood flowing through my limbs and the soft ground beneath my head, looking up at the still blue of the sky.

In the second half both teams tried long shots at goal and eventually we scored after a header of Freddie's bounced off the crossbar. Now that we were one-nil up they attacked more desperately but our defence tackled and headed the ball clear of danger. Steranko seemed to be concentrating on work-rate, charging around in circles.

'Oi, Steranko,' I shouted. 'You sure you wouldn't rather I just threw you a stick so you could chase after that?' He grinned back at me. People stopped and watched for a few minutes. Young boys ran to fetch the ball when it bounced out of play. I looked around. The trees around the park were perfectly still as if time had stopped, as if every second of the afternoon were held in a single moment: Steranko frozen in his running, his feet barely touching the grass; Carlton bent down tying his shoe, the breeze rippling his shirt; the muscles straining in someone's leg; players jumping for the ball, their feet suspended in mid-air, the goalkeeper's hands rising above their floating hair; the ball hanging over them like a perfect moon. And everything around us: the crease of the corner flag, the wind-sculpted trees, the child's swing at the top of its arc, the water from the drinking fountain bubbling towards the lips of the woman bent down to drink, the cyclist leaning into the curve of the path, a plane stalled in the sky, someone's thrown tennis ball a small yellow planet in the distance.

047

THE FOLLOWING WEEK I embarked on a strict régime of spontaneity. It all started with a friend in Amsterdam asking if I wanted to spend a few days there before she moved on to Istanbul. In the event I spent three days changing my mind and dithering about whether or not I could afford the flight. By the time I had finally decided to go there were no cheap flights available. As soon as it became clear that I couldn't go my desire to be in Amsterdam became almost overwhelming. I phoned back the travel agency and said I would take a slightly more expensive kind of ticket but by that time the only available tickets were for ambassador class with free champagne. The ferry was also out of the question: I would have arrived about twelve hours before my friend left. I called her, said I couldn't make it and wished her luck in Istanbul. I put the phone down and after careful consideration decided that I needed to be more impulsive. The first thing I did was buy a pair of badly-fitting brogues from a store in Camberwell. Fifteen minutes after buying them my feet felt like they were wrapped in barbed wire. Undeterred, I resolved that whatever I felt like on the spur of the moment I would do. From now on I was going to live for the moment. I even looked forward to finding opportunities in which I could exercise my spontaneity.

A couple of days later I impulsively went along to a party and spontaneously slurped five or six cans of Shaftmeister Pils. Soon after that I got into some kind of ridiculous argument with a guy of about my age and build. Things got surprisingly heated. This other guy looked pretty feeble and after a couple of minutes arguing I asked him what his problem was. He told me to go fuck myself.

'Listen, there are two ways we can do this,' I said. 'Take it from me, this is the easiest.'

I wanted it to sound full of dangerous calm and neurasthenic menace but it actually came out sounding improbable – like a film buff quoting from a movie – and inappropriate (partly because such a declaration had no logical connection with what had gone before). The guy looked at me. I tried him with an *I know I'm tough and I hope for your sake I'm not going to have to prove it* look. He responded with a *Shit, it's boring having to get into these things so we'd better get it over with* glare.

I gave him back one of the same, an *OK if that's the way you want it*. He responded with a *Right here it comes*; I gave him my *Right now you're really going to reap the whirlwind*. Privately I was thinking exactly the opposite: *Wrong, now I'm going to reap the whirlwind*. Neither of us moved a muscle. Tense seconds passed and I realised with great relief that the other guy had no more intention of fighting than I did. Eventually he shook his head and departed with a *You're not even worth the trouble* and I just had time to get in a quick *Lucky for you, mother-fucker* before he walked off. All in all it was a completely satisfactory encounter, a harmless battle of facial rhetoric – all the thrills and spills of real fighting without any of the pain. Basically we were just two drunk guys who wanted to act tough for a couple of minutes. I bumped into him at the party a few minutes later and we had quite a laugh about it.

A few minutes later somebody offered me a lift back to Brixton. Impulsively and happily I said yes and for the next half an hour I quivered in the back seat of a car with two other passengers while the driver, roaring drunk and sipping Sapporo, squealed around corners and kamikazied his way through the red lights of east and south London. Every couple of seconds I had a precise and frightening vision of a head-on collision, of getting oxy-acetylened out of the wreckage and coming round in hospital a week later while a doctor patiently explained that I was going to have to spend the rest of my life in a brain-damaged wheelchair. I got out of the car about a mile from home and walked the rest of the way, relieved to feel the blood pumping through the muscles of my still intact legs.

Waking up the next morning with the odd sensation of being surprised to be alive I threw recklessness to the wind and abandoned my spontaneity programme then and there. I was fed up with the rigours of impulsive living anyway: I didn't have the application for it. I couldn't cope with being stoned at eleven thirty in the morning and that kind of thing. Spontaneity seemed constantly to tow regret in its wake. Living for the moment was all very well, I decided, but you had to pick your moments carefully. Quite often there was another moment just around the corner which was much more worth living for than the one you were engaged in.

The phone rang. I picked it up semi-spontaneously. It was Fran.

'Hi! How's things?'

'Good. How are you?'

'Fine. Listen,' I said. 'Dad phoned the other day. He said he'd been trying your number for a week and no one knew where you were.'

'Oh shit I've been all over the place. OK, I'll phone him. How are you though? I haven't seen you for ages.'

We talked for a few more moments like that (neither of us really knew how to chat on the phone) and then arranged to meet.

Fran, I reflected when we'd hung up, was much better suited to the spontaneous lifestyle than me. She had a knack for avoiding the consequences of things. Or rather, like Steranko, she was *at ease* with the consequences of things. When we were on holiday with our parents we would go swimming together and afterwards I would always want to get dry fast and change out of my wet trunks; Fran, on the other hand, would be happy to build sandcastles or go for a walk along the cliffs in her wet costume, letting the sun and the wind dry her off. And still, as an adult, she managed to inhabit a world of action and gesture rarely seen outside the cinema, where people walk through streams without taking their boots off, or rush out into the pouring rain wearing only a shirt, or throw plates at their lover across the room in a fit of passionate rage. I'd love to do all those things – but in real life you always have to get your boots dry, or wake up with a cold, or sweep up the broken pieces and fork out for new crockery. It's the same with fighting: afterwards you have to hang around the hospital for three hours waiting to get your nose X-rayed and straightened, or you've got to take your best suit to the dry cleaners to get the blood out and the lapel stitched back on. In the cinema there are only the large consequences of plot; the mess is cleared up off-screen by stage hands; even a real trouncing leaves only a few cosmetic scars.

In cinema or books the climax of the action, however calamitous, simplifies and resolves – brings things to an end. In real life calamity and confrontation always bring chores in their wake. There are keys to return, bills to pay, the milk to cancel, people to tell and arrangements to make. It's like Othello. Two minutes after murdering Desdemona he's expecting earthquakes and eclipses and all he gets is the neighbours banging on the door wanting to know what all the noise is about. Or like a friend of mine who was stabbed and got his dole money stopped because he missed his signing-on day and hadn't filled out a sickness form while he was on a life-support machine.

046

AT THE UNDERGROUND station a group of policemen and women stopped everyone as they passed through the barriers. I joined the long queues at the ticket machines but the police had no interest in fare-dodgers: they were asking everyone if they had been using the tube at this time a week ago when a woman had been killed between Brixton and Stockwell. I shook my head and was handed a sheet of paper with MURDER and APPEAL FOR ASSISTANCE printed in large letters at the top. Underneath was a photograph of a woman. She was smiling; the photo was blurred as if it had been taken at a party where she was laughing and drunk. She was twenty-one, an African, and no one knew anything about her except that she'd been found bleeding to death in an empty carriage when the train pulled in at Stockwell.

And now, exactly a week later, I sat waiting for the train to pull out. Hunched forward and holding it in both hands like a tiny newspaper, I stared at the photo of the dead girl. On either side of me a dozen people were doing exactly the same.

FRAN CAME ROUND the next day in an expensive-looking car. I didn't know what model it was and she wasn't sure either.

'I think it's called a Vauxhall Courgette or something like that,' she said, kicking one of the front tyres as if to suggest casual familiarity with the world of pistons, cross-plys and sump oil.

'Whose car is it?' I asked as we hummed noiselessly past the new riot-proof Tesco's on Acre Lane – it had the look of a place which could be air-lifted out to neutral Vauxhall in under fifteen minutes in the event of trouble.

'It belongs to the guy who goes out with Sal in my house. He lent it to her and she lent it to me on the strict condition that I don't have a prang in it. Apparently that's what motorists call an accident: a prang.'

Fran wore her glasses to drive. They had big plastic frames that made her look almost comically scholarly. She clutched the wheel like she was steering a ship in heavy weather. We moved very slowly in dense traffic; I groaned, complained and swore but Fran, showing no sign of irritation, tapped the steering wheel to the rhythm of a pop song that played on the radio. Over the years my own impatience had become so extreme that I was in danger of becoming incapable of enjoying anything: every activity was an obstacle to the next. This accelerating impatience had nothing to do with being late or in a hurry; it was a condition not a response. I was even in a hurry when I had nothing to do. On buses I watched traffic lights compulsively, dreading a red, loving a green, happiest of all when the bus hurtled past a stop without stopping. On holiday I longed for the train journey to end and the holiday proper to begin, and then for the holiday to end and the normal routine to resume. Fran had always been different. As kids we used to go out for a drive with our parents in their sky-blue Vauxhall Victor. Our father was a very cautious driver and every time someone overtook us he would say: 'he's in a hurry' and our mother would nod wisely. It used to drive me crazy but Fran would continue looking out of the window and sucking her boiled sweet. (I'd already chewed and swallowed mine.)

'What happened to your car in the end?' she asked after a while.

'The car-breakers offered me forty quid for scrap so I traded it in for a second-hand tube pass. I miss it sometimes. The other day I was walking past a motor spares shop and I suddenly had an urge to buy some jump leads.'

'What are jump leads?'

'Don't you know what jump leads are?'

'No.'

'They're those things you lend to people when their car won't start.' Eventually we reached the Common and Fran began manoeuvring into a parking space. You'd have thought we were trying to reverse into a telephone kiosk the way she hauled the wheel first one way and then the other, crawling forwards a few inches and then lurching back after a strangled screech of protest from the gear-box.

'Shall I have a go?'

Fran got out and I slithered over into the driving seat. I twisted and shuffled through the various stages of a three-point turn until the car was parked perfectly between two other vehicles – except that it had its back to the kerb instead of its side.

'It does sort of extend itself unnecessarily at the front and back doesn't it?' Fran called to me through the open window. I extricated the car and got it parallel with the one in front, vaguely remembering that this was what you were meant to do. This time I must have got the lock just right; it started gliding into the space behind without a murmur of complaint.

Fran was directing me back with that circling motion of the hands that I always associated with the adult world of our father. I reversed another foot or so and Fran continued waving me back until I crunched into the car behind. I looked again into the mirror and saw Fran absent-mindedly urging me back.

'Dear God! I do not fucking believe it!'

'What's the matter?'

'Can't you see what's happened?' I said through my clamped, my traffic-wardened teeth. Fran looked down at the cars, surprised for a moment, then put one hand over her mouth and gave a wide-eyed chuckle.

'Ooh!'

'Fran!'

'You silly fucker!' she laughed.

'Fran!'

'What a driver!'

'Fuck sake.'

'You might have been a bit more careful,' she said between laughs. I didn't begin to see the funny side of it until seconds before it stopped being funny, when the man whose car we'd hit came bulging out of the cake shop like meat from a pasty. The first thing he saw was the cars; the second was the smile coaxing its way out of my mouth. He looked like the kind of guy who could get violently angry over something like this: a self-made man who had got where he was through hard graft and wasn't short of a tattoo or two. There was no point saying anything. It was just a question of standing there and hoping that whatever he did wouldn't hurt too much or cause any major structural damage.

'I'm sorry about this,' said Fran. 'I'm afraid we've had a bit of a prang.'

The man still didn't say anything. The bag of whatever it was he was clutching was starting to turn transparently greasy: sausage rolls perhaps. He was breathing thickly through his nose.

'Only a little prang really,' said Fran but as she was saying it the last syllable was already bubbling into a laugh. She tried to stop herself but her eyes were shining with wet laughter.

'Just the teeniest little prang,' she said, holding her thumb and index finger a fraction apart. 'And we'd be very happy to lend you our jump leads. Unfortunately we haven't got any.'

With that she doubled-up laughing. It was OK for Fran. Despite what women claim, in situations like this men are much more at risk than women. The bloke would never hit Fran – he'd hit me twice as hard and twice as often instead.

'Something wrong with her?' the man asked.

'She's my sister,' I said trying not to laugh. Laughing would have revealed my teeth and that might have tempted him to knock them out. I hadn't been hit for years. I could hardly remember what it was like but that only made the prospect more frightening – like getting stung by a wasp: I couldn't remember what that felt like either but the idea of it was terrifying.

The bloke slid into his car and moved it back a foot or two, then got out again, the engine still running. Fortunately the damage was all self-inflicted. As soon as our car had got within six inches of his it had bumpered out our rear light and punched in part of the boot.

'It's people like you,' he said looking at me and not Fran who had stopped laughing by now. 'It's people like you . . .' He left it at that. We never found out what it was that people like us did for him. He just gave me a look that said he could buy me, my sister, the car and everything in it and scrap the lot if he didn't have about a hundred other more important things to ruin first. He had some trouble squeezing the car out of the space we'd boxed him into. Fran was drying her eyes, still chuckling.

'Silly prick,' she said as he drove off.

'Shit, Fran,' I said. 'You've got to be careful with people like that.'

It was a clear but cool day. Fran was wearing a red woollen hat and a grey raincoat which she always called her 'famous blue raincoat' – she had gone through a Leonard Cohen phase a few years back – because it was torn at the shoulder.

'Anyway, it's a good job we hadn't eaten these,' she said,

100

pulling a polythene bag out of her coat pocket. 'Things might have got really out of hand.'

'Are they what I think they are?'

'Yes,' she said pouring out half the contents of the bag and handing them to me. The rest she tipped into her mouth. Wrinkling up her face she pulled a can of coke from another pocket – I was beginning to wonder how many pockets that coat had – opened it and took a big, frothing gulp.

The sky was pale blue as if showing through a gauze of cloud so thin as to hardly be there at all. It was neither summer nor autumn. The sun had none of the intensity of summer but the trees were still thick with green leaves. A strong wind came and went. As we walked by the edge of the Common there was barely a breeze. Then we came up on a large tree hissing and writhing. At our level there was still only the very faintest of breezes, as if the wind existed only in the twisting leaves and rocking branches. Green with time, a large statue of a woman offering a drink to a lame man had been erected in front of the tree. The man was seated; with one hand the woman helped him drink, the other rested lightly on his shoulder. Water ran from the cup and dripped on to their moss-clad feet. Rock, moss, water: the simple ingredients of eternity.

We walked on. The Common stretched out vast and flat before us. Up ahead a line of thin trees cast long poles of shadow across the grass. In the distance there was a clump of fertile trees – slightly hazy as in a landscape by Lorraine or Claude. The sun flung clouds across the sky. Every few seconds the light changed: now the clouds were flecked with lemon or pink; within a few moments they were turning bruise purple. The ground felt hard under our feet. Fran's face and clothes were bathed in the brightness of the light; the light of the sun burned in her eyes.

We watched a man with two young children and a dog take a large model of a Sopwith Camel out of the boot of a car. The plane was radio-controlled; twiddling with his hand-set the man taxied the bi-plane along the ground. We watched for about five minutes during which time he sent his children back to the car for spare parts or oil of some sort. Then he tinkered around with the wings and stepped back, pointing the aerial of the hand-set at the plane. It taxied along the ground for a few more yards but didn't gain any speed. His kids lost interest and were throwing a balsa-wood plane at each other; it caught the wind and looped the loop for a few seconds or just floated before falling quietly back to earth. The man had one more go with his radio-controlled bi-plane but this time it wouldn't even crawl along the ground.

'Can't get it up mate?' Fran shouted.

'Jesus Fran! Honestly you're going to get us killed.'

Clutching it by the tail fin the man dragged the plane back to his car, shouting at the kids to hurry up and making barking noises at his dog. Understandably reluctant to get back in the car – nobody had even thrown him a stick to chase – the dog was still eager to play. The kids were in their anoraks, arms by their side, walking obediently back to the car.

'I'd love it if his car didn't start,' Fran said, tears streaming down her face.

'That would really be the last straw. He'd probably end up shooting the dog and half of Clapham as well.'

We walked back across the Common towards some kind of park buildings – lavatories or storage buildings for the groundsmen. Two young black guys, both carrying smoke canisters of some kind, hopped over the fence and started clambering over the building, every now and then releasing great clouds of red, green and blue smoke. It billowed up in thick palls and then blew away. As the sun sank lower the light became richer and deeper, spreading out in long golden streaks. An angle of honking geese flapped towards these bright strips of light. It was slightly cooler now. I had no idea where I was.

From behind us came the sound of car horns, yelling and bustling. We turned around and saw police scrambling out of a van – first two and then, in quick succession, five or six more – and charging across the grass in the direction of the groundsmen's building, shouting. Then we saw them jumping over the fence by the park buildings, running through coils and plumes of blue and red smoke. More shouting. As the smoke faded we caught sight of the two kids, both still inside the fence and taken completely by surprise. One turned by the edge of the building but ran straight into two cops who pulled him to the ground before he even had time to struggle. A cop lunged at the other one but he swerved just out of reach and started running hard for the fence. The cop was yelling 'Head him off, Ron!' The fence was more than three feet high and the young guy cleared it without breaking stride. Another cop was running towards him as he ran along by the fence, heading for the open park. Running at full tilt the black guy tripped over one of the stanchions and went flying. The cop was only a matter of yards away as he began to pick himself up. By the time he got to his feet the cop was within a foot of him and stretching out an arm. For several seconds they seemed to stay exactly like that but then, unbelievably, the gap between the cop's hand and the kid's back seemed slowly to widen as he got into his stride.

'Go on!' yelled Fran. 'Run!'

The cop ran for all he was worth for a few more seconds but with every second the young guy was another couple of feet clear of him.

'Go on, you'll make it!' called Fran at the top of her voice.

The cop was running out of steam, a few yards more and he was bent over, heaving for breath. The kid looked round, running more slowly now, heading across the field into the bright sun. He looked around again. We waved and shouted to him. He saw us and waved back, then ran on again, silhouetted and getting smaller and smaller until he could hardly be seen against the last crimson scarves of light.

I DECIDED TO buy the trumpet after all. When I called round at Steranko's to pick it up I found only Foomie sitting on the floor of the Blue Room with a mug of tea steaming beside her, reading. She was wearing one of Steranko's sweaters.

'Stay and have some tea,' she said smiling.

'I'm not disturbing you?'

'It's nice to see you. I don't know where Steranko is.'

Foomie's hair was tied up tight in a bun. She was wearing jeans and faded red socks. It was odd seeing her in one of Steranko's favourite sweaters. While Foomie made more tea I trotted up to Steranko's room and brought down the trumpet.

The Blue Room was the main living-room of Steranko's house, so-called because of the painted blue floorboards and the pale blue walls. There was nothing in it except a fire and a small stereo. Foomie put on a record of Flamenco guitar. I poured the tea and opened a packet of biscuits. I took the trumpet from its case and fiddled around with the valves.

'D'you think you'll learn to play?'

'I doubt it.'

We spoke in that relaxed and highly conventionalised way that the friend's lover and the lover's friend tend to when they find themselves alone. We were eager to like each other and laughed too quickly at each other's jokes. We talked about Freddie and about Belinda but the conversation was all the time revolving around Steranko. He both restricted our intimacy and made it possible. There were all sorts of other things we could have said and we avoided all of them.

Instead, Foomie asked what I wanted to do, what kind of work I wanted. I said I didn't know, that for as long as I could remember I had been living from one conversation to the next, going nowhere slowly.

The room echoed with the sharp claps, heel stamps and ringing chords of the music. Foomie wiped away some crumbs that had fallen on her book.

The blue floorboards looked liquidy and wet in the orange glow of the electric fire. The panels in the middle of the door had been painted a dark grey and against the background of blue they formed a cross which, for a moment, seemed like the mast of a sinking ship rising from a blue sea – the bars of the electric fire like the bright stripes of a sunset.

We sat and talked by the light of the fire.

043

BONFIRE NIGHT: STERANKO and I walked back to his house across the park. There was a halo of mist around the moon. A light fog draped the iron skeletons of trees. Fireworks exploded green, red and yellow in the cool mist of the sky. The bandstand loomed stark and empty before us. Paths grew indistinct in the near distance. A rocket arced up into the sky and burst into a bunch of bright petals falling. Some way off to the left there were the shrieking noises and colours of a fun fair. We walked towards it, past the huge pyre that would be at the centre of the firework display later that night. We passed through a thicket of bare trees, indistinct and swampy in the fog. Another rocket asterisked the sky.

On the waste ground outside Steranko's house some kids had built a big bonfire. His room reeled and heaved with the bright light of flames. The window panes were warm, the sky deep blue. The whole room was rolling with orange light swirling around the various half-finished paintings. Writhing shadows. Heat. A portrait of Foomie – the first one I'd seen – was stained red by the light of the flames. Her eyes were startlingly lifelike in the flickering light. Steranko put on a record and propped himself on the window-sill, hands round his knees, to watch the fire, silhouetted by the flames. Music flooded the room which was full of colours moving, full of the light of burning.

042

IT WAS A Sunday afternoon, cold and raining, the sort of afternoon when what you most want to do is spend four or five hours in the cinema, eating cake and taking in a double bill of French films with nice photography and plenty of sunshine. On offer was a triple bill of black-and-white Bergmans so we ended up playing Ludo for money at Freddie's place. Warmed by a gas ring on the cooker Steranko, Freddie and I drank tea and waited for Carlton, picking up bits of the Sunday paper and throwing them down again unread.

'What a lot of shit this paper is,' Steranko said, tossing down the colour supplement in disgust. 'I mean, look at this: part two of a pull-out history of ratatouille through the ages. What a fucking joke.'

Freddie and I didn't bother to reply. That's the kind of afternoon it was. Steranko was wearing a thick and expensive cardigan that a friend of his had ripped off from a shop in Chelsea where he worked. Steranko had the sleeves pulled down over his hands and cradled a steaming mug of tea between them.

There was a ring on the door-bell. Freddie went to answer it and came back followed by Carlton who was wearing a red baseball cap and some kind of thick American-style car-coat. Freddie poured him some tea and Carlton struggled out of his coat, took off his cap and pulled a bright, turtle-neck sweater over his head. Underneath he was wearing another thick sweater.

'You warm enough?' Steranko asked.

'I would be if I could afford a two hundred quid cardigan.'

'I told you: this guy can get you one for fifty quid.'

'I can't even afford fifty quid.'

'You'll have to freeze then won't you?'

'Yes boss.'

'C'mon, let's play some Ludo,' Freddie said.

Freddie's living-room was icy cold so we set up the Ludo board on the kitchen table. After half an hour we'd all put about three quid in the kitty – ten pence every time you threw a six or were unable to move – and no one showed any sign of winning. We were all much keener on sending each other back and forming hindering blocks – at one point Carlton had all his four greens piled intransigently on one square – than we were on getting our own tokens home.

After about an hour, following a fluke throw of five sixes, Steranko – blue – was way ahead: he had three counters home and his last was three-quarters of the way round the board. The only person anywhere near him was Freddie who had a red counter nine places behind. He threw a six ('ten pee in, fuckhead,' shouted Steranko) and a three, sending Steranko back to base. After that Steranko sunk without trace. Unable to move or throw a six he had to put in ten pence every time he threw the dice. He chucked in two pounds in a matter of minutes while the rest of us were skooting quickly round the board.

'Oh for fuck sake,' swore Steranko, rolling his fourth five in succession.

'Ten pee in,' said Freddie, ever watchful.

'Shit, I'll have to change this,' he said pulling out a large coin none of us had seen before.

'What's that man? A Krugerrand?' Carlton asked, wide-eyed.

'I've got a whole load of them at home. They're quite tricky to get rid of these days. People are a bit sensitive about them,' Steranko said, chucking the coin into the kitty and pulling out some small change. 'Jesus, haven't you lot seen a two pound coin before?'

None of us had.

'I'll tell you something else as well,' Steranko said. 'The half crown is no longer legal tender: we've gone decimal.'

'C'mon get on with the fucking game,' I said, throwing a three and thereby forming a pyrrhic block of two yellows.

The game ended up with Freddie and Carlton both needing to throw a one. While they threw a succession of fours, fives and threes Steranko finally succeeded in getting his last counter out and staged a late dash around the board ('Yes! Two sixes! Three sixes – that's eighteen – and a one. Shit!') Eventually Freddie rolled a one and won. The rest of us looked on enviously as he counted his winnings.

'Fifteen pounds twenty!' he said with a big grin.

'What a shit game,' I said.

'Superb game,' Freddie said. 'Tactical – a game of skill.'

'Right Freddie,' Steranko said. 'Now you can go and look for a shop where you can buy some cake. Then you can have a nice little tea party for your friends.'

'Nowhere's open.'

We settled for more tea and digestive biscuits ('probably the most boring biscuit in the world,' Freddie conceded) and sat there slurping.

'God, what an afternoon. The pubs are shut, there's nothing on at the Ritzy, there's not even any football on telly,' said Steranko.

'Isn't there a film on TV?'

'Yes there is,' said Freddie, consulting the paper. ' "Carry on up the Congo": an adaptation of *Heart of Darkness* with Kenneth Williams as Marlow and Sid James as Kurtz.'

'Very funny Freddie,' said Steranko, using his sleeve to wipe clean a patch of the wet, steamy window.

'Is it still raining?'

'Pouring. God, what a piss-bin of a city this is. Why the fuck do we live here?'

'Because we're English.'

'I tell you, this country is getting very close to being uninhabitable. The sheer delight people have in saying "no" to things. It's unbelievable the quality of life you have to put up with sometimes. For at least six months of the year it's virtually impossible to have a good time. I don't know how we put up with it.'

'Nothing else to do,' said Carlton. 'When I was working

at the bakery a couple of years ago – it was a terrible job but I needed the dough –'

'Jesus, I could see that one coming. I was sitting here waving it on.'

'Anyway, I was pissed off all day long. Then one day I just said to myself "Ah fuck it". And then I wondered what to do now that I'd said "Ah fuck it". Nothing. There was nothing to do. It was like having a paralysed leg. In the end you go on and on saying "Ah fuck it" day after day.'

'Yeah, you're right man,' Steranko said, looking out of the window at the rain. 'Shit. I can't think of anything I want to do this afternoon.'

'I just want to stroke my winnings,' said Freddie. 'How much did you say those cardigans were Steranko?'

041

I SPENT THE next week working with Carlton, decorating a house near Camberwell. The job took longer than expected and it wasn't until Friday afternoon as we walked home up Cold Harbour Lane that we found the time to drop in at the dole office to sign on. What with the work and the dole office being open such limited hours we'd both missed our signing days. The woman behind the reinforced plate glass asked me why I was two days late.

'I had a job interview,' I said.

'What about you?' she said to Carlton.

'I had a job interview,' he said. She gave us a warning each, smiling as she did so and not bothering to comment on our paint-splattered clothes. She wrote down our next signing date which was in just under two weeks' time and that was that.

With the exception of my brief period of above-board employment my dole had been running smoothly for years. Once your money is coming through regularly – housing benefit included – the essential thing is to keep your life in a state of perpetual stasis as far as the DHSS is concerned. Avoid any change of circumstance since even declaring a few days work can lead to massive complications. Dealing with that kind of thing makes life more difficult for the people working there so they much prefer you to keep any change in your prospects to yourself. Every now and again I got a visit from someone concerned at the way my career seemed to have made no progress at all in the last two years but I told them I was keeping myself occupied ('I use the library a great deal') and not contemplating suicide and they went off reassured. A couple of weeks previously, though, I'd had to attend some kind of interview down in Crystal Palace – failure to attend, said the notice, would result in my benefit being stopped – where an understanding, polite but suspicious-looking woman grilled me about what I was up to, why I'd been sacked from my last job, and what sort of work I wanted. To each question I gave precisely the answer I thought likely to preclude any further questions but she persisted for about twenty minutes. I persisted in resisting her persistence, assuring her that my attitude towards finding a job had improved considerably.

'I've got my mind straight,' I said, quoting Paul Newman in 'Cool Hand Luke'. 'I've had some interviews and some very encouraging rejection letters. I really think things have started to move.' That seemed to satisfy her or at least satisfied the criteria she had to satisfy in order to bring the interview to an end. She gave me some leaflets and wished me luck. I thanked her warmly and left, less pissed off than I might have been in the circumstances.

Carlton was meeting Belinda in Franco's, the pizza place in the covered market. I was worn out from the decorating and said I'd see him later.

Effra Road felt like a flight of stairs and the closer I got to home the wearier I became. My legs were heavy as rucksacks, my eyes full of hot grit. I envied my shadow for the way it was able to just slide and crawl along the ground.

My neighbour, George, was coming out of his flat just as I was unlocking the door of mine. He was about sixty and lugubrious would be an over-energetic way of describing him. For the last twenty years or so, as far as I could gather, his main ambition in life had been to get out of the rain. Everything else – such as what he did once he was out of the rain – was secondary.

'How's it going then George?' I said fiddling with the lock.

'Oh mustn't grumble,' he said and went on to grumble about anything that came to mind.

'Looking forward to Christmas though?'

'Not really son, not really.'

I opened my door and said to George that I'd see him later.

'Oh well, plod on, son.'

Back in the flat I stumbled into a scene from a low-budget horror film. The mess was too much for the cockroaches: one, the size of a half crown, was in the sink doing the dishes, another was hoovering the floor; a few anonymous amoeba-type things were taking it easy in the bath; dead wasps and flies which I'd swatted over the course of the preceding two weeks but neglected to clear up were petrifying on window sills or glueing themselves to the panes. The airing cupboard smelled like I'd been frying hamburgers in it; the cooker was covered in a solidified yellow ooze which I judged to have come from some mackerel I'd tried to lightly baste in butter a few days previously. Near the black sack that I used as a bin, looking as if it had failed in a last ditch bid to escape from the rubbish and find a more hygenic resting place, lay the partially eaten carcass of a chicken. In tin foil containers the remains of a vegetable curry looked like transparent earth in which could be seen potatoes, carrots and cauliflower, the whole scene garnished with a light confetti of pilau rice. Old peaches in a bowl wore thick fur cardigans of mould.

Stripped down to my boxers, I threw out all the rubbish, piled all dirty clothes into a bin liner and cleaned up everything I could see. I de-greased some kitchen utensils and prised loose some of the cups that had got glued to the kitchen table. In the pantry I found a squelching bag of potatoes which were the source, I now realised, of the odd earthy smell that pervaded the whole kitchen. Close to the potatoes, a bottle of olive oil had sprung a leak and a couple of lumps of meteorite cheese lay basting in a pool of it. Wearing rubber gloves I disposed of a piece of radioactive cauliflower and then threw the rubber gloves out too.

It was not a perfect job but it was certainly an improvement. Even so, it was difficult to see how things had got to quite this state. With each week I seemed to descend another few rungs on the evolutionary ladder. To reverse the process I filled the bath brimful with hot, clear water and plunged in.

I dunked my head under and held my breath, feeling my hair float up like cropped seaweed, and then rose a couple of inches until I could breathe through my nose, hippopotamus-style. I writhed around for a while, then pulled the plug and let the water drain away around me, becoming amphibious, mammalian and then, finally, when there was no water left and only a circle of pond-scum to reveal where it had been, human.

Seconds later the phone rang and there I was, right back in the late twentieth century again.

I DROPPED IN at the Effra and found the lounge bar packed. The only people in the public bar were half a dozen police and a guy lying on the floor, a hole through one of his lungs and bar towels soaking up his blood. A woman crying. It had happened five minutes before I got there. The barmaid was seeing to him, wringing out the towels with red hands. That left only one other person serving. It was quarter to eleven. Nobody grumbled about having to wait.

I asked what had happened but there was nothing to know. These things are always the same: an argument over who's next on the pool table, someone talking to someone else's girlfriend, a spilt drink, somebody looking at somebody else. A scuffle, tables going over, glasses smashing – and suddenly someone's getting their guts cut out.

The ambulance arrived ten minutes after the police. I remembered something Freddie had said one evening when we were both drunk: 'There are two kinds of tragedy: the ones that don't happen and the ones that needn't have happened.'

I thought of the guy being loaded into the ambulance and hooked up to a plasma bag, of the nurses and doctors who would be waiting for him in their masks and gloves, and of all the other people queuing half the night in casualty departments with all their blood and pain and helplessness. I thought of dawn breaking over the broken glass, the indifferent streets and curtained windows.

The regular drinkers talked stoically about what happened. Spend enough time in pubs and you get used to most things.

After a while you're unlikely to see anything that you haven't seen before. Someone said: 'Get into a fight round here and you'd better be prepared to die of it.'

I drank my beer and didn't speak to anybody. I was thinking about my liver and kidneys doing whatever it is they do invisibly and without complaint. I hoped I would never get stabbed. Or get my nose broken, or my jaw, or my teeth knocked out or my face slashed with a stanley knife. But most of all I hoped I would never get stabbed.

At home I watched Mike Tyson smashing the shit out of someone and then listened to Callas singing *Lucia*. As I listened I knew that nothing could be as perfect as the memory of her voice, not even love or betrayal – especially not love or betrayal. Maybe, to her, that was the meaning of tragedy; maybe that was the meaning of all tragedy.

WE WERE TRAVELLING by taxi from a party in north London: Steranko, Foomie, Freddie, Belinda and I. After about ten minutes the driver pulled over and said the engine was fucked. We bailed out over Westminster.

It was one thirty in the morning. The sky was almost purple. A slight mist. We cut through St James's Park, passing a flotilla of ducks. Nothing moving, not even the dappled lights on the surface of the pond. We walked along an avenue of trees and caught dark glimpses of statues. Foomie and Steranko were walking slightly ahead of the rest of us; her arm was through his, her head angled slightly towards him. We passed a bulbous, black statue of Churchill.

A few minutes later Foomie called out: 'Look, Christmas!' and pointed to a Christmas tree decorated with red, yellow and blue bulbs.

We walked through Whitehall, through all the empty architecture of power with its austere ornamentation and inscrutable attractiveness. Wide streets, discreet trees. A sign said 'Churchill's War Cabinet' and an arrow pointed down some steps. The whole area had the feel of a museum. Suddenly we were tourists. There was no one else around.

The windows in the buildings did not look like windows. They shared the same texture as the walls and were not there to be looked in to or out of. What impressed most about the walls was the suggestion of discreet thickness. There was only one impulse behind these buildings: they were built to last – and to last it was necessary not only to be impregnable but also to impress. Vandalism was not even an issue. These buildings created their own time. They did not defy time, they consolidated it. That is the meaning of tradition. Their foundations were deep in an unshakeable past; their walls were the habitation of a perpetual present. The buildings had turned the symbolic power invested in them into an active, brooding patience that rendered surveillance superfluous. The archaicism of the buildings was the chief source of their potency. The buildings had the same weight – the same *feel* – as the war memorials we passed: solid, carefully angled blocks of rock on whose sides the names of men had been scratched. Even the pavement felt more permanent here. We had entered museum time.

The streets commanded respect. Most things were out of the question here. All sound except that of the ministerial clack of steel-tipped Oxfords and brogues briskly mounting steps was inappropriate. Steps. All the time our tread was led persuasively upward. We felt that we were being drawn towards the heart of something without ever arriving there. A sense of conviction grew. Each street or arrangement of steps led to a statue: a rearing horse, a hussar waving a sword, an august statesman surveying the streets and stamping them with unbending authority.

The sound of Foomie's laughter floated back to us on scarves of breath. We walked towards Big Ben. Looking up we saw first the vertical, black railings; then the chaotic branches of bare trees; behind the branches was the intricate decoration of Parliament; above that the sky which, oddly, still seemed purple.

We walked past a square manhole cover. Sharp green light glinted through two small access holes. Curling our fingers through these holes Steranko and I pulled back the cover. Immediately, like the glare from a treasure chest of jewels, our faces were bathed in electric lime-coloured light. A metal ladder ran down from the pavement to the green-bathed room below. A single red dial winked silently in the green room, as obvious as a drop of blood on grass. Extending from this room a small tunnel ran beneath our feet, at right angles to the kerb.

'What is it?'

'I don't know.' We lowered the cover, careful not to trap our fingers.

'What do you think that was?'

'I don't know.' It was impossible to say. My eyes were still recovering from the green glare.

We walked across Westminster Bridge. The river was oily, dark and full of harm.

'Crossing a bridge is always romantic,' said Belinda. 'I wonder why?'

'Whistler,' said Freddie.

'Sometimes when I walk over a bridge I have this fear that I'm going to throw all my money over the edge,' I said. 'I get it on boats too when I'm standing at the back, watching the seagulls and all the litter bobbing around in the wake.' I felt a certain pride in formulating this statement. Big Ben struck two. We were all standing close together and looked back at the huge silvery-white clockface.

'You always know where you are when you can see Big Ben,' said Foomie.

'That's right. Where are we again?'

The Houses of Parliament and Westminster Abbey were slightly hazy in the mist. Except for the river nothing was moving. A jagged crack of lightning flashed over Westminster. The sky flinched and then was still again.

THE WEEKS WENT by quickly. I did some decorating with
Carlton and even got a week's work doing visual research
for a film. At first it seemed a nice job – sitting in libraries
and browsing through catalogues – but the novelty soon wore
off. Even when the novelty had worn off it was still quite nice.
If I wasn't working I spent the afternoons playing squash and
in the evenings I got drunk at parties. It was a good time of
the year. Pubs and buses were full.

One night I came out of the Recreation Centre at about
five o'clock. Beneath the cool night sky a train rushed over
the railway bridge. Through each window I could see the
imploring faces of commuters heading south. The market
traders were packing up their stalls, loading unsold items
and produce into their vans.

Christmas lights hung across Brixton High Street: stars,
lanterns, candles, holly shapes, the smiling outline of a yellow
moon. The tree outside the Ritzy was swathed in blue and red
bulbs. A group of smartly-dressed men, women and children
were singing gospel in front of the library.

A single star was hanging in the sky. I mention it only
because it was there.

037

JUST OUTSIDE MY block was a van selling hamburgers; it looked like a belch in 3D and inside it was a guy toiling away in a tropical drizzle of grease and onions. Walking away from it a lard-faced man threw his empty carton on to the grass in front of the flats.

'Oi! Don't you live on this fucking planet?' I shouted. He turned round, mouth working like the back of a garbage truck, ketchup smeared down his chin.

'No,' he said through a mouthful of half-chewed animal.

Leaving him to it, I walked to the centre of Brixton and spent an hour trawling for Christmas presents before settling down to the sedate and steadily unrewarding activity of reading jazz sleeve notes at the record stall. Holding his styrofoam cup at an angle reminiscent of Lester Young the guy running the stall sucked hot soup through a straw. People were walking quickly along, rolls of wrapping paper protruding from their carrier bags. Some of the market stalls were also draped with coloured bulbs and tinsel. I saw Luther shuffling around with his coffee jar, a piece of tinsel draped festively around it. A police van parked by the entrance to the market played screechy recordings of Christmas carols and reminded shoppers that pickpockets were operating in the area.

Someone called my name. Steranko and Foomie, arm-in-arm, both wearing overcoats and smiling, made their way through the crowd. We stopped and talked about Christmas shopping while people bustled past, our breath forming momentary tangles of sculpture. A hand came down hard on my shoulder.

'Drug squad,' said a voice near my ear. I jumped and looked around.

'I wish you wouldn't do that Carlton,' I said.

'You spook easy man,' he said, laughing. He too was carrying a big bag of shopping. We were all pleased to see each other.

'What time is it?' Steranko asked.

'One fifty seven,' said Foomie.

'How d'you know that?'

As she gestured towards the town hall clock it occurred to me that none of my friends owned a watch.

'In that case,' said Steranko, 'I decree that we abandon our attempts to buy Freddie a Christmas present and spend the money on ourselves in the boozer instead.'

We stayed in the pub until three o'clock. Outside the afternoon reeled into us. After a sleep and some food we returned to the Effra in the evening. It was crowded, people were standing several deep at the bar. Gold streamers, silver balls and coloured balloons caught the warm light of the pub and bounced it around the bar. The large ceiling fan rotated quickly overhead. I squeezed in between Belinda and Freddie. All around us people were drinking and talking. I knew most of them by sight. From the other bar came cheers from people playing darts. Every twenty minutes or so Carlton and Steranko would get called into the pool table in the other bar. Before he went to play Carlton pulled on a pair of wire rimmed spectacles that made him look about fourteen years old.

'How come you're wearing glasses Carlton?' I said.

Belinda laughed.

'You tell him Lin,' Carlton said.

'He stayed at my place last night but didn't have his contact lens case with him so he put them in a glass of water by the bed but he didn't say anything to me. In the morning they were gone. I drank them in the night,' Belinda said before bursting out laughing.

122

'Women man,' said Carlton while everyone else laughed.

'What about you Freddie, has anyone ever drunk your contact lenses?'

'No but someone I was going out with did hit me in the face and break my glasses once. I don't suppose that counts though.'

Someone called Steranko and Carlton again and they made their way to the other bar.

'Did you see the news the other night?' said Foomie.

'Maybe.'

'They had this thing about Halley's comet. You know it's only meant to come round once in a lifetime or something. Well apparently it's due quite soon. I thought it had actually come round last year or the year before.'

'Yes, I'm sure I remember something about it,' said Belinda.

'It seems to be around all the time these days.'

'Maybe what we remember is all the anticipation about it coming.'

'The more I think about it the less sure I am one way or the other,' said Foomie.

'Me too,' I said, wondering if it was possible that the prolonged build-up to the actual arrival of the comet could create a sense of expectation so intense as to make you think it had already taken place.

'Did you see the thing last night about the ghost of Karl Marx?' said Belinda. 'Several people claim to have seen him wandering around Highgate cemetery trying to ponce cigarettes off passers-by.'

'I thought there was a ghost in my flat the other day,' said Foomie. 'I was in the living-room when I suddenly heard a voice say "Do you want a piece of bread and butter?" Then I realised it was the junkies next door preparing their evening meal.'

Steranko had come back from playing pool – Carlton had thrashed him in about three minutes – and was talking to Freddie and someone I didn't know. 'I tell you,' Steranko was saying. 'Anyone who can watch a film of Pele dummying the goalkeeper in the Mexico World Cup or Muhammad Ali beating Foreman in Zaire or see Said Aouita breaking the world record for the ten thousand metres or whatever it was – anyone who can watch those things without tears in their eyes, without being moved in the same way as they are by a work of art is a philistine – there's no other word for them.'

'That's right,' said Freddie.

'Bigot-speak,' said Foomie.

'The voice of reason,' said Belinda and both of them laughed.

'The problem with football though,' said Steranko, 'is that it's its own worst enemy. It's like when England got knocked out of the World Cup by Argentina. If instead of complaining about Maradona's handball Bobby Robson had just come out and said "so we lost the game – big deal. The important thing is that we played our part in staging the greatest goal that has ever been seen" – if he'd said something like that then football might get near to the condition of art.'

This was fairly typical Steranko. His method of arguing was both forceful and feeble. Everything he had to say was compressed into the first couple of sentences, something like: 'I thought that film was utter fucking dogshit. I only stayed five minutes.' That was it. If someone raised an objection he would listen attentively and then say 'yeah, maybe. I wasn't so keen on it.' Either that or he would attempt to marshal some kind of reply but he was a hopeless arguer, really. Easy to out-manoeuvre and catch in contradictions of his own making, he was like a boxer who only has one punch: if he failed to get a knockout with that and bring the conversation to a quick conclusion he was done for. This suited me. I'd never had the patience for elaborate debate either.

In the meantime there was some discussion as to whether or not it was Freddie's round.

'Look I'd love to buy all you people a drink but the thing is it's my wallet: there's a time lock on it.'

'You're not kidding. I remember the last time you bought a round: I kept the bottle as a souvenir.'

'I think it's Carlton's round,' Steranko said, seeing him walk back towards the table.

'I'm skint,' he said, turning his pockets inside out and looking, for a moment, as if he might turn into a snooker table – it must have been the green shirt that did it.

'It's supposed to be Christmas.'

'Have you been to his house recently?' Belinda said. 'He's so mean he's installed a Durex machine in his bedroom.'

'Jesus Lin!'

'No I'm only joking,' she said reaching for Carlton's hand. 'Condoms make him impotent!'

'Me too,' said Steranko while everyone was still laughing.

'He makes nice porridge though,' said Foomie.

'What about you Freddie?'

'Oh, it takes very little to make me impotent. Generally the merest thought of sex is enough to do that.' Everyone laughed.

'Come on, whose round is it?'

'Honestly,' said Belinda, getting up to go to the bar. 'The four Scrooges. What does everyone want?'

By this time the pub was even more crowded. Various other people had joined our table and I began the arduous business of making my way to the toilet. By the time I got back Steranko was standing by the bar talking to Ed, the depressed manic-depressive.

'I'll give you one reason why it makes no difference who you vote for,' Steranko was saying. 'You go on the tube tomorrow and when you get off at the other end there'll be some poor guy – or woman – waiting to take your ticket. And he'll have been doing that all day, all week, all year, and he'll probably be doing it for a good part of his life. I tell you when I see some young guy about twenty doing that it breaks my heart. And those guys about forty or fifty you see who've probably been doing that job since they came over to this piss-bin country thirty years ago. If I had a son I'd tell him to sign on and spend his days down at Brixton Rec or dealing dope rather than do that. Unemployment's not the problem, it's employment.'

Ed rolled a cigarette and grunted that he couldn't believe how naive Steranko was, that he wasn't living in the real world, that he had no involvement in politics.

'That's junk,' said Steranko. 'I'm up to my neck in politics.'

'Bollocks.'

'Listen, I'll tell you how I'm involved in politics: I never eat at McDonald's, I never play electronic games, I've not seen five minutes of soap opera on television or any of the other shit they put out. I try not to listen to pop music, I never listen to Radio 1; I don't read the review pages of Sunday papers. I don't buy any South African goods, I don't own a car and generally I don't spend any money on the kind of crap shops are full of. I've no interest in getting a proper job and I don't care if I never own my own house – when people talk about house prices I don't listen. I don't know any bankers or any people who work in advertising – I've only even been to the City once. If somebody is reading a tabloid newspaper I try to make sure I don't see it. OK? Now we come to the really important things: I spend quite a lot of time painting and thinking about art. In other words I try not to go blind. I don't read shit books and I never go to shit films. I play as much sport as I can and I listen to Coltrane, Sonny Rollins, Lester Bowie, Beethoven and Shostakovitch – in other words I try not to let myself go deaf. You get the picture? I'm engaged in some of the most important political battles of our time.'

I laughed but it was difficult to tell whether Steranko was serious or not. Ed wasn't having it either way.

'You're the most arrogant fucking wanker I've ever met,' he said and trudged off to the other bar.

'I do talk some shit sometimes,' Steranko said.

'You're just a garret radical,' I said laughing, as everyone made room for us back at the table. Freddie was telling Belinda about his book.

'It's all autobiographical,' he said. 'The narrator is an influential jazz critic who sleeps with lots of trendy women.'

'No, what's it like really? Is there a plot?'

'Oh no there's no plot. I hate plots. Plots are what get people killed. Generally the plots are the worst thing about books. It's such a bore the way that in chapter eleven or whatever somebody always has to get hold of a gun. Plots

126

are what you get on television: there's no need for them these days.'

'How much have you written?'

'Not much at all. You don't fancy taking a stab at it do you?'

Steranko had his arm around Foomie's shoulders; Carlton was talking to someone I didn't know. The pub was full of the noise of laughing and chinking glasses and the ringing of the till. There was hardly room to move. People bought each other drinks and no one wanted to fight. Freddie bought a huge round and I realised that I loved piss-ups even more than I did a year ago. I looked up at the Christmas streamers and the balloons, the tinsel lanterns and the brightly coloured balls. The hubbub of the pub was all around me and again I had the odd sense that I'd had on the football pitch, of time standing still for a fraction of a second. Looking up I saw the ceiling fan slow and stop, the blur of movement replaced by the sharp image of its four stationary blades – a spider's web strung taut as a net between them.

036

IN THE POST was a summons to the Magistrates' Court for non-payment of rates I'd already been assured I didn't owe. Four months ago they'd written to confirm that I wouldn't have to pay any rates. Then they asked me for five hundred quid. I wrote back explaining that they'd already told me I didn't owe any rates. Another demand arrived. I wrote again. They sent another demand. I wrote again. None of these letters of mine were acknowledged – as though the place sending the demands didn't actually exist.

When the summons arrived I phoned the rates office but there was no answer. I went down to the office but as soon as I began speaking a man in uniform waved his hand to silence me and pointed to a notice explaining that no enquiries could be dealt with because of an industrial dispute. I sat down in the corridor, wrote another letter and dumped it in a rubbish bin marked 'Post'.

Back home I ate a dismal plate of beans on toast and drank a mug of tea. Under the prison glare of the bare lightbulb, tiny bubbles of grease floated on the brown surface of the liquid.

On the news there was an item about anti-hunt demonstrators somewhere in the home counties. The huntsmen were all decked out sedately in their red riding gear, the hounds all yapping and panting while the demonstrators tried to get in the way and make a nuisance of themselves. In close-up one of the demonstrators was yelling 'Scab! Scab!'

In recent years the word had become an all-purpose term of abuse for any situation in which one group of people wanted to move while another group wished them to remain stationary. So frequently had the word been used that it no longer carried any pejorative weight as far as the scabs were concerned. Its moral edge had been blunted and now it sounded like an aggressive greeting that was also an exclamation of pain, defeat and humiliation on the behalf of the person uttering it. It was something you shouted when the lorries or strike-breakers had already driven past under police escort. There was almost something elegiac about it, a nostalgic appeal to the word's own lost moral and political authority, like a fading echo on a cold day, trying to call its way back to the lost warmth of the mouth.

ON CHRISTMAS EVE Steranko invited everyone over to his house for a turkey dinner. We all sat around the kitchen table which he had dismantled, hauled up the stairs and then reassembled in his room. A fire was burning in the grate and more wood was piled up on either side of the fireplace. All the usual clutter of his room had been cleared away and thrown on his bed or shoved into corners: notebooks, sketch pads, paperback novels. As always the walls were covered with unfinished drawings; canvases were stacked up in a corner. Apart from the fire the only light in the room was from candles on the table and on the mantelpiece. He had even bought some cheap Christmas crackers. Everyone had brought booze and grass and we were all drunk and stoned by the time Steranko emerged from the kitchen bearing the turkey ceremoniously before him like a crown on a cushion. The roast potatoes and turkey had been cooked a deep golden brown. There was gravy, broccoli, peas and boiled potatoes. We ate like pigs and swilled back more glasses of red wine. When we had finished the turkey we pulled the crackers and all put the coloured paper hats on our heads. Freddie announced that the other day he'd met someone who was commissioning editor at a place where they did the mottoes for Christmas crackers and he reckoned he'd be pushing some work his way. Everyone laughed and we all compared the pointless trinkets that dropped out of the crackers: a gondola, a chandelier, a parachutist, a bicycle, a saxophone.

After clearing the plates away we devoured the box of

expensive chocolates that Belinda had brought. We played our favourite records, drank a bottle of port and took it in turns to try and break brazil nuts with Steranko's nutcrackers. The table quickly became congested with empty beer cans, bags of grass, corks, wine bottles, nutshells and screwed-up chocolate wrappers. There were six of us: Carlton, Foomie, Freddie, Belinda, Steranko and me.

Through the window I could see the yellow glow of the street lamp and above that a cold sickle of moon. The fire filled the room with warm light. Propped carelessly on the mantelpiece was a postcard of Millais' 'Burning Leaves': the pale light fading, the leaves burning, the trees receding, the girls' faces touched by the light.

I looked across at my friends, their eyes made soft and dark by the candles and fire.

FREDDIE AND I sat in his kitchen drinking tea. The radio was on. Someone knocked on the door and when Freddie opened it a cold wedge of air rushed in. Foomie stood in the hall, stamping snow off her boots. She was wearing Steranko's huge dark overcoat.

It was winter in the city.

Freddie filled up the kettle and I moved round the table to make room for Foomie. Her face was glowing from the cold. Snow was melting in her hair.

'D'you want a mince pie Foomie?' Freddie said.

'I'd love one.'

'Yeah, I'll have two or three as well please,' I said.

'Honestly,' said Foomie.

'My mother made them at Christmas,' said Freddie, prising the lid off the tupperware container. 'I'll put them in the oven so we can have them hot.'

'What a nice guy eh?' I said to Foomie.

'So you and Steranko both got sacked,' she said after a few moments.

'I'm afraid so,' I said, laughing.

After Christmas Steranko and I were skint and had both ended up applying for temporary jobs in a big department store in Knightsbridge. Each year they took on thousands of extra staff for the January sale and after a very short interview Steranko and I were hired to work in the vast stock and storage area beneath the shop. A good part of each day was spent calling out 'Mind-your-backs-please!' as we charged through menswear with rails of cashmere coats.

During coffee breaks we played cards with two other guys who were only there for the sale. Quite often all four of us would get wrecked at lunchtime and spend the rest of the afternoon pushing stock around deliriously, accidentally taking clothes up to the hi-fi dept, or men's pyjamas into women's lingerie, laughing crazily as we did so. We were sacked after a week.

'All things considered,' I said to Foomie. 'I'm surprised we lasted that long.'

'Me too,' laughed Foomie.

We ate the mince pieces and slurped mugs of tea. The pastry was light and flaky, the mince so hot you had to keep it moving round your mouth so that it didn't burn your tongue.

'I'll tell you what,' Freddie said. 'Let's have some port as well.' He went over to the kitchen cabinet and took down a bottle and some glasses.

'These are nice,' Foomie said, picking up one of the glasses.

They were small, about the size of an egg cup. Each of them had two little corgi dogs on the side and just beneath the pattern on the rim was written: 'Every Dog Has His Day'.

'They're great aren't they?' said Freddie as he began to pour the port. 'It's funny the way you get attached to certain things. In this flat apart from things like the bed and some chairs I've got a stereo, some secondhand suits and other clothes. I don't really care about any of those things. When they get ripped off it's a drag but it doesn't really matter. Then I've got books, two favourite T-shirts, some records, one of Steranko's paintings – those are the things I care about. And then there are these glasses: I think I like these glasses more than anything. An old girlfriend gave them to me when I was about seventeen. I think she won them at a fair somewhere. I played a very big part in her sexual awakening: it was while she was going out with me that she realised she was a lesbian.'

'That's very touching, Freddie,' I said. We all clinked glasses and drank the port like elderly school teachers. Then we talked about what we were like when we were younger.

'I can't even remember what I was like when I was seventeen,' Freddie said. 'What about you Foomie?'

'At seventeen? The same as now. Except I was fatter.'

'Were you?'

'Much. Then I lost it all. And I used to listen to reggae a lot. What about you? What were you like?'

'I didn't have a personality at all until I was twenty-one,' I said. 'I was a late developer. Until I was about sixteen my main hobbies were Airfix models, football and Subbuteo. From sixteen on my real interest was beer drinking. Pretty much like now really.'

Freddie poured some more hot water into the tea pot. He had bits of pastry round his mouth.

'Have you ever been in love?' Foomie asked.

'I imagine so,' I said.

'What about you Freddie?'

'I'm in love with the woman in the health food shop.'

'You don't even know her.'

'Doesn't matter,' Freddie said, shrugging.

'That's not love,' Foomie said. 'It's infatuation.'

'Infatuation is the highest form of love.'

'Good one Freddie,' I said.

'You two: you're like children,' Foomie said laughing.

'And what about you Foomie?'

'What?'

'Don't be so coy. Are you in love with Steranko?'

Foomie laughed: 'What a question!' she said, holding her mug with both hands and taking a big sip. 'Anyway, what does it mean to love someone?'

After a pause I said, 'It means you never tire of watching what someone says.'

Freddie turned up the radio for the news summary. A planned space-walk by American astronauts had been abandoned because of bad weather conditions.

'It's snowing in space,' said Foomie.

The window was bathed in steam, like a perfect memory of home.

134

033

WINTER IN THE city. More snow was forecast but none fell. Sometimes I got to the end of a day and wondered if it had actually taken place. Whole weeks disappeared without trace. I bought disappointing loaves of bread and had conversations with the local shop-keepers. I caught a cold and passed it on to someone else. I went out; I stayed in.

I was on the tube, waiting for it to pull out of Brixton. Three young guys got on. They said something to an older man who was sitting in the other end of the carriage. He said something back – I thought they'd asked him where the tube was going – and suddenly they were all kicking fuck out of him. He was half lying on the seat and half on the ground. Punches and kicks thudded into him. Everyone from that end of the carriage charged up to my end where we all huddled, horrified, like cattle in a storm. Someone called the guard who walked towards the carriage slowly. Two of the attackers walked off but the third was still piling into the older guy. Then he sauntered off too. The guard helped the man to his feet. There were big lumps taken out of his face, bright blood spattered all over the tube floor and on the window behind him.

'Why you all just standing there?' a woman shouted at us all. 'Why no one help him?'

Nobody said anything. No one wanted to sit near where it had happened. No one wanted to look at anybody else.

THE COURT WAS already packed when I arrived: hundreds of people all getting hauled up for non-payment of rates, all protesting their innocence. I looked through a list pinned up in the foyer of the Court but couldn't see my name on it. I mentioned this to the clerk: 'Maybe there's been some mistake,' I said.

'Nobody's name is on the list,' said the clerk. 'You can't get out of it that easily.'

There were so many cases to be heard that we were called into the court ten at a time. I joined an S-bend queue of people waiting to see a weary official from the rates office – the man in front of me was saying, 'Who do you fucking people at Lambeth think you are? Pol Pot persecuting the intelligentsia?'

I took a more moderate line and persuaded the official to adjourn my case. Then I played my trump card and said I wanted to complain to the Ombudsman. I didn't know what the Ombudsman did but Freddie – who knew nothing about these things – had told me I should complain to him. Those behind me in the queue, clearly impressed by this raunchy display of citizens' rights, waited their turn. As I pushed my way through the crowds I heard the person after me in the queue insisting that he see the omnibus man immediately.

I walked home through the park, crossing an empty football pitch and passing through the thin H of rugby posts, noticing the trees and the way the pond endured. Back home there was a letter from the rates office advising me that I didn't need to attend the Court after all.

I CAUGHT BOOMERANG flu, a new bug from Australia – a week after you've shaken it off it comes back more virulently than before. I went out, I stayed in and watched 'The World at War'. During the autumn I'd taped most of the series on a secondhand VCR that I'd picked up in Brixton market and now I often watched two or three episodes straight through: Stalingrad, the Pacific War, Arnhem, the Battle of Britain, the Afriker Korps, B29s, Lancasters, Spitfires, the Eighth Army, an egg frying on the scorched metal of a tank, Orde Wingate, the leeches in Burma, the death railroad, Stukas, panzers, rubble, search-lights dissecting the night sky, the Russian winter, a French collaborator being hit on the legs with a hammer . . .

At night I slept in a deep pit of dreams, familiar scenes tinted by the newsreel images of 'The World at War': Brixton consumed by the black and white fires of the blitz; Steranko, Foomie, Fran – all of us – on a beach where the sand is white and the water Iwo Jima blue, planes bursting into flames in the clear skies overhead, a charred landscape behind us. I am in the water up to my waist. Everyone else is talking on the beach. Steranko has fallen asleep. As the tide moves up the beach the sea laps over his legs and chest and covers the palette of water-colours lying by his side. When the palette is completely submerged threads of colour – red, yellow, green, blue – drift like smoke in the water until it is dyed a colour that I haven't seen before. An American pilot bails out of a damaged fighter plane. The parachute fails to open; he disappears into the sea and then the parachute inflates, a white jelly fish with a man tangled in thin tentacles beneath the waves.

WE WERE SITTING round a table playing poker, a smoky light hanging atmospherically overhead. At first we played five card stud but there were so many hands when nothing happened that we changed to three card brag which was much simpler. After a few hands Freddie began betting blind so that everybody who had looked at their cards had to put in double. Eventually everyone but Carlton dropped out. Freddie kept going: ten blind, ten blind . . .

Alarmed at the speed with which he was having to put money into the pot, Carlton said, 'I'll see you.'

'Can't see a blind man,' snapped Belinda who knew the rules.

'Can't see a blind man? Man, what an idea!'

Noticing how Carlton had panicked, Freddie raised his stake to twenty blind each time. Carlton had no choice but to go with him and eventually Freddie looked at his hand.

'Three quid open,' he said, betting the limit — mutually agreed on at twice the kitty — and very obviously bluffing.

'See you,' said Carlton. He was wearing a green-tinted visor that he'd picked up that afternoon in the market. He felt it gave him an edge on the game.

'Queen high,' said Freddie, tossing down his cards.

'Queen high? Shit man . . .' Carlton threw down his cards: a jack flush.

'D'you have any idea what you're doing Freddie?' Foomie asked him.

'Not really, no.'

We decided to change the game but it was impossible to

agree on one that we all wanted to play. Belinda suggested complex variants of poker: Eight card stud, High-ball, Low-ball with twos wild and no changes; Double Barrelled Shotgun; Anaconda; El Paso Criss-Cross . . .

'How do you know all these games?' Foomie asked.

'I used to play with my brother and his friends in Streatham.'

'Let's play Montana Red Dog,' said Freddie.

'How d'you play it?'

'I don't know.'

The problem of what to play was temporarily resolved by letting the dealer choose the game and rotating the deal after each game. The problem then was that each new game required about ten minutes of explanation (Freddie insisted on attempting some cobbled together version of Montana Red Dog on his deal) and even then a lot of us weren't sure what was happening. After half an hour of letting the dealer choose we reluctantly agreed to Acey-Deucey, a game that was even simpler than three card brag. It was Steranko's favourite game (God knows why, I'd never seen him win at it) and he explained the rules with impatient enthusiasm.

'Ace is high, two is low. You get dealt two cards and you bet on the probability of the card you get dealt next being numerically between the two you've got. OK? So if you've got say a queen and a three you win on four, five, six, seven, eight, nine, ten, jack. If you win you get what you bet. If the card you get dealt is outside the two you've got – in other words if it's two, king or ace, you lose what you bet. And if it's the same as either of the cards you've got – queen or a three in this case – you lose double what you bet. So the best hand is ace-two because there are only six cards in the deck you can lose on. Any money you lose goes into the pot and you can bet as little as you like or as much as there is in the pot. OK?'

Acey-Deucey is a vicious little game and I would warmly recommend it to anyone with a nasty streak. When the rules are explained it seems difficult to lose but within two hours you can be brought to the brink of ruination. The way it tends to work out is that five players win a little and the sixth gets really fucked over.

For the first twenty minutes very little happened. We bet ten or twenty pence and won or lost without caring.

'This is the most boring game yet,' said Foomie.

'Just give it a bit longer,' said Steranko who was dealing.

'I'll bet the limit,' said Freddie, showing king-five and impatient to get the game moving. 'Whatever's in the pot.'

Steranko dealt him a four. Freddie put in a pound and the kitty doubled. Right after him Foomie showed queen-four, went for the pot and got dealt a four.

'Oh no!'

'Good dealing, Steranko.'

'You're going to be sleeping on your own tonight Steranko,' said Foomie, putting her money into the pot and bringing the kitty up to six pounds. In the next five minutes we nibbled away at the pot, winning or losing twenty pence or thirty pence a time.

'Deucey-fucking-deucey,' said Carlton throwing in two twos and asking for new cards – a rule Steranko had forgotten to explain. He got Ace-two.

'Jesus!'

'Ah shit. There's two twos already gone as well,' said Steranko. 'Lucky fucker.'

'The lot,' said Carlton from beneath his green visor.

Freddie was dealing. He took his time and then flipped up an ace.

'Nine quid, Carlton. Get it in.'

'Men are just unbelievable,' Belinda said to Foomie. 'They're so greedy.'

Carlton took out a pound coin from the kitty and threw in a dejected-looking tenner. We were all edgy now and the games got faster and faster as we became more and more desperate for a winning hand.

'What's in the pot,' said Steranko calmly. I was dealing.

'About fifteen quid.'

'Right, let's have it then,' he said, flinging down king-three. I turned up a three.

'Yes!'

'Oh bad luck Steranko,' Freddie said.

'Clean bowled,' Carlton said, slapping my hand high above the table.

'What happiness,' I said. 'The pack's in fine shape. Completely unpredictable and *very* malicious.'

'I thought we were meant to be playing for fun?'

'Fun? Fun?' said Steranko. 'You think this is fun?'

The table was piled high with money. Belinda was dealing.

'It's like a news item about the affluent south-east. This is probably what stockbrokers do to relax at night,' said Foomie, picking up her cards. 'Ooh! Jack-four.'

'Go for the lot!' I said.

'Pot it!' said Carlton. We were very keen on somebody going for the kitty when there was a good chance of their losing.

'I'll go ten pounds,' Foomie said.

'I hope you win Foom,' said Belinda and dealt a five.

'Yes,' said Foomie.

'Shit,' said Carlton.

Belinda leant across and kissed Foomie.

'Ugh, God,' Steranko said. 'Women just don't understand cards. Cards is about malice, greed. Cheats. Dykes . . .'

'Steranko, you are really pushing your luck,' said Belinda, laughing.

'I haven't got any luck to push. If I did I'd be fleecing everybody.'

My deal. Belinda had jack-five, went a fiver and lost gracefully. Next up was Freddie: Queen-two.

'The lot,' he said.

'Sure you can afford it? Could be nearly sixty quid if you lose.'

'Let's have the card.'

Everybody was quiet as I flipped over the top card. A seven.

The rest of the pack I threw across the room.

'Shit! Look what I had: Acey-fucking-deucey.' No one took any notice of this declaration from Steranko.

It seemed a good time to go to the pub and we all hurried off, eager to drink as much of Freddie's winnings as possible.

After the pub shut we bought a stock of carry-outs and went back to Freddie's to continue playing. Steranko rolled a large joint.

'That'll be twenty pee a toke to you,' he said when it got round to Freddie.

'You'll have lost the whole bag before the night's out,' Freddie said.

Once again no one could agree on a game; Steranko wanted to continue playing Acey-Deucey – can you believe it? – but nobody else was up to it; Belinda wanted to play poker but Carlton and I vetoed that (principally so we didn't have to sit through Freddie doing his *the kid's got him, the kid's got him* routine from 'The Cincinatti Kid'). In the end we settled for a dull variant of whist played for high stakes. I was not convinced that the game we were playing was actually a game and nobody else was quite sure of the rules. A major part of it seemed to involve smoking Steranko's dope and making sure you drank your share of the carry-out before anyone else had a chance to. Play was also interrupted by Freddie who was drunk, stoned, flushed by his winnings and wanted to talk wildly about whatever came into his head at any moment.

'You write a delicately observed book about the moral intricacies of human relationships in this day and age,' he was saying. 'That's not a novel: it's an *alibi*.'

'He's been doing a therapy course,' said Steranko: 'beyond self-parody.'

Freddie then went on to give us a white water monologue on a book which nobody had read: 'It's an incredible book. With it Naipaul makes an assault on the highest European literary form: the boring novel.'

'Listen let's just concentrate on the enigma of whose fucking deal it is shall we?' I said.

'No, it's an incredible book,' continued Freddie. 'One of those books where it's a real effort to remember to wonder what's going to happen next.'

'Who's this?' said Foomie.

'V.S. Naipaul.'

'Every sentence a thriller,' Freddie said, coughing on the hot smoke of the joint.

'Listen Freddie, if you could just concentrate now and again on the game. You know, like every ten deals or so, it would be a great help.'

'OK ... OK. Now just remind me what game it is. No, don't tell me − I want to work it out for myself,' he said, picking up the cards from the last deal and fanning them into some kind of order. 'Now let's see. Too many for Acey-Deucey, too many for Brag ...'

'Shut the fuck up Freddie!'

'Isn't it your deal?' Steranko said to Foomie.

'I just dealt didn't I?' Foomie said with that kind of confused smile she had when stoned.

'C'mon somebody deal.'

'God, it's cold in here,' Carlton said.

'Put the Hindenberg on,' said Freddie. Carlton held a match in front of the gas fire which suddenly ignited with an explosive *whuumph!* of flames about two inches from his face.

'Hence the name,' said Steranko, laughing. 'I think it's your deal, Freddie.'

'Alright,' he said, picking up the cards. He shuffled the deck, treating us, in the process, to his full array of card tricks. The first one involved flicking the cards by his ear to count them. 'There's only fifty-one, I think,' he said, flicking through them again and moving his lips as if counting at high speed. 'Ah it's OK. Two stuck together.'

'Very funny Freddie. I never tire of seeing that one.'

Next he divided the cards into two piles, holding their backs with four fingers of each hand and rippling through them with his thumbs. When he'd done that he kept the two halves of the pack separate and stacked them one on top of the other so that the cards were in exactly the same order as when he started.

'Freddie you are definitely beginning to try my patience with that joke. I love it dearly and the first fifty or so times I saw it I even laughed but now I really think you could give it a rest.'

'OK. Here they come ...' he said, dealing out the cards quickly. A mis-deal needless to say.

'Whoops!'

'Freddie give me the fucking cards will you. I'll deal,' said Steranko.

'Everybody put in?' I said when the cards were out.

'Yeah.'

'The kitty's light.'

'Belinda?'

'I've put in.'

'Actually maybe it's me,' I said, unable to remember whether or not I'd put the ante in.

The game got underway. It was a fairly simple game but nobody could quite remember how to play properly.

'What are trumps?' asked Foomie.

'Hearts.'

'C'mon hurry up.'

'I've just played fuckhead.'

'Oi Carlton! Wake up!'

'OK . . . OK . . . Hang on.' Carlton played a card.

'What are trumps?' asked Steranko.

'HEARTS! Jesus.' Steranko played two cards at once, retrieving one of them.

'It's no fun at all, this game,' I complained. 'What's it called again?'

'Maybe this is Montana Red Dog after all.'

'No Montana Red Dog is much more fun than this. I remember it from "Alias Smith and Jones" when I was a kid. In the days when not everybody had BBC2 and nobody had colour.'

'C'mon whose turn is it?'

'Yours,' said Steranko, taking a sip of beer.

'That's my beer,' said Freddie.

'Where's mine?'

'You lost it to Carlton.'

'And your dope,' Carlton said.

Soon after that we abandoned the game of whist and had a few rounds of a game so absurd that no one even knew its name. At first we called it Montana Red Dog but then Foomie suggested we change the name to One-Card Cyclops. It was another simple game: you're dealt one card which you stick to your forehead (you have to be sweating to play this game). You can see everyone else's card but you can't see your own. Ace is high and you bet on who has the highest card. The idea is to force other people out of the game by sheer force of recklessness.

I tried to use some latent function of the brain to see through my skull and glimpse the card that was glued to my forehead. A jack, I felt sure it was a jack, a jack of hearts. Everyone else dropped out except Steranko and me. I stared at the single Cyclopean card – a nine! – in the middle of his forehead. We kept raising each other until eventually he called me.

I took the card off my forehead. It was a ten. I won anyway.

AS I WALKED to the bus-stop a woman I'd noticed off and on for a long time finally spoke to me. I'd first seen her a couple of years ago when she looked very bad, as if she hadn't seen any daylight for six months – thin, white, ill-looking with frightened glasses. Something bad must have happened to her. From time to time I saw her walking along the street; if she had to cross a road she waited on the pavement a long time to make sure there were no cars coming. Once I saw her with a man I presumed to be her father walking beside her slowly and protectively. That was the first time she said hello. A couple of times before that she'd glanced at me timidly but this was the first time she'd actually spoken. I suppose she'd begun to recognise me at about the time that I'd started to recognise her. Since then I'd run into her about once a fortnight and on each occasion she'd said hello more vigorously – more familiarly and confidently – than before. She had pale skin and stunted ginger hair. When I saw her another time she was wearing a little eye make-up. There was something ghostly about her slow regeneration; although she looked much better you could see she was still in a bad way. There are people like that. You see them and your first reaction is 'what happened?' She was recovering from something bad that happened, that was for sure. To find out more would be to become involved. I didn't want our nodding acquaintance to increase.

The last few times we'd bumped into each other she'd taken me completely by surprise and on this occasion, walking to the bus-stop, I didn't notice her at all until, suddenly, there she was, standing a couple of feet away from me. I knew she was going to speak.

'You're very good-looking,' she said, holding my eyes for several seconds before I could think what to do. I mumbled something and walked on, leaving her standing there. Then I crossed the road quickly.

At the bus-stop I watched her walk away and wished I had smiled and said 'So are you!' I thought of calling out to her but it was too late. Instead I concentrated on small things: two milk bottles lying in the gutter, each with a tiny pool of grey milk in the bottom; a car braking hard to avoid a dog padding across the road.

Two other people were waiting for a bus and we took it in turns to stamp our feet and moan. More people showed up. The wind howled as if it longed for the coarse grass of the moor.

Across the road a man in a greasy anorak nipped into the phone booth. He fumbled for change, pressed a few digits which served only to ignite the blue touch paper of his anger and then hurled the phone back into its cradle. While we laughed, he strode off with his anger and rage, tremors of ill-feeling spreading out across the city. Perhaps he'd been trying to phone the Samaritans. In six months' time maybe he'd buy a shotgun and massacre four people in a sleepy town somewhere and no one would be able to say for sure why he did it, no one would know the part played by the broken phone and the people at the bus-stop laughing.

By now there was a large herd of us huddled round the bus-stop, nourished by the thought that when the bus came we were really going to give the conductor a hard time because we were freezing and late and wished we had the money for a fucking taxi even though you hardly saw any taxis round here.

Phones and buses: part of the war of attrition that the city wages on its inhabitants, part of its attempt to purge itself of citizens and become pure, empty possibility.

We waited another ten minutes and then saw a bus barging its way towards us through the wind.

'Come on in,' said the conductor, leaning out to help an

old woman with her shopping trolley. 'It's nice and warm in here.'

As if he was welcoming her into his *home*.

The memory of that gesture warmed me for the rest of the day.

I HAD JUST got back from the paint shop when the phone started shrieking. It was a market research company wanting to ask about my opinions and habits. I asked them to hang on a moment while I took my coat off. These calls started a couple of months ago when someone telephoned and asked about a dismal new product that I'd never heard of. A couple of weeks later they called back and asked if I would be willing to have my name put on their list of regular interviewees. I said I would be only too pleased and after that the calls started coming fairly regularly. Quite often the interview was closed down after a couple of questions because my habits or income cast me outside the research pool they were interested in. I soon learnt that when it came to the second or third question – 'Do you have a mortgage?' or 'Do you have a car?' – I should give whichever answer was most likely to enable me to pass through to the next stage of the questionnaire ('yes' was usually the best response when it came to mortgages and cars).

Shoulders still aching from carrying the cans of paint I got back to the phone and answered an apparently random series of questions.

Have I heard of Sellafield? Do I know what it does? (I'm not sure: something to do with nuclear fuel – these interviews made you feel really ignorant sometimes.) Do I own a carpet cleaner? Would I like to? How often do I shave? Do I use an electric shaver? Do I wish I did? Have I heard of the new butter that you do not have to spread? ('Yes!' I snapped, eager to be of help, 'Yes!') Who would I vote for? What do I think are the most important issues of our time? How many times a week do I take exercise? Would I be interested in using a new tummy flab reducer? How many hours' television do I watch per week? Which programmes?

'About two hours a week – all sport, plus three or four hours of 'The World at War' on video but I suppose that doesn't count.

'The World at War?'

'It's a kind of hobby,' I said, and with that the interview came to an end. I put the phone down feeling slightly bewildered. Usually I felt pleased and happy when I'd done one, as if I'd played my part in shaping reality. It seemed a much more effective form of political involvement than voting. Even in a survey with a large sample I was still speaking on behalf of tens of thousands of other people. My every opinion got multiplied many times over and in the course of time most subjects would probably be broached. Bearing this in mind I usually tried, when asked to express an opinion or preference, to pitch my answers within a broad consensus of approval or disapproval. There was no point in voicing opinions which were so extreme or confessing to habits so insistently peculiar as to consign you to an irrelevant one per cent of hardened eccentrics. As a general rule it was useful to ally yourself with the twenty per cent who dissented mildly on any given issue. If you played your cards tactically you could be influential in preventing a new chocolate bar coming on to the market; or you could be part of a significant minority who thought English newspapers should be printed in Arabic. We were living in an era of strong opinions: anything was possible.

Before getting down to painting my living-room – that morning I had realised quite suddenly that I couldn't stand the piss-coloured wallpaper a moment longer – I made some tea and fiddled with the radio. I wanted to listen to one of those pirate radio stations that play great music all day but I couldn't find one. I couldn't find *one*; I found hundreds, all cancelling each other out: snatches of reggae blending into chat shows, lunch-time plays and chart shows. I got a faint echo of soul music but as soon as I moved the knob the barest fraction I lost the soul and ended up with what seemed to be Belgian Radio 2. So many people wanted to have their say that nobody could make themselves heard. These days it was a twenty-four hour rush-hour on the airwaves, and at certain times it was probably possible to pick up every kind of music: everything from Bach to go-go in one ear-drum bursting roar, the whole of the world's music in a single second.

I settled for silence – for the noise of the traffic – and levered open a can of emulsion. Magnolia: not a colour to get excited about, hardly a colour at all, not even not a colour. It hugged the pot neatly, the very image of soon to be disrupted serenity.

Slapping the paint on the wide expanse of walls was very pleasant – you got extremely good mileage out of those rollers. Unfortunately you also got a thin film of magnolia sprayed over carpet, chairs and stereo, none of which I'd properly covered with rags and newspapers. I only noticed this when someone rapped on the door and I made my way through the wreckage to see who it was.

'Foomie!' She was eating a pale yellow banana.

'What are you doing?' she asked. I kissed her carefully to avoid getting paint over her clothes.

'This is not your lucky day. I'm decorating,' I said, re-boiling the kettle. 'Actually maybe it is your lucky day . . .'

She was shaking her head.

'It's creative, stimulating and great fun. Good practice for when you want to do your flat. I'll give you a few tips.'

'I bet. You're covered in paint – look you must have stepped in some: you're treading white footprints everywhere.'

'Oh fuck. It's not white, it's magnolia actually. See, you're picking up useful knowledge already and you learn even quicker on the job.'

'Not me Michelangelo.'

'Go on.'

'Out of the question.'

In the end she agreed to help on condition that she was able to drink as much lager and smoke as much grass as was 'reasonably possible'.

151

'What does that mean?'

'As much as I want.'

'It's a deal,' I said, handing over money for her to pick up beer from the off-licence. While she was out I sorted out a sweatshirt and some old trousers for her to wear. From then on we were really flying. We drank beer almost continually and stopped for a joint every hour. I slapped on dripping coats of emulsion and she touched up neatly around the edges. In what seemed hardly any time at all the flat was transformed into a bright haze of not-quite white. The thick, fresh smell of paint felt heavy in our nostrils. By the time we finished I was so thickly covered in paint that I cracked as I walked; standing against one of the walls I was invisible except for two dark eyes. Foomie had only a couple of smears of paint on her hands and a small white dot the size of a mole on her face.

When I'd had a bath and peeled off my emulsion skin I cooked some sort of vegetable mush which Foomie ate without complaint. I tipped the dishes into the sink and we sat in the bright-smelling living-room, playing music quietly and drinking tequila. I turned on the main light, dyeing the night outside a deeper blue. The patter of rain.

'Is this the trumpet you bought from Steranko?' Foomie said, opening the case.

'Yes.'

'Have you learned to play it yet?'

'No. I couldn't get the hang of it at all. I was really determined to learn. For a while I practised for about twenty minutes a day. Then it dropped to ten. Then I just practised whenever I felt like it which was about once a week. After that I just left it lying around because it looked nice. Now I keep it in the case to stop it getting dusty. It's principal function now is to serve as a symbol of non-achievement.'

'I'm like that with my self-defence classes. I go for a couple of weeks. Then for some reason I can't go and after that I stop going for about six months. Then I go again and wish I'd kept at it.'

We listened to the music which was only slightly louder than the rain.

'What shall we do this evening?' I said after a while. 'What's Steranko doing?'

'He's having dinner at his brother's. He won't be back till late.'

'So shall we do something?'

'Yes.'

'What would you like to do?'

'Let's go out dancing.'

'I knew you were going to say that.'

'What's wrong with that?'

'I hate discos.'

'We wouldn't go to a disco,' Foomie said. 'We'd go to a club.'

'All clubs are really discos.'

'Have you ever been to one?'

'Several. Hundreds. Years ago I went to loads and I never had a moment's pleasure in any of them. All I did was watch people having what I thought was a good time but which I now realise was simply a highly ritualised form of boredom. Besides I'm allergic to clubs.'

'What shit,' Foomie said, laughing.

'It's true.'

'I swear . . .'

'I swear it's true. I get neon rash, strobe sickness, bass-induced vomiting, funk giddiness, flash-outs, bouncer paranoia . . . I asked my doctor about it. It's quite common apparently among people of my age.'

Foomie shook her head. 'Let's go to the Fridge.'

'I went there once. It was the exact antithesis of a good time: massive, dark, thumping disco, beer that tasted like lager, lager that tasted like water. I tell you, if someone in the 1920s had made an expressionist film of people enjoying themselves like that it would have seemed like a vision of the future as hell. If you saw it today – with poor sound, in black and white – it would still seem like that.'

Foomie pursed her lips and made a long sucking sound that was not intended to be anything like a kiss.

'I love dancing,' Foomie said. 'Don't you like dancing?'

'Hate it. Can't stand it. It's one of those things I'm really

153

glad I don't do. Every time I don't do it I get a small thrill of pleasure. It's like playing chess or doing crossword puzzles. Chess, I don't like to even think about; I can rest easy knowing that it's something I'm never going to be interested in and will never regret not having taken up. As for crosswords . . .'

'We're supposed to be talking about dancing.'

'Right, actually I sometimes have an urge to dance but I'm always too embarrassed to actually do it.'

'It doesn't matter how you dance. It's just whether you do it.' As she finished speaking Foomie started dancing a little, moving slightly to an imagined beat. She held her hands up like fists and moved them slowly and rhythmically, her eyes half-shut.

'See?' she said, rocking her head to the beat. 'Come on: groove that body.'

'Can't I just watch you and imagine you've got no clothes on?' I said.

There was a sharp intake of breath as Foomie prepared to shout.

'I'm joking, I'm joking!' I said. 'Look, I'm dancing, see? My heads nodding, my foot's tapping.'

I went out to the kitchen to fetch the bottle of tequila. When I came back Foomie was standing at the window, looking out.

'Hmmn, chilly,' she said, putting on her cardigan.

The block opposite was invisible except for the angular pattern of windows which appeared as squares of coloured light – warm yellow, mauve blue – hanging in emptiness, capillaried by the scribbled silhouettes of twigs. The room was filled with the cool breath of the rain. The sound of dripping trees, the faint moan of traffic. I poured Foomie another drink.

'We could go to the cinema. What's on at the Ritzy?' I said.

'Oh, it's that stupid Japanese film about a man getting his willy cut off. What's it called? "I'm not a Corridor" or something like that.'

'I'll tell you what we could do,' I said, laughing and

154

reaching for the bag of grass. 'There's a dog fight tonight in Stockwell. We could go to that.'

Foomie shook her head.

'What about badger-baiting over in Essex?'

'Badger-baiting is the pits,' said Foomie. 'What time is it? How much longer before I can go home?'

'It's early yet and we're having a great time . . .'

'Like a house smouldering.'

'Do you really want to go dancing?'

'Not really.'

'You sure.'

'Hmm-mm.'

We ended up going to the Atlantic. Foomie walked straight in; I got delayed at the door.

'You want sinsee?'

'No I'm fine.'

'Black ash?'

'No man I'm skint.'

'How much money you got?'

'I've just got enough for a couple of drinks . . .'

'You want a five pound draw?'

'I told you, I'm skint . . .'

The guy got fed up with me and waved me into the pub. Foomie bought two glasses of beer and we waited for the band to come on.

It was the first time I'd been in the Atlantic for a while. Since the night of the raids on Railton Road the pub had got into that cycle of dealing, arguments, fights and police. Despite this, it had been getting more and more crowded and Foomie and I devoted a lot of our energy to making sure we didn't nudge somebody or spill their drink. Previously it had always been nice to get stoned and listen to music here; now I found myself overcome by waves of gulping paranoia.

Ray, an American who had been living in Brixton for a year, came over to where we were standing. I introduced him to Foomie and he told us how a gang was out to get him. He'd got into a fight after someone had spat in his hair while he was on a bus. When the bus stopped he dragged the guy on to the pavement and cracked him in the mouth a couple of times. By this time the guy's friends had got off the bus too and Ray had had to run for it. Now the whole gang were out to get him.

The purpose of this story was to impress Foomie; he looked at her almost continually while he spoke. He even looked at her when he asked me what I would have done in his shoes.

'On the bus?'

'Yeah.'

'Nothing.'

'Nothing? I can't believe it.'

'I'd rather get spat on than beaten-up.'

'Man, you can't live like that. You've got to have some self-respect.'

'That kind of thing is a question of self-preservation, not self-respect.'

'So you'll let people do anything to you? I can't believe it.'

'Look,' I said, wondering what Foomie was making of all this. 'I don't like the idea of being spat on but apart from the unpleasantness — having to wash it off or whatever — it doesn't really bother me. Obviously I think the guy who does it is a right fucking bastard but I'm not going to do anything about it. It's like a code, that idea of self-respect. Either you buy into it or you don't. That's the one good thing about fighting; it usually takes place between people who share the same values. But I don't share those values. That's not where my self-respect lies.'

'Where does it lie then?'

'That's a good question. Maybe I haven't got any at all — which makes life a lot easier . . .'

I thought of the guy who'd been beaten up on the tube. Nobody had done anything to help him; we were all paralysed by our fear. But there was a logic to our fear as well, a logic that we all shared: better he gets a pasting than I get stabbed trying to help.

Ray, meanwhile, was talking to Foomie who responded to his questions with the same formal politeness that I'd noticed when I first met her. As Ray spoke she slipped her arm through mine. Suddenly, off to the right, three young guys with knives were slashing at a big guy who batted them away with a bar stool. As they caught the bright lights of the stage their knives left gleaming hoops and arcs hanging in the darkness. The four of them gradually carved a path across the floor of the pub and disappeared around the corner of the bar.

'Let's go,' said Foomie.

As we walked up Cold Harbour Lane I asked her what she thought of Ray. Laughing, she formed a circle with her thumb and index finger and shook her left hand slowly.

IN THE NEWSPAPER I read about the death of a violinist in a famous quartet. Like the other members of the quartet he was highly respected as an individual musician but it was the quartet itself rather than the individual members of it that was well known. Anyone who enjoyed chamber music would have heard of them but only a small percentage of these would have been able to name any of the members. Together they recorded complete cycles of Beethoven and Schubert quartets. When the violinist died – he was in his sixties – the quartet decided to disband rather than try to continue with a replacement. They had been playing together for about thirty years.

I got up to put a record on the turntable and listened to Coltrane swinging out in wider and wider arcs, aching on the frontier of the possible.

There was a photo of the four members of the string quartet practising together. They were all in their fifties or sixties, dressed in casual clothes with their jackets hung over the back of their chairs. Two were wearing glasses; one was bald and the other had white or grey hair. They had the look of gentle, considerate men who probably enjoyed a joke together during rehearsals when one of them played a wrong note or lost his way in the score. Probably they all had wives who may or may not have accompanied them when they made tours of England or the United States. What the photograph made most plain, however, was that for four or five or however many hours a day they practised they all shared in an activity that probably constituted their main reason for being alive. Gradually, I imagined, the intricacies of their relationships with each other became expressed and defined entirely by the music they were playing. It was hard to imagine them arguing.

It was equally hard to imagine how great must have been the sense of loss for the three surviving members of the quartet. Perhaps there was some trio for strings by Beethoven or Schubert which they would continue to play from time to time, a piece which, whatever its mood – even in the lightest, fastest movements – would be saturated, in their interpretation, by their longing for their dead friend.

There was something beautiful and poignant about the photograph of the middle-aged quartet: the raised bows, the sharp creases in the trousers, the music stands and the look of relaxed concentration.

The tape was coming to an end, the saxophone choked by its own intensity and drowned by the weight of the drums. I thought of Coltrane who was forty when he died, of Eric Dolphy and Charlie Parker and Lee Morgan – shot in a nightclub where he was playing; I thought of Fats Navarro and Clifford Brown who died in their mid-twenties, and of Booker Little who died when he was twenty-three.

The record seemed to end and then, impossibly, the saxophone emerged again, surviving the tidal wave of drums that had broken over it: the resurrection.

SPRING WAS IN the air: low cloud and faint drizzle alternating with drenching showers and biting winds. Leaves. Here and there a few chinks of light in the dull armour of the sky.

Travel Research and Information – the market research company that I worked for from time to time – was organising a huge survey over several rail routes in the south-west of England. They needed forty additional staff and Steranko, Foomie, Carlton, Freddie and I were all taken on. We had to interview passengers on trains and since some of these trains started from places like Truro, Exeter and Penzance at six in the morning the company put us up in an assortment of hotels in the region. Freddie and I stayed in a vast hotel in Taunton where the towels were thick and white, the carpets silent, and the taps eager to fill clean baths with steaming water. Staying away from home was thought to be a great hardship so they paid eight pounds a day expenses. Once that was used up we loaded as much as possible on to the hotel bill: drinks in the bar, room service, twenty quid dinners, newspapers; even things we didn't want like salad sandwiches at two in the morning.

None of us gave a shit about the actual survey and for most of the week we simply ran riot in unspecified parts of south-west England. By careful manipulation of our rosters – suddenly the word roster loomed huge in our lives – Freddie and I managed to meet up with Steranko and Foomie for a lavish meal in Plymouth where they had a double room in the Fitzwilliam hotel. Another day we completed our quota of questionnaires quickly and hopped on a train to Exeter where we wolfed down a couple of cream teas for lunch and strolled round the Cathedral.

So far the weather had been dull and overcast but bright sun over the south-west had been forecast for the following day. As Freddie and I tucked into a five-course meal at the hotel that night, he said that in the circumstances we were virtually obliged to take off to some coastal resort and spend the day lying on a beach, eating ice-cream and making up answers to the questionnaires. The next day we did a few interviews and then caught a train to Teignmouth where we'd arranged to meet Carlton. By lunch-time the three of us were on the beach, jackets folded up in plastic shopping bags, sipping cold beers and using questionnaires to keep the sun out of our eyes.

'Paradise,' said Carlton, speaking for all of us in a voice that was drowsy from the heat and the beer. 'Three quid an hour for doing fuck-all.'

'Not quite fuck-all,' I said. 'There's still the questionnaires to make up.' Inventing answers was not as simple as we thought; it was very easy to make some little slip which had your imaginary respondent making an impossible journey or travelling on a non-existent ticket. In a way, as Freddie explained from his deckchair, it was a bit like writing a novel: you had to invent a character – a retired school teacher, a business executive – and think yourself into his itinerary and probable opinions.

'We'd better leave it to you in that case then Freddie,' said Carlton, as we rolled up our trousers and paddled in the grey-green ocean.

025

WE HAD ONLY been back in London a few days when I got a call from Freddie. He sounded a little strange and said he wouldn't be coming over that evening.

'How come?'

'I got my head beaten in last night.'

'Oh no.'

'Yeah.'

'Where are you?'

'Home.'

'Have you been to hospital?'

'I went this morning.'

'Are you OK? I mean . . .'

'I suppose so.'

'How . . .? Hey listen, I'll come over late this afternoon.'

'That would be nice.'

'About four or five. Is there anything I can bring you?'

'No.'

On the way to Freddie's I stopped at the record stall in Brixton market and bought an Art Pepper album. Freddie took a while to come to the door – I heard him shuffling along the corridor like an old man – and when he opened it he just nodded slowly. He was wearing dark glasses. His face looked puffed up and purple in places.

'Freddie,' I said, feeling tears pricking my eyes. I put my arm around his shoulder. I closed my eyes tight a couple of times and then stepped back.

Freddie took off his glasses and in the bright sunlight I could see the harm done to his face. One side was swollen out around the cheekbone and badly discoloured; the other was livid and bright-looking. There were small cuts on his forehead and cheek. One eye was swollen shut and purple; the other was bloodshot but basically OK. His lips and nose were swollen. Both nostrils were filled with hard black blood. His voice came out thick and bubbly because the inside of his mouth was smashed and swollen. He looked so bad it was difficult to imagine his face ever healing again.

We walked to his room and Freddie lay on the bed, propped up on pillows.

'I'm so sorry Freddie.'

'Me too.'

'Are you going to be OK?'

'Yeah.'

It didn't matter that this was all we said. It didn't matter that we didn't hold each other and sob, that words adequate to the situation were not there. Tenderness is a matter of inflection, not vocabulary.

'I've brought you a record,' I said. 'I thought getting something for nothing might cheer you up.'

'That was kind of you . . .'

'How d'you feel?'

'I've felt better. My head aches, I get dizzy when I stand up, my nose hurts, my mouth is sore. My ribs hurt . . .'

'What happened at the hospital?'

'I spent the whole morning there. What a shit-hole. I was sitting next to a bloke with a big bloody bandage round his foot, tucking into a bag of McDonald's burgers. Have you been to a hospital recently?'

'No . . .'

'It was like a DHSS waiting-room. The same atmosphere: people driven there as a last resort. Everything old and worn out and not even clean-looking. All the doctors and nurses looking like they were going to drop dead from exhaustion at any moment. I tell you, I'm going to join BUPA.'

'What did they say?'

'They took a whole load of X-rays. Basically I'm alright. My teeth are still all there, my nose and jaw aren't broken. My eyes don't seem to be damaged . . .'

There was a loud knock at the door.

'That'll be Carlton,' said Freddie. I let Carlton in and made some tea while he went in to Freddie.

When I returned with the tray Carlton was very gently dabbing Freddie's face with something.

'It's arnica,' he said. 'It brings the swelling down and soothes everything. How's that feel Freddie?'

'OK. Nice.'

Carlton continued very gently putting this thin cream on Freddie's face. Again my eyes nettled with tears. I poured the tea while Freddie – he couldn't drink, his mouth was too bad – told us what happened. He'd just come out of a party when a young guy asked him the time. Freddie said he didn't have a watch and next thing the guy was hitting him all over the place. He didn't even take any money.

'I don't remember much else,' Freddie concluded. 'Except that just after I'd fallen on the floor he kicked me in the chest but I had a book in my coat pocket and that took the brunt of it.'

'What was the book?'

'Rilke poems funnily enough. It's made me regard him in a whole new light.'

A few moments later Carlton said, 'Did you get a look at the geezer?'

'Not really. I hardly saw him. Just a young black guy, short hair, leather jacket. About twenty I suppose. Younger maybe.'

'Would you recognise him again?'

'No. You know, he was just some guy who was so pissed off he wanted to beat somebody's shit in so he'd feel a bit better,' said Freddie. 'It could've been a lot worse. I wasn't stabbed. Nothing's broken . . . Once in six years, you know? It happens.'

'Yeah.'

We stopped speaking and listened to Art Pepper. It was a recording of a gig he played a couple of years before he died, the music of someone who'd learnt to cherish what he did. Pepper was an alcoholic and a junkie; he served time in San Quentin, but he didn't squander his ability by getting as fucked up as he did. He had to waste his talent in order for it finally to flourish. As an artist his weakness was essential to him; in his playing it became a source of strength.

The room filled up with hurt pity and the tenderness of scarred hands. The music cried out but there was no appeal in it; it had to find its own consolation.

I was still at that age when you do not form friendships but are formed by them, when there is no difference between having good friends and being a good friend. I'd known Freddie for a long time, six or seven years, twice as long at least as I'd known any of my other friends. I hardly ever kept in touch with people for more than three years – Freddie was the only exception I could think of. After about three years of knowing a group of people your identity becomes fixed by their expectations, you become trapped by your shared history; your range of responses becomes more and more limited. After a certain point there's no room for anything but the most gradual alteration in your identity. The past suffocates and restricts and the only way you can breathe and move again is with completely new circumstances, new people. With Freddie it was different. My affection for him exerted no pressure. I mean the kind of pressure where liking someone makes you want to be like them – this was exactly how I felt about Steranko – and then, after a while, that turns into its opposite: you begin to dislike them for not being enough like you. I say 'you'; I mean 'I'.

Freddie once said that friends are the difference between being a spectator and a participant and I remembered how, together with another friend who I'd since lost touch with, the three of us had got beaten up by one guy outside a party in Putney. 'Go on: all three of you rush me,' he'd said after hitting each of us once. 'Right,' he said when we all just stood there, 'now I'm really going to teach you a lesson,' and he proceeded to instruct each of us in turn. Eventually we ran off with no real damage done – a fat lip, a black eye, a bloody nose – and soon the whole episode was remembered only as anecdote fodder. This was about the time when – on the basis of having flicked through *The Dharma Bums* and watched several episodes of 'Kung Fu' – Freddie claimed to be a Buddhist. That lasted about six weeks and soon after we dropped our first tabs of acid. I remembered Freddie, notebook in hand, waiting for something to happen. 'Am turning inside out' was the only entry he made. For the next year we gobbled down micro-dots and blotters by the handful. 'You know,' Freddie said sadly as we were coming down one evening. 'One day we'll look back at these days and we won't be able to remember a thing about them because we were too out of our heads . . .'

The record came to an end. Freddie had fallen asleep and was breathing heavily through his mouth. I looked at Carlton and we smiled. I made more tea and Carlton put on another record. When that one finished we played another, letting the room grow dark around us, hearing the hiss of the gas fire between songs. Freddie woke about an hour later, unsure where he was or what had happened to him.

'Where am I?' He looked at Carlton and me, glad we were still there.

We stayed until nine. We told Freddie we'd phone him tomorrow.

'Thanks . . . for the record and the arnica,' he said as we left. 'Take care.'

'You too.'

Carlton and I walked part of the way home together. Getting done over in some way was just a question of time really. You hoped that when your turn came it wouldn't be anything too bad, that it would just be young kids who were only after your money, that if you handed it over you'd be free to go, that if you got punched to the ground you wouldn't get a kicking too, that if they pulled a knife they'd slash and not stab; and you hoped that you would spot the moment when the only chance left was to run – and that if the worst came to the worst, if all else failed, you would have the presence of mind to lash out with whatever came to hand.

024

LATER THAT WEEK Foomie's flat got burgled. They came in through the bathroom window and took a cassette player and a portable TV. Foomie said it made her feel glad she didn't own anything.

I was edgy and alert as I walked around. The whole area seemed tense but it was difficult to know whether this was a result of my own contingent experience or of my gauging an aggregate feeling that made itself subtly but palpably felt.

I told people about Freddie and the guy getting done over on the tube. They told me about things that had happened to them, that they had seen or that other people had told them. Ripples of panic and suspicion and worry spread out and intersected.

I went to dinner with some people in Kennington whom I vaguely knew and quite liked. I took beer; everyone else brought wine but wanted to drink beer. When someone asked what I did I said 'odds and ends, bits and pieces, nothing really' and felt pointless as a broken bulb.

The food was nice and there was plenty of it. When we'd finished eating and had drunk all of the beer and most of the wine somebody started telling a story about how he'd recently been involved in a car accident. Someone else told of an injury they'd suffered a few years ago. I told the story of how my leg got smashed in at the factory. We talked about a programme that had been on TV about self-defence. Someone told of how they'd recently been burgled and after everyone had told their burglary stories we talked about mugging, rape, trouble at parties, stabbings and broken bottle fights in pubs.

These subjects were our currency, the common denominator of our experience; they were subjects of interest to us all, topics on which everyone had something to say.

The dinner came to an end – it was a Monday night and people had to get up for work the next day – and I caught a late bus home. A storm was building up and by the time I got off the bus at Brixton a steady rain was falling. Walking past Freddie's house I saw a light in his window on the second floor. I stood beneath a street lamp, threads of yellow rain falling around me. I saw a face framed by the window in the warm light of the anglepoise above Freddie's desk, looking out into the night. Suddenly there was a flash of lightning like a jagged crack in time. A shudder of bleached rain.

I glanced up at the window once more and walked on, the sound of my footsteps lost in a low roll of thunder.

023

I SPENT THE rest of the week in Court. A friend of mine who knew a solicitor asked if I wanted to do some court clerking. All you had to do, he said, was sit with the client and take a few notes to remind the barrister of what was going on. It paid twenty-five quid a day, cash.

'Oh and don't forget to wear a suit,' he said before putting the phone down.

The case was being heard at the Crown Court in Croydon and I was quite looking forward to it as I travelled down there on the train: meeting the defendant, piecing together a story from the unfolding catechism of the court, weighing up the truth and falsehood of witnesses, seeing the judge and lawyers in action . . .

I met up easily with the barrister – a puppy-fat Oxbridge graduate – and he introduced me to the client. He was a sad half-caste kid, an eighteen-year-old no-hoper who wasn't much good at anything, not even looking sympathetic in Court. He was accused of breaking and entering some offices in Lewes. His story was that he'd gone to look for his friend Trotsky who was living down there. He called in at various bars and asked where Trotsky was but nobody had seen him. In the end he got pissed, missed the last train back and was picked up while trying to find somewhere to crash for the night.

The judge didn't look at him sternly or savagely; he hardly looked at him at all. The whole thing was conducted like a bored ceremony that had considerable power but which no longer had any meaning. Clarifying points of legal procedure for the benefit of the jury, with a bored impatience he made no attempt to conceal, the judge made it plain that he had no interest in either the judicial or human aspects of the case – the only time he showed any alacrity was in arranging adjournments for lunch. The members of the jury were bored too; they wished they were involved in something more interesting like armed robbery or rape. There was nothing about the kid being tried to threaten the indifference or rouse the interest of anyone in the Court. The proceedings left him with only two options: insolence or submissiveness – and since there was nothing to be gained by either of these he looked bored. The nominal object of the court's attention, he played a part in its proceedings only to the extent that someone getting stitched up by doctors participates in surgery.

If he got convicted, he told me during one of several adjournments, he'd probably end up back inside. He could handle that if he had to. Maybe he'd get off with a suspended sentence in which case he'd have the summer to look forward to.

The case dragged on. Each day I commuted down to Croydon in my suit. The longer the case went on the more money I earned (I'd already begun to think like a lawyer). Somehow the elaborate indifference of the court proceedings coloured – or rather, they did exactly the opposite, drained all colour from – my feelings for the boy. He became simply 'the accused', an abstraction, a legal term. Both his case and the circumstances in which he was being tried were dwarfed by the lofty ethics of justice in whose name they were being carried out. In the praxis of the Court all that remained of the ideal it embodied was the shabby paraphernalia of robes and wigs, the elaborate hierarchical etiquette with which only the officers of the court were familiar.

After a brief adjournment the jury proudly delivered their verdict of guilty. It was as if by announcing his guilt they had negatively affirmed their own freedom from civic wrongdoing, demonstrated to the Court their own harmlessness. The judge looked gravely over his glasses and handed out a suspended sentence, pointing out to this sad eighteen-year-old (the accused, the defendant, the client – or did he have some new title now that his guilt had been established and proved beyond reasonable doubt?) that the suspended prison term would be there, hanging over his head like the sword of Damocles. Unimpressed by the classical reference the defendant didn't even blink. I walked with him back to the station. He borrowed a pound for the train fare to London and bought a pack of cigarettes. That was the last I saw of him. I called in at the solicitor's office, claimed half a day more than I'd actually worked and multiplied my claim for travelling expenses by improbable complications of route. They didn't seem bothered one way or the other.

SUDDENLY, LIKE A submarine breaking the surface of the ocean after long months beneath the waves, it was summer. From open windows, radio chat tinkled to the street. Carlton and I walked round the market, ostensibly to buy vegetables but really just for the pleasure of seeing bare arms and legs, women in dresses, sunglasses, the sun on people's faces. The market was clogged up with smiling people. Coins glinted in the sun as they were handed over. The stallholders had something to say to everybody. No one wanted potatoes or turnips. It was oranges that compelled attention, piled on top of each other, two halves cut open and glistening freshly at the bottom of each stack. Apples, lemons, grapefruits, tomatoes swelling redly in the heat. Next to the fruit-seller the man who ran the china stall pinned up a notice – 'Please don't stand in front of my stall. It's not a waiting-room for the fruit-stall' – and was happy to let the sun polish his wares. Winding through the noise was the sound of an ice-cream van; today was the first day of the year he was selling more ice-creams than hotdogs. I bought a can of coke that tasted like being hit in the teeth gradually. A group of young guys, heads almost shaved and wearing Raybans, trainers and black leather jackets moved fast through the crowd. Heavy women were clinging to their shopping and laughing with their friends. There was the smell of coconut oil in hair, glistening. Music from shop doorways mingled and remixed in the open air. Splotches of ice-cream on the pavement. A car went by, trailing a loud exhaust of hip-hop.

'Greenpeace,' said Luther shaking his coffee jar suggestively in front of an American tourist with a camera and wide-angle check trousers. A mad guy with locks and a walking-stick was shouting 'let me out! let me out' as if he was locked up inside himself. A tall rasta in a blue tracksuit strode past taking no notice of anything except where he was going. At the Recreation Centre a BBC news team were stopping representative-looking people and asking how Brixton had changed since the riots. Other representative-looking people shrugged through the heavy doors, struggling under a bulk of muscle which, until they got to the weights room, looked awkward and inessential as a diver's tanks.

'I'd give my right arm for biceps like that,' I said to Carlton.

We made our way along the crowded pavement, the elderly moved cautiously along in jackets and ties, in cardigans and coats. I saw Freddie's bike, locked up to a lamp-post by the tube station. A young punk with grey arms and eyes so pinned you wondered how any light got in asked Carlton for money.

'I'm always giving you money, man.'

'I'm always skint.'

Carlton handed him some coins. We crossed the High Street where the traffic was hardly moving. Bus drivers, shirt sleeves rolled up to their elbows, sat it out; conductors hung from the back platforms of their buses. From somewhere in the congealing traffic a police car wailed pointlessly.

We stopped off at the Trinity and sat outside, our beer warming quickly in the sun. It was like a little bit of Islington, estate agents said of this square, with its pub and restaurant. The small forecourt of the pub was packed with people who looked like they worked for the council, arguing departmental politics, getting a few down them and loosening their ties. I felt sleepy drunk after one pint but still only just resisted the temptation to have a couple more.

'It's riot weather this, perfect riot weather,' said a shiny-faced white guy, holding his beer up to the sun as if reading the future in the dregs.

Slowly, dragging our bags of produce, we walked along the High Street past the smearily opaqued front of a large shop that was being refitted. This often happened: a shop selling mass-produced beds and furniture started up with an opening sale that lasted for a couple of months. Then there was a closing-down sale and as soon as that finished the windows were whited over and signs saying 'New Shop Opening Soon' appeared. Then a new shop – called Price Slasher, or Cost Buster – opened on the old premises, selling exactly the same thing.

'That must be the worst shop in London,' said Carlton. 'The only decent thing you can buy in there is a black bin-liner.'

A few yards further on was the new, refurbished Woolworths where they used to stock nothing except security guards and empty shelves. We walked past the Ritzy and the library where round-the-year alcoholics stuck with the Tennants Extra that served as anti-freeze through the long months of winter. A few steps further on we passed a place called Brixton Fashion. For a long time no one knew what it was supposed to be: there was only this elaborate designer façade with nothing going on behind it. Then Freddie pointed out that our confusion was due to wondering what was happening *behind* the façade when what was going on here was, precisely, the façade. The whole thing existed solely in the realm of display. The front wasn't the outward display of a concealed function: the façade *was* the function.

'What sort of architecture is that?' I asked Carlton.

'Mock something,' he said.

A little further on someone had sprayed DON'T CATCH IT on a clean white wall.

021

WITH THE GOOD weather everything changed for the better. Boredom turned to leisure. People with no work were glad once again that they didn't have jobs to go to. What to do was no longer a problem. Everyone felt bouncy and fresh as new tennis balls.

Freddie was getting better too. The bruising had come out and the dizziness had passed. Apart from some discolouring around one eye you could hardly tell that anything had happened to him. I ran into him late one morning as he bought a paper from the stall outside the Prince of Wales on the corner of Cold Harbour Lane. A couple of years ago the man who ran this stall had handed Freddie his paper with the words: 'Now you look like what I'd call a radical intellectual sir.' It made Freddie's day – it made his year – and since then he'd always bought his paper from the same bloke.

'You're looking great Freddie,' I said as we strolled around the market, enjoying the smell of the new season. He was wearing a crumpled linen jacket and had the look of someone who might go on to write novels set in south-east Asia.

'You bet. I'm thriving both physically and financially.'

'You've sold a story?'

'Not exactly. But I did sell Steranko my bike.'

'How much for?'

'Sixty quid.'

'This calls for a celebration,' I said, offering him a wine-gum.

'What about you?' Freddie said. 'What have you been doing?'

'Fuck all really. I take each day a little easier than the previous one. I've started the long slow fade to retirement and senility.'

'You were saying that three years ago.'

'I was joking then. Now it's really happening. I didn't realise it at the time but those jokes were just a premonition of what was to come.'

'What is the past though,' said Freddie, 'if not an intense premonition of the inevitable?'

We walked past the side of Woolworths, past one of those badly painted murals depicting a multi-racial society where women are the equal of men, where no one is discriminated against because of their age or race or sex, where work looks like play and play looks like work because it's all painted with a childlike simplicity and the sun never stops shining. Across the road, like nothing in the mural, guys hung outside the Granada Car Hire or sat chewing in the Acapulco. An old man came out of the door, dragging a leg that was heavy and useless as a sledgehammer.

We ate a pizza in Franco's in the covered market. It was a tiny place with room for only a dozen people inside, either on stools or at tables. Outside in the Arcade there were more tables but these were always full too. It was the sort of place where it was nice to hang out but because it was so crowded and there were always so many people waiting to get served you had to do your hanging out quickly. With people eating or queuing for tables or waiting for takeaways there was hardly room for the waiters to move. There was hardly even room for the opera which tumbled to the floor from two speakers high up on the wall. After ten minutes we got a table outside which was fine because the sunlight and warmth fell through the high glass roof of the Arcade.

'I heard a gunshot last night,' said Freddie, cutting his pizza into meticulous slices.

'How do you know it was a gunshot and not a car backfiring?'

'You can tell.'

'How?'

'A gunshot sounds exactly like a car backfiring. A car

backfiring sounds exactly like a gunshot. It's called a paradox lieutenant.' He said it in a kind of fast drawl, the whole sentence coming out like one long corrugated word.

We left Franco's and walked to the health food shop so that Freddie could gawp miserably at the woman who worked there.

Inside there was a long queue of people waiting to pay. You always had to wait here. Learning to roll joints in the back of the shop with the right proportion of hash and herbal smoking mixture was a higher priority than mastering mental arithmetic as far as the staff were concerned. Not being in a hurry was part of the underlying ideology of the whole place. What really made the staff happy was a customer asking if he could see the boss – then they could point out that there was no boss, the shop was a collective.

'Excellent,' said Freddie, seeing the size of the queue and picking up a pack of wholewheat spaghetti. 'Bigger the queue, longer the look.'

I picked up a big bag of brown rice and then, after a moment's hesitation, another.

'What d'you want all that rice for? You'll never eat it.'

'I know. I've got a big jar and I'm trying to fill it up. It's my ambition.'

We shuffled towards the counter. The woman Freddie claimed to have been in love with for almost two years was wearing a black vest; her hair was tied up in a scarf. Her arms were tanned; she looked energetic and full of health (in sharp contrast to the rest of the staff who looked like they could use a plate of steak and chips). Freddie quietly quoted a line of Rilke – he was definitely feeling better - 'Beauty is only the first touch of a terror we still can bear . . .'

As luck would have it we got served by the man behind the counter. Once the guy had grappled with the addition for a couple of minutes Freddie handed over an irritable five pound note and paid for everything. We both said hello to the woman who was laughing with the person she was serving.

'Things really seem to be hotting up between you two,' I said as we headed away from the counter.

'Beauty is an idea,' he said after we'd stepped outside and

clumsily held the door open for a young woman with a pram and a heavy bag of shopping. 'That's the beauty of it.'

As we walked towards Effra Road we saw the green, black and gold flag of the ANC fluttering over the Town Hall. Further on we saw workers hurrying out of a small factory. They carried lunch-boxes and tool bags. Some were in a hurry to catch buses, others walked slowly, talking and joking in groups or in pairs.

'That's one of the nicest things you can ever see isn't it?' said Freddie.

'What?'

'People coming out of a factory into the sun.'

We crossed the road to my flat and for the first time that year sat drinking beer on the roof. Every now and then a plane passed overhead.

020

I RAN FOR a bus and hauled myself on as it accelerated away from traffic lights. The bus swung round a corner as I lurched to a seat just behind the driver's cabin. It wasn't until I looked up that I noticed the driver: a beautiful black woman, her face in profile as she looked out across traffic filtering in from the right-hand lane. She was wearing a pale blue T-shirt, gold earrings; muscles moved in her arms as she hauled the wheel round. When the bus was held up at lights or in heavy traffic the conductor leaned across me and spoke to her through the tiny strip of open window just above my head. To speak to the conductor the driver had to twist round in her seat and lean out the open door of the cab. As soon as the traffic cleared the bus accelerated smoothly away. Some kind of race was going on with another bus. If we were in front and slowed down to pick up passengers the bus behind would pass us quickly; and then, a few minutes later, we would overtake again. Every time it happened our driver laughed at the man driving the other bus. Whenever we approached a stop where no one wanted to get on or off the conductor gave two sharp tugs on the cord to tell the driver not to stop and in this way we gradually pulled clear of the other bus.

Every couple of minutes our driver waved to drivers in other buses, grinning at them. An elderly white couple got off while the bus waited at lights and gave the thumbs up sign to her and she waved and grinned back. I watched her and wondered about her life, about where she lived, and if she was married.

Executives complain of stress and fatigue but it's as nothing compared with the effort involved in conducting or driving buses in rush-hour traffic five or six days a week. No businessman in the city worked harder than this woman. Driving this bus was something to be proud of – and it was a pride in which everyone who saw her shared – for a few minutes, a few stops. Watching her heaving the bus around so easily you sensed that what she was capable of would always transcend her circumstances and for once, rather than being a source of frustration, this certainty was a kind of affirmation; an affirmation of human potential of the same order as that glimpsed in a work of art or in the performance of any kind of sport, or in the playing of a musical instrument.

019

AS I GET off the tube broken glass crunches under my feet: the remains of a wine bottle. A few steps further on there are large curved triangles of green glass in a pool of deep blood. Slumped on a bench is a middle-aged man with blood over his shirt and a gash down one side of his face. An ambulance man bandages him sternly. I am walking behind two rastafarians: together the three of us sprint up the escalator. By the time we get to the ticket barrier, like a photographer whose finger presses the shutter by reflex, I have already drafted these words.

This book is like an album of snaps. In any snaps strangers intrude; the prints preserve an intimacy that lasted only for a fraction of a second as someone, unnoticed at the time, strayed unintentionally into the picture frame. Hidden among the familiar, laughing faces of friends are the glimpsed shapes of strangers; and in the distant homes of tourists there *you* are, at the edge of the frame, slightly out of focus, in the midst of other peoples' memories. We stray into each other's lives. In the course of any day in any city it happens thousands of times and every now and again it is caught on film. That is what is happening here. Look closely and maybe there, close to the margin of the page, you will find the hurried glance of your own image: queuing at the bar, hurrying for the bus, drinking beer on a roof, bleeding on the floor of the tube (I wanted to help you but was too frightened; I'm sorry, I really am).

Often what happens accidentally, unintentionally, at the

edges or in the margins of pictures – the apparently irrelevant detail – lends the photograph its special meaning. What is happening in the foreground in sharpest focus seems somehow unimportant or meaningless compared with – or at least is leant meaning and importance only *through* – the accidental intrusion of detail: the glimpse of someone's shoes; a car in the background; a furled umbrella; the tilt of someone's hat; the child eating a lolly. These details absorb and transform – and are themselves absorbed and transformed by – the principal action; the main subjects become saturated by the accidental inflections of attendant details. The distinction between foreground and background collapses; the subject is usurped by his surroundings, by the momentary pattern of clouds, by other faces in the street; his shadow is lost in a blur of others – the shadows cast by accidental gestures.

018

FOOMIE'S TEETH CRUNCHED into a huge apple, its skin so dark that the inside, marked by the tracks of her teeth, looked dazzling white.

'You want a bite?' she said, holding it out to me. I shook my head.

'You're missing a great apple.'

Foomie had a knack for buying nice fruit that I could only regard with astonished admiration. When I bought fruit it was always either over-ripe or under-ripe, never just right.

'The other day I bought some cherries,' I said. 'They were like little sacks of rotten black blood; the day after that I bought some bananas that were so soft you could have chewed them quite comfortably within ten minutes of getting your teeth ripped out without anaesthetic.'

'Ugh, shut up. You're making me feel sick . . .'

We were on the roof. Foomie was sitting back in one of the deckchairs she'd spent the winter making. She'd bought a whole load of them from seaside resorts, painted the frames black and replaced the canvas with brightly coloured prints of her own design. She had given one to each of her friends and was trying to sell the rest at Portobello market for fifteen pounds each. I leant against the railing and looked at my own deckchair as it lounged contentedly beneath the blue sky.

On the roof of the lift-housing rested the finished sculpture of the woman that someone had worked on throughout last summer. Freed from the block of stone she was propped up on an elbow with her head back, one leg bent at the knee. Though only two or three feet in length, the sculpture was so life-like that it made the roof seem much bigger than it was, as if what we saw was a life-size figure, lounging in the sun some way off.

'I've got some grapes in my bag,' Foomie said after a while. 'You want some?'

'No thanks. For me the pip destroys the pleasure of the grape.'

'They're seedless.'

'Are they?'

'Not exactly.'

Foomie was wearing a vest, shorts and a battered straw hat that shaded her face. I was wearing shorts too. Looking at Foomie made me feel very white.

'Am I going brown?'

'You look like you've just stepped out of a microwave. You ought to put some cream on. You'll burn.'

'I never get sun burn,' I boasted.

'I wish Steranko would hurry up with those beers,' Foomie said, excavating another crisp apple.

'Me too.' Until he'd been persuaded to go to the off-licence Steranko had spent the afternoon painting up on the roof — since the good weather began he'd kept an easel, brushes and paints at my flat — while Foomie and I read or talked or just sat around.

'Here he is,' I said, looking over the railing and seeing him walk along the street with a brown bag full of beer.

Steranko had only been back a short time when he reached for his jacket to relight a joint that had gone out. The jacket was lying on the concrete and as he pulled it towards him his keys, resting on the jacket, rolled off and disappeared down the drainage hole which had been lurking there unseen. A few seconds later there was a loud splash from several floors down.

'Shit!'

The drainage hole was only a little bigger than the plug-hole of a bath. There was nothing to see as we gathered round and peered down it.

'Where does that pipe end up?'

'In about three foot of filthy water underneath the block.'

'Shit. Is there any way to get at it?'

'No. But it's not a problem is it? What about the other people in your house?'

'Fuck. They've gone to Thailand. They're not going to be back for three weeks.'

'Has no one else got a key?'

'Foo – oh shit you gave them back to me the other day didn't you?'

'Can you get in somehow?' Foomie asked.

'Oh there's no fucking chance. That house is like Fort Knox.'

'Why didn't I get a spare set of keys done? I just do not fucking believe it. I may as well just throw myself off the roof now. Oh shit.'

Foomie put her arm round Steranko's shoulders.

'And I'm just beginning to feel stoned as well.'

'Maybe that'll help you see the funny side of it.'

'There's no funny side *to* it. It's total head-fuck.' Steranko tugged a handful of hair with both hands. 'That grass is so strong as well. I can't think straight.'

Foomie and I started laughing.

'It is not fucking funny,' Steranko said.

'No, I know it's not,' I said laughing. 'Just the thought of it makes me feel quite faint. I'm not sure I could bear it if it had happened to me.'

'I'm not sure I can either.'

The sky was full of the motorway sound of Concorde passing overhead. As the noise faded Foomie said: 'I've got an idea.'

'What? Don't tell me: I go down to the ground floor, pull the manhole cover off with my bare hands and then crawl around in two foot of shit using a bent straw for a snorkel. Or better still I persuade someone else to do it. That might be a bit difficult.'

'It's just an idea but it might work,' Foomie said calmly.

'Right what is it? I'm willing to consider anything.'

'OK. What we need is a long piece of string . . .'

'I've got that in my flat,' I said.

'And a magnet.' There was a slight pause then Steranko leapt in the air.

'Brilliant! Brilliant!' he shouted. 'Have you got a magnet?'

' 'Fraid not. Hard luck.'

'Shit.'

'Maybe we can buy one.'

'Where?'

'Mr Patel's is the best bet but he shuts at six.'

'What time is it now?'

We stood and counted quietly as the town-hall clock struck four . . . five . . . six.

Steranko hurtled towards the door. We heard a crash as he tumbled down a few steps and then looked down into the street and saw him sprinting along the pavement.

'Poor Steranko. I'd laugh if the shop was shut,' Foomie said and we both giggled. I went down to my flat and hunted out a ball of string.

Anxious minutes passed. The sky was still beautiful. Steranko's easel cast awkward shadows across the roof. Birds chirped and sang.

Steranko came back through the door, grim-faced and breathing heavily. Then he grinned hugely and pulled a magnet out of his pocket. It was shaped exactly like a magnet in a children's comic: U-shaped, painted red except for a quarter of an inch at each end.

'Foomie if this works I'll buy you the biggest meal you've ever eaten,' Steranko said, tying the string around the magnet in a fierce knot. 'And if it doesn't you'll be on bread and water for six months . . . Right, now comes the difficult part.'

The three of us crouched round the drainage hole. It was like a scene from Mark Twain rewritten for the late urban world when all that remained of lakes and rivers was this one tiny plunge hole leading to a pit of sewage. Steranko paid out the string. When he had let out about fifty feet there was a faint plop. He continued letting out the string. Every now and again he tugged it to check that it was still taut. He paid out several feet more until the string hung loose in his fist.

'Bring 'er up,' I said.

Steranko gently pulled at the string, careful to ensure that

186

the magnet didn't bang against the sides of the pipe. He kept pulling. The string was tense. Eventually it became wet and dirty. Foomie and I looked on expectantly as Steranko stood up and pulled the magnet clear of the hole. And there, clinging precariously to it, was a small bunch of keys.

'Rejoice! Rejoice!' Steranko exclaimed, hugging Foomie and kissing her loudly. 'The ingenuity of the human mind!'

'You couldn't have done it without my string,' I whined and we all laughed.

'Superb string,' Steranko said, beaming and putting his arm around my shoulder.

The sound of the evening rush-hour rose up from the streets. From overhead came the deep clatter and thump of a police helicopter tracking the convoy of prisoners on its way back from the courts to Brixton prison. The three of us stood with our arms around each other, laughing loudly at the sun.

I TURNED ON the TV to watch Wimbledon for a few minutes and ended up watching for two days. Since I'd last watched tennis a couple of years previously the players seemed to have attained new, almost superhuman standards. Not that this made it more interesting – on the contrary it was the sheer tedium of the game that made it so compelling. If you tuned in for five minutes you wouldn't see much at all, especially in the men's game where a thunder-flash serve had become so essential that the players had to put themselves in a state of deep trance before they could even think about hitting the ball. One guy took ten bounces of the ball, two finger sniffs, a couple of forehead wipes and a dozen racket twists before smacking the ball into the net. After pausing for two minutes he repeated exactly the same ritual and sent the ball flying into his opponent's service court. Unfortunately the ball was judged to have touched the net en route and so, to complete what was perhaps the most elaborately time-consuming double-fault ever attempted, he went through the whole routine again before thumping the ball down the opposite tramline. No wonder he was angry.

No wonder, either, that some of the line judges found it difficult to stay awake and had to take pot luck on close calls. It actually seemed that the conflict between players and officials had reached such a pitch of animosity as to constitute the chief interest of the match. As far as the line judges were concerned their job was to goad a given player with unjust decisions until he was forced to concede sufficient penalty points for bad behaviour to leave the match hopelessly beyond reach. Once that had been achieved the officials switched their attention to the other player. As for the players, their behaviour had degenerated to the point where the commentator found himself looking back fondly on John McEnroe as quite a gent. Even unseeded players were now quite capable of the kind of sustained *F*-ing and *Are-you-fucking-blind*-ing that used to be the preserve of only the most talented players. I imagined some young player plumbing new depths of unpopularity by threatening the umpire with his racket or taking a swipe at a docile ballboy who'd had the misfortune to hand him an unlucky ball. The stage-managed nastiness of one or two players was almost as ritualised as wrestling. I half expected to see someone whipping up the crowd with a chant of Ea-sy! Ea-sy! after a particularly vicious forearm smash.

Inspired by all this tennis I called Steranko to see if he fancied a game but he was out. So was Carlton. As a last resort I tried Freddie.

'There's no point. I can hardly even hit the ball. The only bit of the game I'm any good at is the drinking afterwards – as long as the barman keeps serving I can keep knocking them back,' he said, laughing enthusiastically at his own joke. 'Let's just go out for a drink instead. We can take our rackets if that makes you feel better.'

IT WAS ANOTHER perfect blue day but I didn't have a chance to get on the roof until the early evening. The sky was turning lemon where the sun would later set. Overhead it was pale blue with a few air-brush splashes of light cloud. I was sitting at the end of the low wall at the edge of the roof, one arm hanging over the railing, dangling into the blue air like it was a lake. I'd adopted this posture of exaggerated relaxation because of the book I had propped open on my knees: Italo Calvino's *Invisible Cities*. Freddie had lent it to me on the strict understanding that I didn't squander it by reading it on the tube, that I read it only in ideal conditions, when I could savour each sentence 'like a hammock slung between full stops'. (Freddie tended to wax lyrical about Calvino; he once said that he knew exactly how he was going to meet the woman of his dreams – they'd be sitting opposite each other on the tube, both reading *If on a Winter's Night a Traveller* and that would be that.) Sticking more or less to Freddie's strictures I'd been reading it off and on for about six months and was still only halfway through.

Perched up there on the low wall, I'd only read a couple of pages when I caught a glimpse of someone moving on the opposite block, a blur in the corner of my eye. I looked over and saw a woman leaning on the rail, looking across my roof at the pale yellow of the evening light. I knew I'd seen her somewhere before but had no idea who she was. She was wearing dark glasses and a T-shirt that had been washed so many times it was hardly red at all. Her skin looked tanned and calm in the evening light. Her brown hair was tied back loosely. She glanced towards me as I looked at her.

I shouted 'Hi' and smiled. She waved, smiling.

'Nice isn't it?'

'Wonderful . . .'

'I'm surprised there's not more people up here,' I said.

'What?'

All around us was the faint rumble of the evening traffic. We threw words across the street and sometimes they were difficult to catch and fell unheard into the space between us.

'I said I'm surprised there's no one else around.'

'Yes.'

I nodded. Behind her I could see a red armchair that someone had recently dragged on to the roof.

'You live here?' I called. She nodded.

'You too?'

'Yeah. I've seen you around, I think.'

I smiled. She bent over the railing and looked down into the street then pulled her head back so that the sun touched her throat. She looked back, a sparkle of light bouncing off her dark glasses.

'What are you reading?' she said.

I held up the book. She leaned forward a little, raised her glasses and squinted into the sun.

'I can't see,' she said, leaving the glasses perched up on her forehead.

'You're too far away. Maybe you should come over, then you could see it better,' I said, grinning widely. She was smiling too, but not as much as I was.

'Couldn't you just tell me?'

'It's one of those books you really need to look at closely.' Again I had a smile the size of a slice of melon.

'Is it?' she said, laughing.

'Yeah, ideally while drinking a cold beer . . .'

'Cold beer?'

'Like ice.'

She paused for a moment, smiling and looking around the sky.

'It's a great book,' I said. She looked back, smiling and nodding.

'Well . . .' She tapped her fingers along the railing and then added: 'I'll be about five minutes.'

'Fine.' She paused for a few seconds then turned and headed towards the stairs.

'Hey!' I shouted as she was about to open the door to the stairs. 'Don't forget the beers!'

Her laugh floated across the street invisibly.

'Don't push your luck.'

A little while later I saw her walk out from her block into the street.

I heard her feet on the steps and then she appeared from behind the door. She held her hand up against the glare, trapping a blue triangle of sky in the crook of her arm. She was wearing pale trousers rolled up above her ankles which were thin and tanned. A red sweater was draped around her shoulders. Draped around that was the sky.

Her name was Monica and I was sure I recognised her from somewhere. For a few moments we stood awkwardly and tried to work out where we might have met before. I handed her the Calvino, open at the passage I'd been reading, and went down to get some beer.

If you choose to believe me, good. Now I will tell how Octavia, the spiderweb city, is made. There is a precipice between two steep mountains: the city is over the void, bound to the two crests with ropes and chains and catwalks. You walk on the little wooden ties, careful not to set your foot in the open spaces, or you cling to the hempen strands. Below there is nothing for hundreds and hundreds of feet: a few clouds glide past; farther down you can glimpse the chasm's bed.

This is the foundation of the city: a net which serves as passage and as support. All the rest, instead of rising up, is hung below: rope-ladders, hammocks, houses made like sacks, clothes-hangers, terraces like gondolas, skins of water, gas jets, spits, baskets on strings, dumb-waiters, showers, trapezes and rings for children's games, cable cars, chandeliers, pots with trailing plants.

Suspended over the abyss, the life of Octavia's inhabitants is less uncertain than in other cities. They know the net will last only so long.

'Would you like to live there?' asked Monica when I came back with the beer.

'Where?'

'Octavia: the spiderweb city.'

'It would depend on what the licensing laws were like. What about you?'

'It would depend on the weather.'

'I sometimes think I'd like to live in the country.'

'The country's OK from a distance but close up it's just gnats, flies and mud and damp houses. The best place to see the country is from a city. I'd like to live beside the sea.'

'The sea is pretty disappointing in most places too.'

'Not in some though.'

'No?'

'It's great in Cornwall. And in Brighton.'

'Brighton?'

'I love the sound it makes on the pebbles,' she said, leaning over the railing. 'If it was sea down there instead of road, this would be Paradise.'

'I don't know where I'd like to live,' I said. 'I prefer to think of all the places I wouldn't like to live and then work my way upwards.'

Evening sounds were all around us: birds, church bells, dogs barking, not much traffic. A vapour trail thin as cotton chalked itself across the sky, the plane so high that it was hardly visible. I could smell dinners being cooked and kept thinking I could hear a Bruce Springsteen song being played on a transistor radio. Confirming this suspicion, Monica said, 'This country is turning into America.'

'I'd like to live in America.'

'I thought you didn't know where you wanted to live.'

'I don't. That's why I said I'd like to live in America. America has always been a synonym for anywhere that might be better than where you are now. If you know where you want to live you say Australia.'

'I hate America.'

'Me too.'

'It doesn't matter what we think or say about America anyway. Whatever we say about America we keep buying American products and that's all that counts,' she said, sipping a can of Budweiser.

'I'd like to live in a place where you could walk everywhere,' I said. 'A city where it was warm all night and you could walk down narrow streets, past people of all ages and all races, where there were lots of jazz clubs and cheap beer.' This sounded less impressive than I had hoped – fucking silly in fact. I was tempted to suggest we got stoned. Instead I asked how long she'd lived in Brixton.

'Three years.'

'In the same block?'

'No I've only just moved in there. Before that I was travelling.'

'Where?'

'India, Thailand. I went to lots of islands.'

'Did you go skuba diving?'

'Snorkeling.'

'I'd like to go skuba diving more than anything else in the world.'

'Why don't you?'

'I don't know. I haven't even been skiing.'

'Nor me.'

'I'd love to go hang-gliding and I've never done that either. What was the snorkeling like? Tell me a snorkeling anecdote.'

'As it happens I've got a very good snorkeling anecdote.'

'Has it got sharks in it?'

'Yes.'

'Great.'

'OK,' said Monica after swallowing some beer. 'One of the places I went to was a small island near Bali. On the first day there I went snorkeling. Then I found out that none of the natives ever went in the sea. Imagine that – an island people and they never go in the sea. There's some odd convergence of currents so that sharks, octopuses, rays and stingy star-shaped things end up there. So the sea is quite dangerous but they also throw the ashes of their dead into the sea so it's a place of evil spirits.'

'Incredible. And this fear of the sea is a centuries-old myth, right?'

'That's the great thing about it. This age-old myth has only been around for twenty years,' said Monica. 'It's their way of coming to an understanding of nuclear waste.'

I laughed: 'Travel, it broadens the mind doesn't it? D'you like travelling?'

'Yes, I love it. Don't you?'

'It bores me rigid,' I said.

'Me too actually,' said Monica. 'Something funny always happens when I'm travelling. I go to a place to see certain things and then when I get there I suddenly don't really care whether I actually see them or not. Just the proximity is enough. When I first went to Paris I didn't quite see the Eiffel tower; in the Louvre I suddenly got fed up of looking for the Mona Lisa. When I was in Cairo I almost didn't see the Pyramids.'

'I know that feeling. When I was young my parents took my sister and me to London. We queued up for about six hours to see the treasures of Tutankhamen. We actually saw all the Tutankhamen stuff in about twenty minutes. In retrospect I think we went for the experience of queuing. In many ways it gave me my first sense of allegory.'

High up a bird – some kind of hawk – was swooning and gliding through the empty air.

We talked for a while about people we knew in Brixton. I mentioned Foomie and Monica clapped her hand over her mouth and laughed.

'That's where I know you from.'

'You know Foomie?'

'Not really. I went to a party of hers last summer.'

'You were the woman with the phone number.'

'You never called,' she said, laughing.

I fetched two more cans of beer and we leant against the rail, not speaking. Our shadows appeared as two climbers flattened out against the wall of Monica's block. As the sun sank they inched their way a little higher.

A plane climbed overhead, the sun glinting off its wings. Without our noticing it the vapour trail that had slashed the sky had spread out, thickened into a scar. Monica put on her sweater.

A flock of small birds, lunging quickly after one another, flew a few feet above our heads – agile specks that soon vanished.

'Do you know what sort of birds those were?'

She shook her head.

'Nor me. I don't know the names of any birds anymore. It's like trees. When I was a kid I could recognise all sorts of trees. Now I can only recognise two.'

'Which ones are they?'

'A weeping willow and a conker; three if you count Christmas trees. Apart from those when I see trees that's all I see: trees.'

The vapour trail had broadened out further still and now looked like the print left by a thick tyre. A few minutes later it became still more diffuse, almost indistinguishable from the thin spray of clouds. The sun was casting long strips of shadow on to the red-gold colour of the bricks of the low rampart. Our own shadows had climbed to within a few feet of Monica's roof.

A wasp hovered on blurred wings a few inches from my face and then disappeared into a crack in some cement. Another plane cut its silhouette into the sky.

'Are they from Gatwick or Heathrow, the planes?' Monica said.

'I'm not sure. They seem to come from all directions at once. On a clear day you can see five or six near-misses.'

Monica laughed: 'I wonder where they're going?'

'Paris, Bucharest, Venice . . .'

'It's nice just saying the names of cities isn't it?' said Monica.

I nodded and smiled and watched the laughter in her eyes. Sipping beer, we looked up at the planes climbing through the sky and took it in turns to say the names of cities.

'Stockholm.'

'Aleppo.'

'Detroit.'
'Athens.'
'Marrakesh.'
'Jerusalem.'
The moorings of words were coming adrift, their sense floating free of meaning.

'Octavia,' said Monica finally.

A child's balloon floated up from the street and was blown away by the breeze.

015

NEXT MORNING, FOR the first time since I'd moved in, I cleaned my windows, flooding the flat with blond light that bounced off the walls and skidded along the floors. Suddenly the flat seemed twice as big. The magnolia walls looked a pale yellow in the sunlight. I was still admiring the effect when I heard someone calling up from the street. I leant out the window and saw Steranko propped up against his bike. He was wearing a T-shirt, old rugby shorts and tennis shoes.

'Let's go out cycling,' he shouted. Ever since he'd bought Freddie's bike he was always wanting to go out cycling.

'Come on,' he shouted. 'Let's go.'

'Two minutes,' I said.

Outside the hot blue sky had seeped into every crack of the streets, fitting precisely into every angle of roof and building, even finding space between the agile leaves of trees. The sky encased chimneys, washing lines, car aerials perfectly. Here and there it was swallowed by the open windows of bedrooms. The light slid from the red roofs of buses and the chrome bumpers of cars. The road glittered with shards of glass. We cycled past a block of flats, almost completely obscured by scaffolding and flapping sheets of blue polythene.

'Scaffolding: that's the real architecture of the age,' called Steranko.

When we turned into Railton Road it was as if we had accidentally strayed into a para-military coup. Suddenly we were surrounded by a renegade army of guerillas, all dressed in the same para-military uniform of camouflage fatigues,

DMs, green bomber-jackets and army caps. Some wore sun-glasses, most carried truncheons. Steranko and I got off our bikes as two jeeps, crowded with men, sped past and pulled over to where a group of five or six uniformed men were lounging against another vehicle.

There was a mixture of frantic activity and casualness about the scene. Some of the uniformed men were standing around talking, others scanned the street vigilantly, someone else was shouting instructions. I expected to see them kicking down the door of a house or dragging a deposed dictator out into the streets. Steranko and I were the only other people around. No one paid any attention to us.

'What the fuck's going on?' said Steranko.

'It's the Rats, that big security outfit,' I said quietly. 'I've heard of them but I've never seen them before.'

'It's like we're in Angola or Guatemala or something.'

From behind us two more guys, dressed in the same gear, trotted past, their boots heavy on the pavement.

'Let's go.'

We crossed Railton Road and cycled past white-fronted houses with bars on the ground-floor windows and security gates on the doors. A few moments later we were in Brockwell Park where the wind-flattened grass rippled in the heat. There were a few white clouds but they only emphasised the deep petrol-station blue of the sky.

People lay in the park in groups of two or three. A young white guy was doing martial arts training in the generous shade of a conker tree. A handsome black couple came past, their child tottering along beside them, a big smear of ice-cream down one side of his face.

Where the paths were busy we cycled slowly and then I raced Steranko round part of the park, standing up on the pedals and throwing the bike from side to side. The black path rushed by beneath us, the grass a blur of green on either side. By the time we got to the tennis courts and slowed down I was sweating. On one court a young couple rhythmically whacked forehands and backhands from one baseline to the other without keeping track of the score. The ball spun yellow through the air; there was a deep loud pock whenever it was hit. On the other court a black guy and a white guy were playing a proper game, hitting hard serves and rushing the net to volley or scrambling back to try to lob their way out of trouble.

Round the other side of the park, past the aviary and the pond, we got off our bikes and sat down on the soft grass. The park stretched away in easy slopes. In the distance there was a spire and a gentle sound of church bells.

'Now it's like we're in Suffolk or something,' said Steranko.

I pulled my T-shirt off, draped it around my face to keep the sun out of my eyes and stretched out. Through the blue fabric the sun formed molecular cross-hatches and pearls of light. I could feel the insect itch of the cool grass on my back.

'Right. Keep your eyes shut and listen to this,' Steranko said after a few minutes. 'Ready?'

'Yes.' Next moment there was the unmistakable sound of a beer can being opened. I took the T-shirt off my face and Steranko handed me the can, laughing and opening another one for himself. I took a big gulp of beer which crashed into my throat like sharp ice. Our bikes glistened metallic red and yellow in the grass. We basked in the sun like sharks. I could hardly even remember what winter was like.

After a while we cycled back; Steranko set up his easel on the roof and we chatted while he worked. The painting was of a view from the roof but at this stage it was difficult to tell how it was going to turn out. Even in his straightforward representational work, scenes that would have been clearly identifiable were so dramatically transformed by perspective and colour – distorted, intensified or muted – that they became at once alien, strange and familiar, haunting. Almost always in these paintings some strong source of light cast long Chiricoesque shadows through the heart of the scene.

His paintings resembled Chirico's in one other respect (though their atmosphere and feel were totally different): each painting felt like a brief detail of a total imaginative world that extended far beyond the three or four square feet that you were privileged to glimpse there.

The human figures in his paintings were anonymous and indistinct except for some detail of clothing (a pink T-shirt,

200

the shape of a jacket, a hat) or something about a gesture (a way of smiling or the tilt of someone's head) that made them instantly recognisable. He had recently finished some nudes of Foomie: her face and body were shadowy and indistinct but from the way her limbs arranged themselves on a sofa or on the floor, by the swelling hint of a bicep, the angle of a crooked knee – by the way gravity played uniquely on the figure – it was unmistakably her. What struck me as remarkable about Steranko's paintings was that I immediately recognised the figures by things like this which, until then, I hadn't noticed in real life. It took the pictures to make you notice the delicate, unremarked inflections of the actual. In much the same way, in his abstract paintings, you felt the insistent tug of the distinct and specific reality in which they had their origin. Maybe all that remained of it was a colour – a particular shade of yellow, the texture of a red – but that was enough to bring back very precisely the incident or moment that the painting addressed. Alternatively something about the way two colours sat next to each other, some felicitous relationship of blue and red – or the way a yellow touched an adjacent brown – made you aware of the relation and angle of sky and brick – or grass and pavement – that he had in mind. In this way his paintings came close to abolishing the distinction between the abstract and the physical. They worked on you in the same way as a *déjà vu* which instead of remaining tantalisingly beyond the reach of memory and formulation was suddenly brought unmistakably back – as if the past were a perfect memory of the present.

OI4

WELL, IT FINALLY happened. Walking back from Carlton's one night I got mugged. I'd just got through the entry door to my block when I heard somebody come up behind me. I held the door open for him. He said something I couldn't understand – at first I thought he was asking for directions. Then several little details made it all clear. First, I realised he had a scarf up round his face Jesse James style and it wasn't even cold. Second I worked out what he was saying: 'What you got cunt? What you got?'

Third (the clincher), two accomplices shouldered their way in, pushed me up against a wall and tickled my nose with a rusty stanley knife. Typically I'd gone out without that dummy wallet I told you about – the one I always carry in case of a situation like this – but I did have some loose change and a screwed up five pound note. Finding it was the problem. My pockets were full of junk they didn't want – glasses case, empty crisp packets, a book – but after much ferreting around they grabbed the fiver and some coins from my pocket and scrambled out of the door: three kids, all about sixteen and all looking like they were shitting themselves. Mugging is hardly even the word for it; it was more like begging by force. An intense exchange of gestures between comparative strangers, it was closer to a charade than an assault. It didn't seem worth calling the police.

013

I WOKE EARLY with yellow sunlight blazing through the windows and then drifted back to sleep and dreamt of a red postbox noisily vomiting the as yet unfranked contents of its stomach. Slowly realising that the dream had been set off by the sound of the mail cascading through the letterbox and crashing to the floor I lay in bed and let the sound settle after this welcome intrusion of the outside world. It was amazing the amount of mail I received, especially considering that virtually none of it – with the exception of a few postcards each summer – was from friends (I never wrote to anyone, nobody wrote to me: fair enough).

The room was full of hot light. I could hear the police helicopter overhead. Still unfocused from sleep I carried a pile of letters back to bed and began tearing them open without enthusiasm. With the exception of a query from the TV licensing centre my letters were all disguised circulars. Addressed to me personally they were all about money, urging me to borrow some and get the things I'd always wanted (pretty much the things I'd never wanted). AbbeyLoan, American Express, Daleyloan, Faustbank – they were all dying to lend me money. One just asked straight out if I'd like ten thousand pounds.

Receiving this kind of mail was a fairly recent development in my life and there was no accounting for it. Perhaps I'd been chosen at random or maybe they just trawled through the phone book and mailed everybody. Certainly it wasn't as though my career had made any spectacular jump forwards. Maybe it was just that I was at the age when, according to some complex actuarial logic, my career would normally have been expected to take shape. Either way they were beginning to work on me, these letters, starting to make me think of myself as a pretty well-heeled young man, a good credit risk, a man with prospects, a man people were keen to invest in. Perhaps they'd heard that I was no longer signing on the dole, that I'd managed to carve out an even cosier niche for myself in the poverty trap: I was on the Enterprise Allowance Scheme. I'd set myself up as a self-employed market researcher but the bit of legitimate money I made from that wasn't anything like enough to disqualify me from housing benefit. Any other money I earned was strictly in cash. I didn't even keep track of it.

Most of this money came from painting and decorating, a state of affairs which had its good points and its bad points. The worst thing about it was that it was so fucking boring. The good things were that it required virtually no skill and we got the run of people's houses for however long the job took. Most people who wanted their house decorating had one facility or another to make the work bearable: a good collection of records maybe, or a Compact Disc player.

Mainly I worked with Carlton but if the job was big enough Steranko, Foomie or Freddie would work on it too and at the end of the day we would all travel home together in high spirits. We earned less money working together like that but since so many people were buying places in south London there was always plenty of work. Besides, none of us wanted to do it all the time. Ideally I worked just enough to make me appreciate the days when I didn't. I had vague plans to try to write film scripts but I didn't really know how to go about it and didn't have the concentration to find out. In the meantime decorating suited me fine. It was summer and after that, in the winter, maybe I'd leave England and live abroad or something. For the moment everything felt fine.

LATER THAT MORNING I bumped into Monica outside the Pie and Mash shop on Cold Harbour Lane. She had just come from her acrobatics class and was on her way to sign on. I walked down to the dole office with her and after that we wandered round Granville Arcade. Painted red and yellow, it was bright with the light that showered through the glass roof. We walked past a shop where huge silver trunks were stacked on top of each other like the speakers of a powerful sound system. At the wig bazaar Monica tried on a hairpiece that made her look like Charles II. We watched bloody-smocked butchers chopping pink meat and walked past pet shops and stalls selling kiddies' clothes – cardies and tiny shoes – or toys wrapped in Cellophane, the sort that get featured on the local news around Christmas because a toddler could easily swallow bits of them and choke; either that or they're highly inflammable and give off noxious fumes when burnt. Round a corner from there the Back Home Foods stall gave off the roots and earth smell of yams, sweet potatoes and plantains.

A lot of the people working in the Arcade were quite old. They'd seen a lot of things change and they'd seen nothing change.

'I'm starving,' said Monica as we walked past Franco's.

'Me too.'

'Come on, I'll buy you lunch.'

We got a table quickly. Monica was wearing a ripped tracksuit, her hair was tied back with a blue scarf. She tilted her head slightly to adjust an earring. For a moment her gaze became abstracted as fingers performed the work of eyes. The sound of opera was all around us.

'D'you know who this is?' I said, angling my fork vaguely in the direction of the music.

'No. All opera's the same though,' said Monica. 'Man, woman, stab, stab. I'm hot.'

She pulled her tracksuit top over her head, one hand holding down the T-shirt that had begun to ride up over her slender stomach. I drummed on the table with my knife and fork.

As we ate our pizza Monica asked if I did anything for a living.

'Odds and ends. Nothing specific,' I said. 'I missed my vocation in life.'

'What was that?'

'What I'd really like to have been is a third division footballer, a fairly solid player for a team that tended to end up in the middle of the table each season without ever being close to getting promoted or relegated. That would have suited me nicely. Maybe one lucky cup run that climaxed with a goalless draw at home to Everton before getting hammered 6-0 in the replay at Goodison Park, just something to tell the kids about. When I was at school I spent all my time longing for lessons to end and football to begin. At that age I knew what I wanted. I wish I'd stuck at it.'

'Were you a good footballer? You don't look like a footballer.'

'Not really, but I'm sure it's not that difficult, not as difficult as some things anyway.'

'A girl at school wanted to be an astronaut; she said you only needed two O levels. I bet it's much easier to be a footballer. You probably don't need any O levels at all.'

Laughing, I said, 'And what about you?'

'No, I wouldn't like to be a footballer.'

'I meant do you have any way of earning money?'

'Three nights a week I do some waitressing.'

'What's that like?'

'Awful. Let's not talk about work. That's all people ever seem to talk about in this city: jobs and house prices. I read somewhere that by the year 2000 two out of three people will own their own estate agent's,' said Monica. 'God, you eat fast.'

'Got to. There's not much of the century left,' I said and thought back to an afternoon in Paris when Freddie and I were there a couple of years ago. Outside the Pompidou Centre there was a huge electronic row of numbers. When we started watching the number was about three hundred and seventy million. Then with every second that went by the last digit went down one. Neither of us could work out what the point of it was. Then somebody explained that it was counting down the number of seconds to the year 2000. Freddie thought it was terrific ('hi-tech millenialism – the sort of thing Baudrillard would shit himself over') and made a note of the exact number of seconds left: 376,345,060. It didn't seem that long at all – in fact it seemed quite possible that you could just sit there and watch the digits click their way back to a long line of noughts. I liked the idea of time getting denuded like that instead of simply piling up – a countdown to nothing, to an apocalypse that would last only for a second. A new kind of time. It was both awe-inspiring and, at the same time, absolutely pointless: pure anticipation.

'And what would happen after it worked its way down to zero zero nothing?' asked Monica. 'What would happen then?'

'I don't know. Maybe nothing. Or maybe the whole process would begin all over again. The funny thing about it though was that it actually seemed like a reasonably rewarding way of spending your time, standing there watching the seconds clicking away and waiting to see what happened.'

Monica chewed and digested this information. 'Frightening too.'

'Yes.'

'It reminds me of something I saw on TV the other night,' she said after a while. 'A programme about a prisoner on death row. Half an hour before he was due to go to the electric chair he was picking out a new tune on his guitar. One of the guards asked him what good it was going to do him, learning that tune?'

I was coming to the end of my pizza. After a pause Monica said, 'Do you think about dying?'

'No. Do you?'

'Yes.'

'So do I.'

All that remained on my plate were a few olive stones. I could think of nothing to say and had run out of things to eat. The table was splattered with cheese and tomato. Monica still had over half her pizza left.

'Your table manners are appalling,' she said without malice.

'I know. It's something I've never quite got the hang of.'

When Monica had finished eating we ordered two coffees — Franco is a master of the disappointing cappuccino — and asked for the bill. Monica insisted on paying for the meal and leaving a huge tip.

Carlton and Belinda arrived just as we were leaving. Belinda and Monica kissed and talked enthusiastically while Carlton, unseen by them, raised his eyebrows, grinned and gave me a blokeish nudge in the ribs.

After Carlton and Belinda had got a table Monica took my arm and guided me across to the fishmonger's.

'I love the man who works here,' she whispered as we waited to be served. 'He's so amphibious.'

He had glistening grey hair greased back from his forehead and ears stuck flat against his head. His hands were icy from handling cold fish and there was no hint of sun anywhere on his smoothly shaven face as he darted and glided round the slippery floor of his stall. The expression in his black, unmoving eyes was impossible to fathom.

'It's a great place that,' said Monica as we walked away, two pieces of newspaper-wrapped cod nestling in the bottom of her red string shopping bag. 'I once bought a fish there that had been extinct for two hundred years.'

MONICA AND I were up on her roof talking about our eczema. I sat on an arm of the red chair while she practised her acrobatics. We talked about hydrocortisone and Betnovate and compared ways of keeping it at bay. Monica had had it very badly as a child but since puberty her eczema tended to do little more than threaten. I admitted that as a child, in addition to eczema, my fingers were covered in about fifty warts – I had to go to a hospital to have them burnt off. Monica said her occasional bouts were set off by stress and worry.

'Do you worry a lot?' I asked as she did a perfect back flip.

'All the time.'

'What about?'

'Everything.'

'Like what?'

'Like whether my eczema's going to reappear,' she said, doing another flip. 'What about you?'

'It varies. In the summer I worry about the weather. For nine months of the year I pay no attention to it, I expect nothing from it. Then during the summer I shadow-watch and monitor weather forecasts obsessively. D'you think it's going to rain this afternoon?'

A hot desert wind was blowing across the roof. Monica was wearing shorts and a washed-out white vest that showed the sharp angle of her collar-bone and the hollow at the base of her throat. She shook her head and did a handstand, her tanned legs wavering slightly.

'I worry about my flat too,' I said, holding her ankles to steady her and noticing the way her legs slid down into her shorts.

'What about it?'

'Things snap at me in it.'

Last week I'd been cleaning the flat and instead of sucking up dust from the floor the hoover had blown a full lung of dirt all over the carpet. I turned it off, poked around for a while and thought I'd solved the problem (a sock caught in the mechanism). I turned it on again and gave the brush mechanism one last poke with the screwdriver which was tugged from my hand and hurled across the room by the whirling brushes. It was only luck that I'd used the screw-driver rather than my hand. For the next ten minutes I lay on the sofa imagining myself searching for my fingers in the hoover's dusty stomach or trying to pry them loose from the twists and turns of its metallic digestive tract – with one hand while in considerable pain.

Even the telling made me flinch.

'Surely you wouldn't have put your fingers in the hoover like that,' said Monica, back on her feet again.

'I could have done, quite easily,' I said, enjoying the sound of my own voice. 'It didn't occur to me that it was dangerous. Then, yesterday, my reading lamp went wrong. I took the bulb out, saw what the problem was and started trying to twist the metal back into shape with a pair of pliers. Next thing I knew I'd been thrown across the room. The appliances in my flat are on the brink of revolting.'

Monica cartwheeled along the length of the roof.

'That's fantastic. Such a beautiful thing to be able to do. Are you listening to me by the way?'

'I catch the odd word here and there,' said Monica walking back towards me.

'That's ample. Can you do a somersault?'

'Not quite.' Just then I heard someone calling my name. From the roof of my block Steranko and Foomie were waving to us. They were shouting and laughing, both wearing T-shirts and shorts. Steranko was holding a tennis racket. The sun bounced off a ridiculous green sun visor – the one Carlton had been wearing when we last played cards — that made him look like an American student in a fraternity house.

'Tennis?' he shouted, holding up a yellow ball for our inspection. He was about twenty yards away.

'Rough or smooth?' he shouted, twirling the racket fast in his hand.

'Rough,' I called back.

With his thumb he stopped the racket spinning and looked closely at the head. 'Smooth it is,' he said, smiling again. 'My serve.'

He adopted a serving stance, bounced the ball a couple of times, sighted along his racket and then threw the ball high above his head and served hard from my block to Monica's. High above the street, the ball sped towards us, just cleared the low wall we were leaning against, hit the roof a couple of yards to our right and bounced against the wall behind us. I watched the ball ricochet on to the door of the stairs and roll quickly along the roof. Before it came to rest I heard Steranko guffawing and Foomie laughing wildly on the opposite roof. I had to admit, it was a good serve.

'That guy's a headcase,' said Monica. 'Either that or he's a very good tennis player.'

'Ace!' Steranko shouted. 'Fifteen love!' Foomie was laughing. Steranko had one arm on her shoulder; with the other he waved the tennis racket triumphantly above his head.

I picked up the ball and threw it back across the road. Steranko caught it in one hand. Jesus.

'We're going to Brockwell Park for some proper tennis,' he shouted after a few minutes. 'See you later. What're you doing?'

'Nothing,' I shouted. 'I'll be around.'

'Later then, yeah?'

'Yeah.'

Monica and I waved and watched Steranko and Foomie walk towards the roof door.

'Who is that guy?' Monica asked when they had disappeared from view.

'That's Steranko,' I said. 'A friend of mine.'

OIO

MONICA ACTUALLY MET Steranko and Foomie a few days later when we all went to a party on Ladbroke Grove. It was an afternoon party and by five o'clock people in the living-room were packed as tight as a deck of cards – there wasn't room to dance but you could shuffle your feet. I moved out on the balcony with Freddie who was trembling so much that he was having trouble lighting a joint.

'Jesus Freddie, you're shaking like mad.'

'I know.'

'Shit: you're practically vibrating. This has got to be your greatest affectation to date. No doubt about it. It's even better than that stutter you put on sometimes.'

'You like it do you?'

'It's terrific. You look like you might fall apart at any moment.'

'I think it's got something to do with last night. I was power-drinking over in Finsbury Park.'

'Oh yeah, you went to that party? Did you have a good time?'

'I got blind drunk. I definitely saw the midnight rat. No question about it.'

'It's a shame about the shaking though,' I said. 'I was hoping the shaking was pure affectation.'

Deep tan and shadow from the wavering match flickered over his face. I could see the interior of the kitchen reflected in his eyes like a tiny party in his head.

'And what about the writing? How's that going?' Freddie

212

liked to be asked questions like this when he was wearing his corduroy jacket.

'Oh I don't know. The time I most feel like a writer is at exactly the moment when I'm too out of it to even write my name.'

Monica joined us on the balcony.

'That was good timing,' I said. 'Freddie was about to start on his Malcolm Lowry routine.'

'Oh I'd like to have seen that,' Monica said.

'Me too,' said Freddie, drinking white wine from the bottle. They'd met earlier that afternoon and Freddie had instantly reeled off a list of his favourite writers. Monica had responded by asking if he worked in a bookshop. I could tell they liked each other.

I pushed past the people in the living-room and queued up for a piss. When I came out Foomie had joined the queue.

'Have you seen Steranko?' she said.

'He went out to score some grass about half an hour ago,' I said. 'He's probably been arrested.'

Someone touched me on the shoulder. I heard a familiar jangle of bracelets and turned round.

'Fran! I don't believe it,' I said, hugging her.

'I was sure you'd be here,' she said, laughing. 'Look I only dropped in for a moment to see if you were here. I've really got to rush.'

'How come?'

'Oh I've had such a weird day. I was waiting for a tube and the sign said "Next train ten minutes". When I looked again it said fourteen minutes. About five minutes later it said sixteen. I thought time was going backwards. I was already late so I thought "fuck it" and went to get a bus. Then the bus broke down in the Wandsworth triangle where all public transport mysteriously disappears. Luckily some friends drove past in a car – on their way to the same place I was going – and winched me to safety. And then since we were driving past here I persuaded them to stop for a moment.'

There were dark smudges round Fran's eyes. She looked beautiful and worn out – that was another thing about Fran: looking tired actually suited her.

213

'Hey this is Foomie,' I said, seeing her come out of the bath-room. 'This is Fran, my sister.' They smiled and laughed. 'And this is Carlton,' I added as he joined the queue. 'Freddie's over there somewhere too. You remember him?'

Fran ended up staying about twenty minutes. She talked at high speed with Foomie and Carlton, smoked a joint and met Freddie and Monica out on the balcony. She was still there when a stationary car began hooting.

'I've really got to go,' she said, laughing. 'I told them I'd only be a minute and we're about two hours late already.' With that she said goodbye to everyone, promised she'd come down to Brixton soon and left.

Steranko arrived back just after Fran had left and for some reason I felt vaguely relieved that he hadn't got back a few minutes earlier.

More people were crowding out on to the narrow balcony, pushing Monica and me up into the far corner. There was still some brightness in the sky but beneath us the street was shaded and dark. On the pavements families, couples, young women with kids, middle-aged West Indian men, awkward punks and some teenagers on skateboards passed by. Most cars had their lights on. To the left, heading north, the traffic thinned out; to the right it congealed as it passed under the Westway and disappeared from view. The car lights formed a shifting red and yellow stream that flowed in both directions at once. As the volume of traffic increased to our right it became a thick river of volcanic colour that hardly moved. On the Westway, spanning this red and gold medal ribbon of colour, the grey shapes of cars, vans and lorries whizzed past, blurs of rapid motion against the deepening grey of the sky. Every five minutes or so the traffic on the flyover would be blotted out by a train moving slowly across the railway bridge from Ladbroke Grove station.

Over all this, over the pedestrians and cars in the street, over the traffic on the flyover and the train on the rail-way bridge, luminescent storm clouds were moving slowly towards us, moving even more slowly than the heavy pas-senger plane climbing through the thick grey air in the distance.

We waited for it to rain. Someone's beer can toppled from the balcony. It took a long time to fall and then slopped noisily on to the damp concrete yard below. From inside came the thump of music and the heat of bodies dancing. I felt the cooling evening on my face.

Looking down at the steady flow of people, traffic and trains I became aware of an odd quality of calm in the hurtling kinesis of the city. By repeating itself over and over, day after day, this same configuration of traffic – the precise pattern of lights varying according to the season – had acquired the constancy of sky and clouds, day and night.

We waited for the rain. The sky was like a tarpaulin sagging beneath the weight of water. The air was full of the damp crackle of electricity. Thunder prowled the sky.

Monica and I said goodbye to everyone and made our way through the trashed kitchen and the beer cans, bottles and glasses. Down in the street we waved to the people on the balcony and they waved back. After we'd walked for a couple of minutes I looked back and waved again.

We could hear the traffic rumbling overhead as we passed under the Westway. Cars swarmed past. There were a lot of people around. Cyclists in bright shirts and shorts pedalled past. It felt warmer in the street than it had up on the balcony. The pavements were warm. The street-lights, the neon lights of shop signs and the harsh glare of their interiors, the red stream of brake-lights – all of these intensified the blue night of the sky. A group of teenagers, one of them with a big ghetto blaster on his shoulder, moved apart to let us walk between them. My arm was around Monica's shoulders; her hand was around my waist resting on my hip. She sipped from a last can of lager, warm now. Some strands of hair had come loose from under her scarf. Our hips bumped accidentally from time to time. When I turned to speak to her I could smell her neck and her hair.

'That shirt!' she said.

'I know. It's terrific isn't it?' I'd bought a shirt from Freddie, pale yellow and very big with splashes of a black print.

'Don't you like it?' I said.

'Well I don't think I've ever seen one quite like it before.'

'Yeah I was thinking maybe it wasn't such a good buy after all. I overheard Freddie at the party saying to Foomie: "No, I *sold* it to him" and laughing.'

Monica shook her head and smiled, 'That's some shirt.'

We turned left and crossed over All Saints Road. My skin felt warm and dirty from the sun, my feet sweaty in old sneakers. Monica sipped her beer again and I noticed how small her fingers were, hardly big enough to get round the can.

Some trees still had blossom on them. Two women jogged past in shorts and running vests. A sports car was caught up in the traffic. An Asian family with several smartly-dressed kids walked past. A black couple, the man carrying a sleepy child wearing a big red baseball cap walked slowly by.

'As soon as we've put Marcus to bed you get in the bath and I'll bring you your tea in,' she said to the man. He said something and she laughed and hit him lightly on the arm. I think they were almost home.

It was an evening when no one wanted to do anyone else any harm. No one wanted to fight or hassle anybody. When people bumped into each other they said sorry and smiled because it didn't matter. It was an evening when people wanted to notice the trees and the stars that shone through them, they wanted to smell the blossom in the night air and feel the heat coming off the earth. People were in no hurry to be home but when they got back they'd take a bath and go to bed with the warm night air blowing through the windows and touching the curtains, remembering other times like this.

After the tube ride we walked to the door of Monica's block. I kissed her cheek and touched the back of her neck with my hand. She touched the buttons on my shirt and smiled.

THE FOUR OF us – Carlton, Steranko, Freddie and I –
walked over to Brockwell Park for the second day of the
Country Fair. Trees fanned the wind under a blue and white
Battle of Britain sky. When the sun passed behind a cloud it
was disappointing and slightly chilly; when it emerged the
grass flared up brightly again from under the dull carpet of
shadow.

On the edge of the park we saw a young family: the man
and woman were our age, maybe slightly older; the kid was
about three or four or however old they are at that age. The
couple hid from the child in the long grass and then – when
he was wondering where they were and was probably on the
brink of tears – they sprung up from behind the long grass
and shouted 'Boo!' so that instead of bursting into tears the
child let out a delighted shriek of happiness.

'Jesus,' said Steranko. 'How can any intelligent adult enjoy
the company of children?'

'There's a baby boom going on right beneath our eyes,'
said Freddie as we continued on our way.

As the fair had expanded over the years so its rustic element
had been getting smaller and smaller. There were pigs, donkey
rides, horses and other farm animals but in a few years' time
it seemed likely that a couple of piles of plastic dung and a
hologram of a tractor would be all that remained of the fair's
rural impulse.

We walked round stalls for local associations and societies,
political organisations like the Nicaraguan Solidarity Cam-
paign, the Anti-Apartheid group, El Salvador support group,

all selling T-shirts and pamphlets, badges and books. Various bits of Lambeth Services had lots of stalls and displays: a group of young black and white guys in blue overalls sipped beer from cans and knocked together the wooden frame of a house. Two rastafarians sold prints of Bob Marley and Burning Spear and red, yellow and green patterned T-shirts and wristbands.

Inside a long, bright marquee the more sedate societies had their stalls: the Lambeth Chess Club (Carlton played a game and lost in about eight moves), the Painting Group, Photographic Society and Bridge Club (Carlton claimed he was a good bridge player too). At the end of the tent was the Lambeth Literacy Society.

'Here you go Freddie,' Carlton said. 'The Lambeth Literary Group – just your scene.'

'If you weren't illiterate you'd see it says Literacy not Literary.'

'Even better I'd've thought.'

We made our way over to the main stage where a high-life band were playing, accompanied by twenty women in kangas who danced to the music. It was gentle, catchy music. A few people in the crowd were dancing and swaying. The brightness of the sun and the blackness of the stage made it difficult to see the band clearly except for a guitarist and a couple of men playing elaborate banks of percussion instruments. By the side of the stage a giant video screen the size of a terraced house showed close-ups of the musicians and dancers. The camera zoomed in on their faces or their hands and then panned back a little to show three or four dancers at once. I found myself spending more time watching the video screen than the stage. The video looked more real, more authentic than the people on stage. The dancers and musicians looked as if they were playing at the Country Fair in Brockwell Park; the pictures on the video screen looked as if they were being broadcast live by satellite from Harare or Lagos.

When the band finished their set we walked to the beer tent which had an atmosphere all of its own. Impatient to get to the bar people waved fluted fivers at the bar staff; the smell of beer sank slowly to the ground. Steranko bought four pints of real ale in imitation glasses and we sat outside where people were crashed out on the grass or arguing about whose round it was. When we'd finished these I bought four more and then we lay on the grass and argued about whose round it was.

'It's so nice acting like yobs isn't it?' said Freddie. Hungry after the beer, we wrapped our faces round large portions of falafal and walked on. Feeling sluggish and drunk we took turns on stalls like Soak the Bloke and Test Your Strength. Carlton and Steranko bought balls for the coconut shy. Steranko's second ball flew over the back of the stall.

We waited for a scream. Then we waited for someone to come round the corner with a bloody grimace where his teeth used to be. Steranko gave the balls back to the guy in charge of the stall and we sloped shyly off, making our way through the throb and hum of shaking generators to the fairground rides where the grass had turned to downtrodden mud. Everything here was a blur of yellow and red and kids' screams whooping in and out of the loud music. Most of the rides were fairly gentle, the sort that make kids laugh and screech but not cry: merry-go-rounds and unfrightening ghost trains as opposed to the psycho-death trips or Vietnam gunships that some fairgrounds offered. It was nice standing there watching the black and white kids on the rides, the brothers and the sisters with their curls and pigtails, the happy-looking parents talking to each other and reaching willingly into their pockets for more coins. Some of the men sipped from cans and kept an eye on things. A few thin white gothics were slumped over unicorns on the largest merry-go-rounds but no one took any notice of them.

Leaving the others at the rifle range I went into the flower tent where the light was thick and still, saturated with the fragrance of flowers. The sun beat heavily through the white canvas and made the air humid and tropical. It was bright in the tent but the flowers and plants seemed to absorb light from the air, making it both luminescent and dusky. The plants also soaked up the noise of the fair, creating their own quietness. The flowers were perfect with sleek stems, broad leaves and heads dangling heavy as fruit, their petals shiny purple, dust yellow, poppy red and labile pink. At the far end of the tent the flowers blurred into a haze of rippled green with soft splashes of dull orange, frail white and pale blue, flame-bursts of yellow and red. By one batch of flowers the air was syrupy, sweet and cloying, by another, musky and dense. It was like breathing through a sponge whose pores were clogged with pollen. After a couple of minutes I felt intoxicated, bewildered by the tendril leaves and the quiet blooms. The tent was filled with fragrant air but beneath it was the dark, heavy smell of damp earth.

Someone touched my arm, so softly I hardly noticed. I turned round and saw Foomie. Her hair was tied up in a brightly coloured scarf. I kissed her on the cheek.

'I wasn't expecting to see you here, Foom. I thought you were selling deckchairs.'

'Oh there were all sorts of problems. The van wouldn't start and then – let's not even talk about it.'

'OK,' I said and touched her shoulder, feeling the light film of sweat on her skin. There were small pearls of sweat above her lip. The hair beneath her arms was tangled and damp. 'It's nice to see you here anyway.'

'You too,' she said, smiling and slipping her arm through mine. 'Is Steranko around?'

'He's over by the rifle range,' I said as we walked towards the bright square of daylight at the end of the tent.

Outside, the air felt cool, the sunlight raw on the grass – the flower tent like a dream that was already fading.

'WHAT'S THIS DRINK called again?' I said. 'A daktari?'

'A daiquiri. Strawberry daiquiri,' said Monica rolling the icy glass across her forehead.

Earlier in the day I'd bought a blender from a stall in the market for three quid – the guy let me have it cheap because he couldn't guarantee it would work. I picked up a bottle of rum and an assortment of fruit and when Monica came over we mixed up a jugful of cocktails with crushed ice and lots of strawberries. Monica did the mixing and I cleared up the mess – there was a lot of mess.

The drinks gleamed pinkly in the bright sun. The sky was as blue and still as paint in a pot. Monica was wearing her favourite T-shirt. We were sitting against the low wall of the roof and listening to 'Sketches of Spain'.

'Nice?' asked Monica.

'It's giving me a throbbing pain behind my left eye like ice-cream used to when I was a kid. I love it.' I upended my glass, poured another for myself and topped up Monica's. We were both wearing the same cheap sunglasses. Monica took off her plimsolls.

'Sorry, I bet my feet stink.' She bent forward, grasped a foot with both hands, pulled it easily towards her nose and sniffed. 'Oh, that's not so bad,' she said, rocking backwards slightly. I saw the muscles in her legs straining faintly until she released her foot. It was a supple gesture.

I read a few lines of my book but even with sunglasses the

glare of the pages was too bright. The trumpet dissolved in the air.

'Given a completely free choice,' I said after we had smoked a small grass joint. 'What event would you most like to see enacted in the sky in the next half hour?'

'I don't know.'

'Think.'

'You suggest things to me and I'll pick one,' Monica said.

'OK. Wait a second. OK: An airliner, a 747, exploding in mid-air and sending a shower of wreckage and people all over Stockwell while leaving Brixton completely untouched.'

'No.'

'No problem. What about a Spitfire and a Messerschmitt 109 from a nearby air display staging a mock dogfight directly overhead, climaxing with the German pilot bailing out of his damaged plane and eventually landing here on this roof where we torment him with pitchforks until the arrival of the home guard?'

Monica shook her head.

'I can see you're after something really spectacular. A fleet of Flying Fortresses flying overhead in dense formation to execute a daring daylight raid on industrial targets in the Rühr Valley.'

'Definitely not.'

'Oh come on . . . What's wrong with you? That would bring a shiver to anyone's spine. OK. See that air balloon over there advertising Goodyear tyres? What about that exploding in a ball of flame and then slowly floating in tatters to earth while a dense cloud of black . . .'

'Nope.'

'How about me making a spectacular escape from this roof by a rope-ladder dangled from a helicopter which hovered dangerously close to the TV aerials?'

Monica yawned.

'Come on then. Think of one of your own.'

'OK.' Monica thought for a moment. She had a slight smile on her face like someone doing a jigsaw who sees the puzzle is complete but still holds one more piece, uncertainly, in her hand. After a while her smile broadened.

'I know what I'd like to see,' she said. 'A rare and beautiful bird – a heron, a flamingo or a golden eagle – gliding overhead on warm thermals, dawdling, circling the roof on its long and lonely flight south.'

007

WE HAD JUST finished a lavish breakfast. Carlton was sitting in one of Foomie's deckchairs with a newspaper folded over his face; Foomie was stretched out on a rug. The sun flashed off dishes and glasses of orange juice and melted ice. Someone's sheets were hung out to dry and flapped in the wind, making a noise like the sail of a yacht. With the sky all around us the block felt like the opposite of a swimming-pool where a blue cube of water was enclosed by concrete; here a solid block of bricks was surrounded by the liquid blue of the sky.

I glanced over at Freddie who was sitting on a small cushion, writing in a notebook.

'What you writing Freddie?' called Carlton, taking the newspaper from his face and heaving himself out of the deckchair.

'Nothing really,' said Freddie without looking up.

'I bet,' Carlton said. ' "Pound of tomatoes, loaf of bread, tin of corned beef, bag of potatoes . . ." Have a look Steranko: I bet it's his shopping list he's working on. Just shout if you need any help with the spelling Freddie. Only one M in tomatoes . . .'

'You just concentrate on reading your comic,' Freddie said.

Steranko was fiddling with the cassette player, unable to find the track he particularly wanted to hear. He spent the next five minutes rewinding and fast-forwarding, ejecting tapes and putting in new ones but whatever he played he became dissatisfied with quickly. Eventually he went charging down the stairs in search of another tape. Ten minutes later he resurfaced empty-handed and tried to find the track we'd been listening to originally.

This kind of behaviour was not unusual. Steranko at this time had developed the exhausting habit of constantly trying to improve the happiness of any given situation. In his efforts he frequently managed to disrupt and even destroy exactly the situation he was trying to improve. He would suddenly decide that we had to have some booze and at two minutes to two on a Sunday afternoon would run off in pursuit of an off-licence where he could beg and plead with them to sell him a couple of six-packs of lager. Freddie termed this constant attempt to nudge the moment a little closer to perfection the dilemma of the late urban romantic.

'Let's go swimming,' Steranko exclaimed enthusiastically after a while.

'Hey relax, man,' Carlton said. 'Take it easy. All this fucking around is really interfering with my quietness.'

'Mine too,' I said. I was barely awake. Carlton's voice had floated thick into my ears; I had a book over my face and breathed in the sharp wet smell of the ink.

'Steranko, what's the matter with you?' Foomie asked, laughing. 'Why don't you calm down, just for a few seconds?' She said it with that tone of endless patience she had when she felt most affectionately towards him.

'Why don't you do something useful like roll a joint?' suggested Carlton.

'OK.'

'Am I going brown?' I said from beneath my book.

'No.'

Later in the afternoon Belinda and Monica came over, giggly and stoned and wearing pale dresses.

Steranko suggested we get some beer and he and I walked over to the off-licence. Trudging back, clutching an American-style brown bag full of booze, I saw Fran walking up the road towards us, waving and smiling. I shifted the weight of the cans so that I could wave back.

'Who's that?' Steranko asked.

'My sister, Fran,' I said when she reached us. Fran held

my face between her hands and kissed me. She was wearing sandals, shorts held up by braces and a large blue T-shirt.

'This is Steranko,' I said. 'And this is Fran.' They shook hands and smiled. 'You've come just at the right time. There's a lot of people here. It looks like turning into a party.'

'Shall I buy some drink?'

'No there's plenty here. It's great to see you Fran.'

We were standing at the edge of Effra Road, waiting for a break in the traffic. Seeing a slight pause Steranko and Fran dashed to a bollard in the middle of the road. A car sounded its horn in an angry warning and then they walked to the opposite pavement. For the next thirty seconds the traffic was even heavier. I saw Steranko and Fran talking and laughing on the opposite side of the road but then a steady stream of lorries and buses blocked them from view completely. I crossed the road a few moments later. Fran put her arm through mine. We smiled at each other. Steranko walked slightly ahead. On the road behind us a police car roared past at high speed, siren wailing.

Back on the roof Fran kissed Monica and Foomie and said hello to Freddie and Carlton and soon she and Belinda were laughing together like they were old friends. Planes glinted in the sun as they passed through the perfect sky. A short time later, when we were all stoned and not wanting to do anything, Steranko declared that since everybody was here and the light was so spectacular we ought to take a photograph. He and I went down to the flat to look for my camera. It took us five minutes to find it and another five to discover that there was no film in it. Undeterred, Steranko borrowed my bike and set off looking for a shop that sold film.

He got back about a quarter of an hour later, a yellow cycling cap tilted back on his head. He was sweating, breathing heavily and snapping pictures without remembering to adjust the focus or the light setting.

'Let's take one with us all in,' he said after wasting half the film. 'It's got a self-timer hasn't it?'

Setting up the picture took a long time. To get us all in the frame the camera had to be placed on the low wall at the other side of the roof. To see through the viewfinder and check that we were all arranged properly Steranko had to hang from the railing over the side of the building while Freddie moved the camera fractionally in accordance with Steranko's grunted instructions of 'left a bit, right a bit'.

'I feel like Bernie the Bolt from "The Golden Shot",' Freddie said.

'Hurry up Steranko,' Foomie said anxiously. All we could see of Steranko were his white knuckles gripping the railing and his cycling cap above the camera. We began to wonder how much longer he could hang there.

'Are you alright Steranko?' Freddie said, looking down anxiously.

'No, I'm. I can't . . .' Suddenly the hands slipped from the rail. There was a long scream and then a dull thud from the other side of the wall.

Freddie's face mirrored the shock on all our faces.

'Oh Jesus fucking Christ,' he said quietly as we rushed over towards him. I was the first to get there. I looked over the wall and saw Steranko, grinning and standing on the narrow ledge that ran just above the top windows of the block. The others crowded round. There was a collective sigh of relief which turned immediately to a groan. Freddie and Steranko were laughing crazily.

'What a wrister,' said Carlton and then we all took up our positions again on the other side of the roof. Once he had hauled himself back over the rail Steranko shouted 'Ready?', depressed the timer and scampered over to rejoin the rest of us. Foomie was peeling an orange. Freddie and Carlton were trying to push each other out of the picture. Monica and Belinda posed with their arms around each other. I was standing between Fran and Foomie; Steranko was crouched down in front of everyone. We waited, smiling.

'It's not working,' Freddie said.

'Yes it is, you can hear the whirr of the thing going round.' I took a sip of beer – and at that moment there was a sharp click from the camera.

'Maybe now we can get some peace,' Carlton said as

Steranko walked over to pick up the camera and wind on the film.

I heard the drone of a propellor plane making its way nostalgically across the sky. Squinting into the bright sky I saw a plane circling slowly overhead.

'Look!' said Steranko suddenly.

Gradually, red, yellow and then green and dark blue smoke trails appeared in the sky like Christmas streamers. A few moments later there were two sudden twists of even brighter colour, ballooning out into perfect parachutes, one striped red and yellow, the other quartered into segments of black and gold. There was a third brief flicker and then another full canopy blossomed, a sudden poppy of colour in the blue sky. Up until this point the smoke trails had been stretched fine by the speed of the free-falling parachutists; now, with the parachutes stalled in mid-air, the smoke curled out thickly and lazily. Then the bottom of the fourth and last smoke trail ignited in a sudden flame of colour, twitching and falling through the sky – but this time it failed to burst into a perfect canopy. The sheet of colour was just hanging there, a faint speck tumbling away from it and dragging a stream of smoke like a scream. A huge second passed. There was another brief pinch of colour turning instantly to a bright parachute, clinging tight to the sky.

The four parachutes rocked and pendulumed slowly downwards, smoke trails aerosoling elaborate and curly signatures on the wall of the sky. As they descended it was possible to see the parachutists themselves, hanging beneath their canopies on invisible strings. One drifted out wide from the rest and for a moment it seemed possible that he might land here on the roof. Gradually the radius of descent narrowed and he drifted away from us, heading with the others towards Brockwell Park. Two disappeared behind trees, their smoke trails exhausted; then the third and fourth until there was nothing left except fading loops and wisps of smoke: pink, faint lemon, pale green and blue. Soon there was just a mist; and then only the haze of memory.

006

LATE THAT NIGHT we all made a drunken arrangement to meet up at Brockwell Lido at eleven o'clock the next morning but it was gone twelve by the time Fran and I set off. We walked the long way round, past the old garage on Effra Road that looked like a painting by Edward Hopper with its faded red and blue petrol pumps and the people and cars no longer there. A little further on there was a white building with a sign for 'Cool Tan'. Fran thought it was advertising some technique for getting brown without getting hot but it was for a fizzy drink in the fifties or sixties that never really caught on. All that remained was the sign.

Brockwell Lido was built in the 1930s. The pool itself was an unheated rectangle of blue water surrounded by wooden changing huts and two high chairs for lifeguards. With the barbed wire on the surrounding walls the whole place looked like a camp, converted for leisure now that the refugees or prisoners had gone. It was a nice pool but I could never quite rid myself of the feeling that it was the kind of place where you got issued with verrucas when you exchanged your wire basket of clothes for a faded rubber ankle-band with ink-smudged number. Toes curled up reflexively, I splashed quickly through the disinfectant footbath. Fran emerged from the women's changing-room, thin, tanned and wearing a blue one-piece bathing suit borrowed from Monica. Wrapped around her shoulders, a brightly striped towel soaked up the sun. The pool was already fairly crowded but there was no sign of any of the others. A group of dripping adolescents stood about five yards from the edge of the deep end, watching attentively until someone walked by fully clothed. Suddenly they rushed towards the pool and plunged into the water, sending drenching waves over the unsuspecting passer-by. The lifeguard whistled and shouted.

We found a space to spread out our towels and books on the warm paving stones. There were cigarette butts lying around, impossible to ignore. The air was full of the tinsel shimmer of radios playing pop music. The sun shuddered overhead like a bronze gong struck. Nearby three young white guys in boxer shorts passed round joints of strong-smelling grass.

'Oh shit I left my grass at your house,' Fran said, arms around her knees.

'Maybe the others'll bring some. If they don't we can send Freddie off to the frontline in his swimming trunks to score.'

After a moment Fran said, 'It's lovely here isn't it?'

'Yeah. Last year it had only been open for a couple of weeks when some kids threw a load of toxic chemicals in that turned the water purple. It was closed for the rest of the summer while the bottom was scraped and cleaned.'

'What a shame. It's not as nice as the Lido at home though is it?'

I shook my head. It was funny hearing Fran say 'home' like that.

'I remember getting the bus from school down to that pool,' I said. 'It was a big old double-decker and the branches of trees used to whack the top of it. On the journey there this bus used to have to go round a very steep bend and when it did everybody on the top deck used to charge over to the left-hand side to try and topple it over. About fifty kids all crammed into the front four seats on one side of the bus. "Come on – one more push and it'll go!" We really wanted the bus to go over.'

A guy in tourniquet swimming trunks strolled past, his body a dark map of muscle that the sun navigated easily. A few yards away a woman with spiky bleached hair was reading an old Penguin Modern Classic. At the edge of the pool a young punk was wondering whether to take off his pyramid-studded wrist-band before getting in the water.

'Am I going brown?' I asked Fran.

'Yes.'

'Good.'

'Shall we have a swim?' Fran said.

'We could have a bit of a paddle.'

'Come on.'

I was still a couple of feet from the edge of the pool when Fran dived past me and entered the water in a low, perfect arc. I saw her shape, wiggly beneath the water. After several seconds she came to the surface, smiling and rubbing her eyes. She swam back to the edge.

'Come on!' She flicked an armful of icy water on to my shoulders.

'Fran, please don't. I hate being splashed.'

'Sorry,' she said, smiling and kicking up another freezing scoop of water. I did a scorching belly-flop into the cold shock of water. Still gasping from the cold I thrashed my way up the pool. Fran swam alongside in long easy strokes and then pulled away, straight and fast as a torpedo. The shock of the cold faded quickly and I did a couple of lengths as fast as I could. I'd never really liked swimming – I'd never got the hang of breathing properly and the idea of doing fifty lengths a day or whatever it is you need to do to keep fit bored the crap out of me.

After four lengths I climbed out and wrapped myself in a towel. After a few minutes Fran clambered out of the pool too. A hand slapped my shoulder – 'Drug squad!'

'Shit!' I jumped and turned around. 'Approximately how many times have I asked you not to do that Carlton?'

'Ten or twelve,' he said grinning. Beside him Foomie was doing the same. She and Fran kissed and held each other; Carlton and I just stood there. Foomie was wearing a loose white T-shirt and a pair of Steranko's shorts. Her hair was pulled back tight, making her eyes look large and oval. Carlton was in a vest, shorts, red baseball cap and tennis shoes. We expanded our encampment of bags and towels and sat down.

231

'Nobody else coming?' I asked.

'Yeah, Steranko and Freddie should be. What about Monica?'

'She's got to do a lunchtime shift at the restaurant. She'll be down later.'

'There's Freddie look. Yoh!' Carlton called, waving. 'Freddie!' He saw us and, just too late, just as he was waving back, he saw the three kids running to bomb him. The next moment he was lost in an explosion of water. Everyone laughed.

Wrapped up in the towel I slithered out of my wet trunks and pulled on my shorts. Freddie picked his way between towels and people and eventually stood before us in dripping shirt and trousers.

'Good job you didn't have the corduroy jacket on, Freddie,' said Carlton.

Foomie was reading the paper. Freddie was carefully rolling a large all-grass joint. I picked up my book but lost concentration after about five lines. It dawned on me that I was actually becoming more badly read as I got older. Fran was stretched out on her front, absorbed in the book she had curled up in her fist.

'You read so quickly Fran,' I said. 'You must have read about a hundred pages of that since we got here.'

'D'you speed read?' Freddie asked, always interested in other people's literary skills.

Fran shook her head. A few drops of water fell on to the open pages. 'No, I just miss out the boring bits.'

'I did a speed reading course once. I read *War and Peace* in two hours,' Carlton said, slowly. 'It's about Russia.'

Freddie laughed and asked if anyone had anything to use as a roach.

'Here you are,' Fran said, tearing a large corner off the back cover of her book.

'Jesus Fran. For a bad moment I thought that was my book,' I said. 'That's why she reads so fast. She has to get through them quickly – before they fall apart. Look at that: it's got about two hours' life left in it at most, that book.'

Fran put down the book and smiled. Freddie lit the joint and passed it to her. When it had gone round once more she got up and asked if anyone was swimming.

'My head is,' said Carlton.

Fran walked to the edge of the pool and dived smoothly into the water.

Steranko showed up a few minutes later, a large bag slung over his shoulder. He grinned and said hello to everybody and kissed Foomie. Freddie said he could finish the joint.

'Well Steranko, you must have quite a hangover.'

'That's putting it mildly. Jesus, was I ever fucking drunk.'

'Did you see the midnight rat?'

'I must have done. I can't remember what it looked like though.'

'If you'd seen it you'd remember it.'

Foomie put her arm around Steranko's shoulders. A man bounced towards us, his Hawaiian shirt fully inflated by a wrap-around gut.

'That guy looks so much like a beach-ball I'm surprised nobody's taken a kick at him,' Carlton said. The lifeguard nearest us blew his whistle, shouted something at two kids and then leant back in his chair. Nice job, just sitting there, telling people off and getting tanned.

By the time Fran pulled herself out of the pool we were all stoned. For a moment she stood by the edge of the pool, smiling, her wet hair dripping. The sun caught her earring. No one was speaking. Steranko looked at her, at her neck and shoulders, her waist, her legs. They held each other's eyes and then Fran looked away quickly, conscious suddenly of the way her feet were moving over the warm ground. Foomie saw the way Steranko was watching Fran as she walked towards us, pearls of water clinging to her short hair.

For a moment we were all trapped by the chains of our gaze. Then Steranko looked down to the trail of wet footprints stretching towards us from the blue pool, turning quickly to damp smudges and then melting away to nothing.

Fran reached for her towel and draped it around her shoulders. A pair of kids flicked their towels at each other like whips, soaking the corners so they stung more.

Someone had to speak.

'What's the water like?' Carlton said.

'Lovely,' said Fran, clearing her throat. 'You should go in.'

'He can't swim,' Freddie said and everyone laughed.

Fran stretched out on her towel and stared at her book. I glanced at Foomie who looked quickly away. Steranko put on a pair of sun-glasses.

The sun slipped and slid over the blue water.

ON FRIDAY CARLTON and I went to a bad party near the
Elephant and Castle. We left early and sober, grumbling
about the party as we walked along. We turned a corner
and almost bumped into three young white guys. One of
them mumbled something to Carlton who said nothing, kept
walking. It looked like nothing would happen. Then they
trotted after us and blocked our path.

'What was that you said?' one of them said.

Carlton said nothing.

'I'm talking to you.' All three of them were looking at
Carlton; nobody was paying any attention to me. They all
smelled of beer and had the same look of tabloid malice.

'I didn't say anything,' Carlton said. 'I was just going about
my business.'

I took a step nearer the guy.

'Come on mate. He didn't say anything . . .' I said but
it was pointless. Whatever you say in situations like this
becomes part of the ritual of provocation which is a necessary
prelude to violence. There must always be some excuse.

'Stay out of this you,' the guy said. The same guy was doing
all the talking. He'd been through this scene so many times in
his head – maybe in real life too – that he now spoke his lines
without any real enthusiasm or threat. The other two hadn't
said a word yet. The talker and the one to my right were both
thick-set and ugly. The third one, standing slightly behind his
mates, looked wiry and spiteful. The other two looked like
thumpers; this one was the potential slasher, the vicious kid
who was also a little scared. He would wait till you were

on the ground before getting stuck in. He was the one who would end up killing somebody one day.

The smell of booze in the night.

I was starting to tremble. There was no one around. I looked at Carlton.

'So what was it you were saying?' The bloke walked towards Carlton, the other two watching. I took another step forward.

One of the other guys – the other big one – pushed me in the chest with the palm of his hand: 'This isn't your fight. Unless you want it. Stay there and you won't get hurt.'

He half turned away from me and faced Carlton while the other guy also started crowding Carlton. Jesus fucking Christ, Jesus fucking Christ, was all I could think, over and over. I tried to control my trembling, tried to remember stuff I'd read about the way that everyone is frightened by violence, about how you master fear, but all I could feel was the fear of getting hurt. How to turn all that fear into adrenalin or whatever it is that makes you able to fight? I started breathing deeply. Whatever happens, you've just got to help Carlton, whatever happens Jesus fucking Christ. Carlton glanced at me and I don't know what he saw. One of the white guys had moved to within inches of him.

I thought: whatever happens is going to happen soon. It was too late to stop anything now. I tried to steady myself again, to gain control of my limbs, to make myself not be scared.

The guy spoke straight into Carlton's face: 'I'm talking to you, you bla –'

Suddenly Carlton's head snapped forward into the guy's face, his fist into his stomach, his foot into the guy's knee. He was already turning when he shouted: 'RUN!'

Carlton was a couple of feet clear of me when I started running. As soon as my limbs began moving my fear ignited all at once in a burst of energy which took me to just behind his shoulder. We were both running flat out. My head was thrown back so that my lungs could take in more oxygen which my heart pumped out all over my body. I didn't look back once. My feet flew over the pavement. Without realising where we were we charged into a main road. The yellow light of a cab came towards us through the dark. Carlton waved frantically, looking round fast to see if we were being chased. We were still running and the cab drove past, not wanting to get involved in whatever it was we were running away from. I glanced round quickly. About twenty yards back I saw the three of them running.

'Carlton!' He looked round. Up ahead there was a bus at a stop, indicator flashing, waiting to pull out into traffic. Without speaking we sprinted for the bus. By the time we were close to it it was out in the road and gathering speed. With a final burst of acceleration Carlton leapt on. I was a few steps behind – the bus was going faster and faster, in another few seconds it would be accelerating away. I lunged for the hand-rail. My grip slid down the pole but I got my hip on the platform and slithered on board. The conductor started bawling us out and for a moment it looked like he was going to throw us off the bus.

'Don't stop,' I panted. All the passengers were looking at us, wondering if we were running from the cops, unsure what to do. We were breathing like we were trying to suck every drop of oxygen out of the bus. The bus stopped and an old woman got on but the conductor didn't give the starting signal. There was blood on Carlton's forehead. I looked out of the back of the bus. I could still see the three of them, a good way back down the road.

Something about the way we looked – maybe he could see the ashes of all that burnt fear in my eyes – convinced the conductor that we weren't running from the scene of any murder except our own. He tugged the cord twice. The bus groaned and pushed its way again into the night traffic.

004

I KNOCKED ON Foomie's door and watched her shape swim
and lurch toward me through the pebbled glass. I kissed her
on the cheek and followed her inside. Her hair was wet and
she showed me into the kitchen while towelling it dry. The
flat was full of the warm smell of cooking. Her eyes looked
big and clear.

'You OK?' I said, leaning on the back of a chair. She
nodded, smiling. I walked into the living-room. She had lots
of plants; they created a fresh, restful atmosphere.

'I've got to get some more plants,' I said.

'Hey?' she called from the kitchen.

'Your plants are nice.' I walked out to the kitchen again
and clambered into the small gap between a chair and the
kitchen table. The kitchen walls were painted a yellow that
was bright but very easy on the eye; all the woodwork
was green. Foomie had the white towel wrapped around
her head.

'D'you want some tea?'

'Shall I make it?'

'That's OK.'

She pulled the kettle over to the sink and filled it without
unplugging the lead.

'Very handy,' I said. 'That's something I'd really like to do
– except I don't have the first idea of how to go about it.
Design the ergonomically perfect kitchen.'

Foomie smiled and leant back against the sink. Behind
her the window was pearled with steam. The shelves were
crammed with herbs and spices. Pots and pans were piled

up to one side of the sink. Cups hung from the undersides of more shelves. The noise of the kettle working started.

'It's just you and me. I hope that's OK.'

'That's perfect. I feel quiet.'

'Me too . . . I hope you're hungry; there's a lot of food.'

'I'm always starving. The more I eat the hungrier I get. Is there something I can do?'

'No, I'll just do the salad. You could put a record on,' Foomie said.

In the main room I crouched down and flicked through Foomie's records. She had all the latest funk and hip-hop, a few jazz albums. From the kitchen came the sound of chopping. The sun was angling through the blinds. Tiny diamonds of dust danced over the stereo; a golden caterpillar of light inched its way along the sofa.

Foomie came in and leant against the door frame. I stood up with a click in my knee so loud it sounded like a couple of bones had cracked. Foomie's eyes widened. 'That sounded painful.'

'Not really.'

'We can eat in about five minutes,' she said after a slight pause. The sun arranged thin racks of shadow on the wall.

Back in the kitchen I sat at the table and pulled four cans of Red Stripe out of a carrier-bag.

'D'you want a beer, Foomie?' I asked.

'Hmmn, please.' On one hand she had a quilted oven-glove made to look like a crocodile, four fingers forming the head and upper jaw, the thumb making the lower jaw. She held up her hand and snapped the jaws together a couple of times. I laughed; like Freddie's 'Every Dog Has His Day' glasses, a crocodile oven-glove struck me as one of those objects for which you could develop quite a strong affection.

Foomie had cooked vegetarian lasagne. I tried to eat slowly but it was too delicious and I ended up, as always, shovelling it away by the forkful. We talked about nothing in particular, sentences and topics following each other on a faint thread of sense and then disappearing as if they'd never actually taken place. The punchlines of jokes evaporated before we got to them. It was strange being like this with Foomie. Judging by the conversation you would think we hardly knew each other but it was because we knew each other well that there was this odd evanescent quality to what was said. Neither of us mentioned Steranko or Monica or anyone else.

The yellow walls glistened with a light film of condensation.

It was a warm evening and after dinner we took Foomie's cassette player on to the roof of my block. Silhouetted by the slanting light the TV aerials threw long strips of shadow on to the red bricks of the low wall. Sheets hung out to dry on the opposite block shrugged like flags in the breeze. There were a few lights on. While Foomie rolled a joint I put a tape of Schubert's fourteenth string quartet on the cassette player.

We passed the joint back and forth and listened to the music, saying nothing.

For a few moments the horizon was a damson smash of clouds. Then the sun sank behind the flats in the distance, leaving the roof in shadow. I went down to the flat to make coffee and fetch some candles.

When I came back up the sky had deepened to indigo with a few ink-dark clouds. I handed Foomie her coffee and lit the candle.

Foomie leant back against the railing, a slight breeze combing her hair. Steam was floating from the dark surface of her coffee; when she sipped from the cup there was a slight movement of muscle in her dark arms. She was wearing a sleeveless dress that came to her knees, blue with tiny white splashes like stars in the dark sky. It was still warm. The red and white lights of a plane flashed above us. Clouds slipped past the early moon. To Foomie's left I glimpsed the frail pattern of a spider's web stretched between railing and wall.

The second movement of the quartet slid into the night: desire and dread circling, coaxing, and turning into each other; the sound of longing generating its own momentum, finding its own form.

Listening, Foomie tilted her head to the sky. Warm candle-light touched her throat. Half her face was in shadow. The dress moved faintly in the breeze; the music swaying. She was still leaning against the railing, her feet slightly apart.

The candle flame twisted and writhed, recoiling from the touch of the breeze that would extinguish it.

As I moved towards her, my shadow, agile with the light of the flames, disappeared into Foomie's and then climbed slowly up her legs. I touched her neck and a few strands of hair. The light of the candle glowed in her eyes. I bent my face towards her until there was only breath and then nothing at all between our lips.

003

FREDDIE CAME ROUND when I was in the bath. While I got dry and put on some clothes he made a pot of tea. We sat in the kitchen and talked about boxing. After a while Freddie said, 'I've come to a momentous decision.'

'You're going to kill yourself?'

'No.'

'You're going to pay me that money you borrowed four years ago?'

'No, I'm leaving England.'

'When?'

'In about three weeks. I booked my ticket today.'

'Jesus.' I looked at the jar of marmalade and the teapot. 'Why?'

'There's no point staying here.'

Then, as if offering an alternative answer, he said, 'The fable's got to run its course.'

002

THAT NIGHT THE weather riots.

Dreaming that the door of the flat was being kicked down I woke to the sound of the wind hurling itself at the walls of the block. A strong wind lunged around the room, flinging the curtains aside and then sucking them back through the gap of the open window. Above the surge and shriek of the gale came the sound of breaking glass. I closed the window and looked out as another gust began thumping at the windows and walls. The air was full of dark shapes. Branches flew through the air like shrapnel. Burglar alarms were ringing in the distance. Street-lamps rocked and swayed. A section of fencing was catapulted into the road. A piece of corrugated iron floated through the air and clattered against a wall. Someone walking along the street was battered to the ground. The grass was flattened and glassy like a wave swept back into the ocean by the receding tide. Trees lunged at each other. The air was thick with leaves. From across the road there was a deep *kurrump* as a tree thrashed clear of the earth, hovered for a moment like a rocket on the point of take-off and then tottered and crashed to the ground. A few seconds later a clump of bricks crashed through the windscreen of a parked car. All around was the sound of the gale breaking the branches of trees and pounding the walls of buildings.

I was still staring out of the window when, suddenly, everywhere was plunged into darkness. The ringing of burglar alarms died instantly. In place of the faint rust-coloured glow that had hung over the city there was only deep night.

Next day the air was fresh as a shaved face; the walls of buildings looked sore and clean as if a layer of dirt had been razored off by the wind. Uprooted trees were everywhere, scattered across the roads like barricades, vast craters where their roots had been. Here and there were piles of masonry, the debris of houses looted by the wind. A fresh breeze ran through the grass. Everywhere seemed lighter. Where before the light had filtered through clumps of trees now only bewildered daylight lay like a flood across junctions and road. The sky was an innocent blue, washed clean by the wind and rain with no sign of contrition or knowledge. These things happen sometimes – that was the only message written on the blank sheet of sky.

MONICA AND I were standing on her balcony, drinking beer and watching the setting sun carve deep canyons into the clouds. From the stereo in the living-room I caught snatches of Callas singing of love and betrayal, her voice like a promise so vast it could only be broken.

Monica went inside to get more drinks. As I turned to watch her go I found myself looking straight into her bedroom. On other occasions when we'd been on the balcony the curtains had been drawn and I'd not noticed the room behind us. This evening the curtains were wide open and the light was on. Clothes and jeans were piled on the bed. A dress was hanging on the back of a door. Odd shoes were scattered over the floor. Magazines, cassette tapes and books. On her bedside table were a full roll of pink toilet paper and an old clanger-style alarm clock. Two pillows. A stack of LPs and her old music centre. No posters on the walls. The door of her wardrobe hung open, revealing coloured dresses on hangers, the silver rectangle of a mirror. In the window was a well-tended pot plant. The window was very clean and because of the darkness of the balcony the room looked exceptionally bright. There was a stillness about the interior that made it look like one of those installations in museums showing rooms and furniture from different periods of history. It was easy to imagine a small discreetly printed placard just below the window-sill: 'Young Woman's Bedroom, Council Flat, South London: Late Twentieth Century'.

What will survive of us?

Monica came back on to the balcony carrying two more

cans of beer and a small grass joint that gave off a thin drift of smoke. She had put on a red and blue turtle-neck sweater. Over the blocks of flats in the distance, thick crimson light welled up behind the last dark rags of cloud.

OOO

THE SUN WAS watery and faint. The long trunks of mottled trees were scattered across the Common. A slight mist. Gangs of workers piled branches into the back of a lorry. Any trees still standing were bare and broken; high branches hung at angles that couldn't have grown. The grass was strewn with wet brown leaves. Smoke drifted in the distance.

Steranko and I walked on until we came to a part of the Common that had been cleared and scraped flat. Large piles of wood were smouldering and burning. A lorry dumped a load of branches and then rumbled off. The soil was heavy, soft and criss-crossed with the marks of large tyres.

We followed the tracks into the bare stretch of ground where all the trees uprooted in the gale were being slowly burned. The ground here was covered in a layer of grey-white ash. With each step a small cloud of ash was kicked lightly into the air, like sand on a beach from which a tide of fire had receded. All around, piles of ashes and embers were still smouldering, some two or three feet high. Nearby, a mechanical digger scooped up thick loads of black earth, swivelled round and buried the trees' ashes beneath a dark drizzle of falling soil.

We walked towards a fire that was burning fiercely. Expertly made, it was banked up so that the lower slopes glowed red and white hot while new wood thrown on the top burnt easily and steadily. Another lorry juddered past and deposited a load of wood. Two workers threw the wood on to a slow burning fire, their faces touched by the light of the flames. There was a rose tint to the sky. The smell of burning wood. Through the waves of heat rising from the fires, lorries and buses on the nearby road melted and rippled as they passed by. Behind them were the bare branches of tall trees and, still further off, a few lights in large Victorian buildings. To the right a long line of trees that had survived the storm receded into the distance.

Unnoticed, the sun had disappeared behind the Victorian houses. The fires burnt quietly but all around was the clatter and roar of the lorries and the digger, the traffic on the road. The light from the fires made the hazy sky a pale golden blue.

The pale light fading, the leaves burning, the trees receding.

We walked on and there, hanging in the wide gap between two rows of houses, was the sun: a perfect crimson disc, thin branches silhouetted against it like broken veins. Smoke from the fires drifted across the bare ground. Buses shimmered along the road, the blood-coloured sun suspended only a fraction above them. High above the sun a red vapour trail, razor-thin, cut the sky.

Another lorry arrived, this time dumping a load of pallets, hardboard sheets, chairs, tables and desks. Steranko asked the man driving the lorry if we could borrow a couple of chairs.

'Help yourself,' he said.

We dragged two large armchairs to where we could watch the sun shiver through the heat and flames of the largest fire. Flames reached high into the air, staining the sky a thick blue. The lorry trundled off and we sat back in our armchairs, surrounded by the waste ground, the slow-burning fires and the sound of the digger mechanically returning the ashes of the trees to the soil. Smoke from the fires behind encircled and drifted past us. Slumped in his armchair, long legs stretched out in front of the fire, Steranko's face was bathed in the deep red light of the flames. More wood had been thrown on to the fires behind us and they erupted suddenly in bright flames. Two more workers from the parks department came along.

'Are you supervising the fires?' one of them said.

'We're just sitting here,' Steranko said. The man limped off and then he and his mate began throwing the hardboard, chairs and tables on to the fire. They caught immediately and bright yellow flames reached higher into the air. The heat scorched our eyes and we pulled the chairs back a little way. At the base of the fire the burning mass of wood from the trees glowed and pulsed. On top, tables and chairs perched for a few moments at odd angles and were suddenly engulfed in flames. Something thrown on the fire bounced off and landed with a clatter at my feet: a record player, smouldering.

The heat was so intense now that the two men had trouble throwing stuff on to the top of the fire. Their faces were stained deep red with gold and black shadows. The sun had sunk from sight as if consumed by the bonfire. My face felt scorched, my eyes watered. I touched the arms of my chair to make sure that it was not about to burst into flames beneath me. The burning frame of a chair toppled down the slopes of the fire and rolled, still burning, to the ground. There were shadows everywhere. Steranko's face and clothes were lit bright orange and yellow. The sky had turned a deeper blue than either of us had ever seen. Another table caught light and I moved back still further, angling my chair to the left, looking away from the flames. High up in the frozen sky was a full moon, bathing the flattened ground and the trees in calm light. Half of my face was still scorching hot from the fire, the other half chilled by the evening air. Steranko had also turned his chair round; the left side of his face was pale and silver-grey in the cold light of the moon. Burning more slowly now, blue-grey smoke from the other fires curled slowly past us. There was another whoosh of flame from the main fire and we turned away from the moon and the empty sky as a mattress went up in a gush of flame. The two workers walked over and stood watching the fire with us.

'Hot eh?' one of them said, wiping his smoke-blackened face with a piece of rag.

'Throw them chairs on when you've finished will you?' he said a few minutes later. We said we would and they walked off into the night. We continued sitting, watching the worsening flames subside into molten red embers. Alone in the waste ground, in our armchairs, we were reluctant to break the elemental pull of the fire.

Eventually we got up to leave. Together we swung first Steranko's and then my chair on to the fire. For a few minutes they sat there as if untouched by the heat and then suddenly erupted in a rush of flame that flung back the cold of the night once more. We walked back through the waste ground, fires dying all around us.

IT WAS TWO *in the morning by the time I found the apartment. At first I thought I had been given the wrong key. It turned in the lock but the door refused to budge. For five minutes I stood on the dark landing, pulling and pushing the door, turning the key first one way and then the other. Then, suddenly and unexpectedly (some fluke of the mechanism) I heard the easy click of the key engaging the levers and the door opened. I ran my hand up and down the wall, found and flicked the light switch. Nothing happened. It was too dark to see anything. Lighting a match I entered the apartment and while the light flickered I made out a small kitchen. I lit another match and made my way into the main room. By the light of the match I could see a bed, a table, a desk, the blurred square of a window. Striking my last match I walked towards the desk and tried the lamp there. To my surprise it worked. In addition to the bed and table there were some hard chairs, a book-case and some kind of sideboard. Paperback books and clothes were scattered here and there.*

The room smelt of stale time.

Back in the kitchen I noticed a cup and a plate in the sink. On the table was half a loaf of bread, solid as stone, surrounded by scattered crumbs. There were some greyish milk bottles, a towel, a small glass with silhouettes of dogs and 'Every Dog Has His Day' printed just beneath the rim. I turned on the hot tap and immediately the water heater humphed into life. By now my eyes were used to the dim light. There were some spots of mould at the end of the tap. Cracked tiles.

Lying by the door were a couple of Airmail letters, covered by the smudged postmark of a shoe – I must have trodden on them as I came in. I picked them up and saw immediately that the address of one was in my own handwriting. Post-marked six days ago, it had arrived too late; as I posted it his own last letter was already making its way towards me.

I went back into the main room. On the wall, attached by yellow sellotape, was a familiar, faded poster for an exhibition of an artist's paintings. An identical poster hung in my own flat back in England.

Time had settled on everything like dust. I picked up a sweater with a shirt inside, taken off at the same time – how long ago? – and thrown carelessly on a chair. By the skirting-board was a pair of shoes, the outside of each heel worn down almost to the sole. How much meaning was contained in the accidental arrangement of these things? How far back would you have to go to decipher the simple creases of that shirt, to establish how it came to be lying there, like that?

I walked over to the window and looked down at the wet street. Through the threads of rain I saw someone hunched up in a raincoat beneath a street-lamp. There was a brief flash of lightning and in the sudden bleaching of the rain I saw the figure in the raincoat look up at my window and then walk on. A shiver passed through me. A moment later he disappeared from sight, the echo of footsteps hanging in the damp air.

Be near me when my light is low.

Near the desk was a small electric fire with a frayed flex. I plugged it in carefully and immediately both bars began to glow orange. Arranging my coat on the back of the chair I sat down and looked at the mess of papers and odds and ends that covered the desk. There were a few cassettes, pens, an empty glass. On the back of an envelope was written FRIDAY and a neatly printed list of things to be done. All of the other papers were in his usual chaotic scrawl. I picked up odd sheets but most were incomplete. Many paragraphs had been crossed out; there seemed no discernible continuity.

One by one, I pulled open the drawers of the desk. The first was empty except for pencils, an old diary and a small dictionary. In the next there was a stack of unused paper and some more sheets covered in writing, much of it crossed out. In the last drawer there were more sheets of unused paper and, underneath them, a large notebook. I opened it in the middle and flicked through a few pages. Though much neater than any of the other pages – as if he had been copying from an earlier draft – the handwriting was still unmistakably Freddie's. The pages were bathed in the yellow light of the reading lamp. I read a few phrases at random, flicked through some more pages and then turned back to the beginning and read the first sentence:

'In August it rained all the time . . .'

Skipping here and there, impatient to get to the end, I read all the way through, remembering incidents that I had totally forgotten, recognising many episodes despite the distortions and dislocations. By the time I came to the end the first grey light of day was coming through the window.

The text stopped about twenty pages from the end of the notebook. I flicked through these last pages in case there were some more paragraphs but all were blank.

Reluctant to break the spell of the past, I took off my glasses, rubbed my eyes and sat back in the chair. As I did so I noticed a couple of postcards taped to the wall above the desk. To one side of these cards, propped up against the right-angle of the wall was a photograph that I recognised immediately in spite of its age. I reached for it and saw that a few words had been written on the back: '. . . that terrible thing which is there in every photograph: the return of the dead.' Then I stared at the image on the other side.

We are all there on the roof, crowded together to get into the picture frame. Spreading across the ground are the thin shadows of TV aerials. Surprised by the self-timer some of us are caught at unexpected angles as we jostle for a good position in the photograph but because the light is so bright everyone is in sharp focus and is clearly recognisable. Most of us are laughing or smiling as we squint into the glare. Freddie is drinking from a red can of beer. The colours are striking: there are the reds, blues and whites of T-shirts, shorts, dresses; a half-peeled orange; a halo-yellow cycling cap; the wide stripes of a deckchair. And over all of this is the deep blue of the empty sky — the colour of memory.

ACKNOWLEDGEMENTS

I WOULD LIKE to express my thanks to Xandra Hardie and Frances Coady for their encouragement, advice, good humour and invaluable editorial suggestions. Without their help this book would not have been written.

———————————

A few lines in the text were suggested by or (mis)quoted from the following sources:

p.16 Sentence beginning 'His desk was crammed . . .' cf. Walter Benjamin, *One Way Street*, p.90, Verso, London.

p.57 'People tended not to run like that . . . running away from something.' cf. Theodor Adorno, *Minima Moralia*, p.102, Verso, London.

p.68 'People of our generation . . . when we were still kids.' John Osborne, *Look Back in Anger*, p.84, Faber & Faber, London.

p.82 The lyrics from the fourth movement of Mahler's third symphony are from Nietzsche, *Also sprach Zarathustra*.

p.151 Sentence beginning 'So many people wanted to have their say . . .' cf. Jean Baudrillard, 'The Ecstasy of Communication' in Hal Foster (ed), *Postmodern Culture*, p.132, Pluto, London.

p.165 'He had to waste his talent . . . a source of strength.' cf. Theodor Adorno on Verlaine in *Aesthetic Theory*, p.58, Routledge & Kegan Paul, London.

p.165 '. . . having good friends and being a good friend.' cf. Nietzsche, *Human, all too Human*, p.145, Cambridge University Press.

p.245 'What will survive of us?' From Philip Larkin, 'An Arundel Tomb' in *The Whitsun Weddings*, p.46, Faber & Faber, London.

p.252 'Be near me when my light is low.' From Tennyson, 'In Memoriam A.H.H.', *Poems and Plays*, p.242, Oxford University Press.

p.253 The quotation on the back of the photograph is from Roland Barthes, *Camera Lucida*, p.9, Hill & Wang, New York.